"Just one dance. . .

"That is all. I promise I won't get any ideas."

She gazed up at him. Too bad she couldn't explain why she was so hesitant. She was wasting her life, letting this fear hold her back. There was a handsome man before her who had shown her nothing but kindness and all he wanted was a dance. The truth was: she yearned in her heart of hearts to dance with him.

"All right," she said softly.

The last time she placed her hand in another man's like this it had been the beginning of the end.

Prue forced her breath to be even. In. Out. In. Out. She willed her heart to beat in a steady rhythm as she tried to reclaim power over her emotions and fears.

Castleton's gaze settled on her face. She peered up at him. This time she really looked at him, focusing on his mouth, which was firm, sensual, and smiling encouragingly. His blue eyes had darkened in the candlelight.

"Are you having fun yet?" Castleton asked her affectionately.

Her gaze flew up to his. Ah, those eyes. Knowing. Dark.

MAYA RODALE

What a Wallflower Wants

AVON

An Imprint of HarperCollins*Publishers*

This is a work of fiction. Names, characters, places, and incidents are products of the author's imagination or are used fictitiously and are not to be construed as real. Any resemblance to actual events, locales, organizations, or persons, living or dead, is entirely coincidental.

AVON BOOKS
An Imprint of HarperCollins*Publishers*
195 Broadway
New York, New York 10007

First Avon Books mass market printing: October 2014

Avon Trademark Reg. U.S. Pat. Off. and in Other Countries, Marca Registrada, Hecho en U.S.A.
HarperCollins® is a registered trademark of HarperCollins Publishers.

Printed in the U.S.A.

10 9 8 7 6 5 4 3 2 1

For girls like Prudence and men like Roark

And for Tony

Acknowledgments

I AM INDEBTED TO Sara Jane Stone, Aimee H, and Tony Haile for reading early versions of this manuscript and offering brilliant feedback. Many thanks to my Facebook fans for helping me determine the title of this book; my friends, family, and the Lady Authors for their encouragement; and my editor, Tessa. I am especially indebted to the brave people who shared their stories of sexual assault and recovery, which helped me in writing Prudence's experiences.

Introduction

Dear reader,

Sometimes a story seizes an author and won't let go. *What a Wallflower Wants* is a departure from my usual lighthearted romances. This novel is darker, it includes a graphic depiction of sexual violence, and it's deeply emotional. It is also a novel that ends happily.

Though set in a historical time period, this story was influenced by all too frequent accounts of sexual violence against women in the news today. These heartbreaking and enraging stories impelled me to put pen to paper (or fingers to keyboard) to write about a girl, Prudence, who suffers the worst thing imaginable but finds love and acceptance anyway; a hero, Roark, who defies conventions but is heroic in all the ways that truly matter; and a villain who gets just what he deserves.

Above all, *What a Wallflower Wants* is a romance novel, which means that this is a story about a hero and heroine falling in love, saving each other, and living happily ever after.

Yours,
Maya

What a
Wallflower
Wants

Prologue

"Are you there, God? 'Tis I, Prudence."

Her voice wavered. Her knees buckled and she sank to the ground, her back sliding down against the wall.

God didn't answer, which was just as well. Prudence didn't have the words to describe this *thing* that had just happened to her. One minute she was waltzing and the next—

A sob caught in her throat. She drew her knees against her chest and wrapped her arms around them. Slowly she rocked on the ground, back and forth, back and forth, holding herself close. Her memories were hazy, with a few sharp, piercing moments. She could still smell him on her skin—a noxious mixture of stale smoke and wine.

She was faintly aware of the sound of the orchestra mingled with the dull roar of hundreds of people laughing and chatting. They had no idea that just down the hall a girl had been stripped of everything. Only eighteen, she was an innocent girl on her first season with her life stretching out before her, rich with possibilities.

Was.

Everything was different now.

Just an hour ago she had believed in love, romance, and happily ever after. She had believed in God's mercy and trusted that heroes came to the rescue. But that was *before.* No one had answered her pleas. No one had come to save her.

From now on, Prudence would be on her own.

Chapter 1

If a young lady is traveling west on the London road and a young rogue is traveling east on the London road, at which point shall they meet?

EVER SINCE HER first season, Miss Prudence Merryweather Payton had known that she would never marry. By her third season, she had made peace with the sad truth that love and marriage were not in the cards for her. Which was *fine*. FINE. Truly, she was not bothered in the slightest at the prospect of a long, boring spinsterhood. Why, think of all the needlepoint or charity work she might do.

Or so she had thought.

But that was before the invitation had arrived. A delicately worded missive, written in an elegant script, inviting her to the one-hundredth anniversary of her finishing school, Lady Penelope's Finishing School for Young Ladies of Fine Families.

With that invitation had come the mortifying

and heartbreaking truth: no graduate had ever taken more than four seasons to land a husband.

Except Prudence.

Until recently, she had not been alone in her matrimonial failures—her friends Emma and Olivia had also been wallflowers with hardly any suitors amongst them. Prudence had envisioned a future for the three of them, living happily in a cottage by the sea. She had known this invitation, this ball, this moment would come, but Prudence had always thought she'd confront it with her very best friends by her side. But then Emma had landed a duke and Olivia had found love with the most unlikely man. Prudence was happy for her friends—truly. No one deserved love and happiness more than Emma and Olivia.

Now Prudence was on her own.

The last wallflower.

Given that marriage was not an option for her, this put her in something of an indelicate position. By *indelicate*, she meant angsty, stomach-knotted, quietly panicked, a constant state of terror.

She could either be the one failure in one hundred years, or she could face her fears and make one last attempt to secure a husband. With a spark of hope that surprised her and a fortitude she didn't know she possessed, Prudence embarked on one last-ditch effort to wed.

Thus, Cecil.

Prudence stared at the sleeping man across from her in the mail coach. Convinced that there was no one for her in London, Prudence had left for Bath with her aunt and guardian, Lady Dare. It was in the Bath Assembly Rooms that she'd struck up an unlikely acquaintanceship with Cecil, Lord Nanson, who tended to seek refuge in the wallflower corner during balls. They came to the realization that a quick, clandestine marriage of convenience would suit them both.

Thus they were traveling to his estate, where they would marry by special license.

It was almost the stuff of romance, except that he had no romantic interest in her, nor she in him. Cecil wanted two things: his mother to stop plaguing him to marry, and Lord Fairbanks. After their perfunctory wedding, Prudence and Cecil planned to promptly return to London, where she would prove to everyone that she wasn't the sole failure in the one-hundred-year history of Lady Penelope's Finishing School for Young Ladies, and then . . .

She didn't know what then.

She knew only that she had to attend and that she could not face that ball without a ring on her finger. Otherwise The Beast would have won.

In the years since, Prudence had become rather adept at pretending that the awful thing had never happened. She'd told no one and had proceeded to pretend with Emma, Olivia, and Lady Dare that she was the same girl she'd always been. Sometimes she almost believed it.

But then The Beast was there—a shard of a

memory, or at the same party—reminding her that she had no future. No man would ever want her or love her. Which no longer mattered, because she had no interest in being with a man intimately. Yet every so often she felt a hot flare of determination to prove him wrong.

Thus, a husband for Lady Penelope's Ball.

Cecil, with his round, pale cheeks and floppy blond curls, would never hurt her. Of that she was certain. As he slept, he breathed faintly through his parted lips. Prudence tried not to be immensely irritated by this. She deliberately avoided thoughts of a lifetime sleeping next to a man who breathed through his mouth. Beggars could not be choosers.

Besides, knowing her and knowing Cecil, they would keep separate bedrooms. Cecil, she suspected, had as little interest in bedding her as she him. The way his gaze had strayed to Lord Fairbanks when they'd all conversed in the assemblies at Bath hadn't escaped her notice. He wouldn't hurt her. Nor would he touch her. That suited her just fine.

The prospect of a marriage of convenience didn't provide the relief she had sought. This wasn't what she had dreamt for herself. She had wanted love: all-consuming, passionate, can't-stay-away, shout-from-the-rooftops, die-without-you kind of love.

But at least she wouldn't be a spinster. At least she wouldn't be the one failure in the hundred-year history of her school.

She could *do* this.

It was her best option. It was her only option.

There was no reason for her stomach to be in knots. There was no reason for her heart to ache a little more with every beat. And there was no point in being sad for what she'd lost.

Everyone else in the mail coach slept. Everyone else included a portly middle-aged man and his equally portly wife, one wiry young man with spectacles, and a vicar. None of them breathed through their mouths.

Prue looked out the window and watched the countryside roll by in the moonlight. Fields gave way to a thicket of forest. Instead of the usual luscious green of old trees and expansive meadows, a drought had made everything dry up, stiff, crackly, and brown.

They ought to have arrived at Chippenham hours earlier, but the journey had been fraught with delays. First, Cecil's private carriage had broken irreparably. Her insistence that they return to London in time for Lady Penelope's Ball had meant that travel by the mail coach was their only option.

Her maid and his valet had taken the first coach, having been sent ahead to prepare the household. Prudence and Cecil had remained behind for lunch whilst he'd written a letter to his mother in town announcing their imminent marriage. An hour later, they'd been on the road again, this time stuffed into the mail coach with strangers.

Unfortunately, her bad luck had continued. Someone had failed to properly secure the luggage, and somewhere around the village of Corsham it had all tumbled off with a great rumble. Valises, trunks, and some of their contents—a man's unmentionables, a crushed bonnet, leather gloves—had been strewn about the dusty road.

They were delayed.

It was now late.

Her small valise hadn't made it back on top of the carriage and was now nestled at her feet. She longed to stretch her legs. She really wished to lie down on cool sheets in a dark room. Perhaps wash the dust from her limbs and face with a cold, wet cloth. She wanted to be alone, behind a locked door.

The carriage stopped abruptly. A few passengers stirred, blinking their eyes sleepily. Beside her, Cecil woke up. The night was dark, quiet. Because they were all silent, waiting, they could hear the highwayman's voice loud and clear.

"Stand and deliver!"

The occupants of the carriage stirred awake to the sound of someone approaching and nervous horses pawing at the ground, whimpering.

They started to argue then—the carriage driver and this highwayman—their low, angry voices like a threatening rumble of thunder in the night. Prue's heart started to pound. She wanted so badly to reach for Cecil's hand. Instead, she reached for her valise and hugged it to her chest.

The matron started weeping. The vicar started mumbling under his breath. Prayers, presumably.

"Cecil, do something," Prudence whispered fiercely. He was a man, her protector in the big bad world, and danger was approaching. She needed him. Everyone knew that no good came of encounters with highwaymen. It was rare to walk away still in possession of one's valuables and virtue. Prudence was not a lucky girl.

"You ought to go out there," Cecil replied. It was a moment before the shock wore off and Prudence could speak.

"Are you mad?" she hissed. Sane men did not send women out to battle ahead of them. They didn't sacrifice their intended. She knew this wasn't a love match. But really! "I will not," she said, her chin trembling.

"It's you he wants," Cecil said, driving a nail in chivalry's coffin.

The driver and the highwayman continued to argue loudly, their voices a thick, heavy, rolling thunder punctured by a sharp crack of lightning.

Followed by a thud. Then silence.

It wasn't lightning. It was a gunshot.

"I am a *mother*," the matron sobbed, heaving heavily and pressing a handkerchief to her mouth. She didn't need to say anything more for them all to understand: the young, unmarried woman's life was worth less than hers. The highwayman would want the young woman for whatever nefarious pleasures he had in mind.

"He wants our valuables, not me," Prudence whispered quickly, trying to reason with them. "If we just hand them over, perhaps he'll leave us undisturbed."

"But what if that's not all he wants?" Cecil replied, his face pale with terror. "Besides, I need my valuables."

Prue frowned. His father had five thousand a year. Cecil needed his valuables less than anyone in this carriage.

Prudence glanced at the vicar. He caught her eye and hastily bowed his head and resumed his prayers. She wanted to tell him not to waste his breath. She wanted to tell him to have mercy on *her* in this moment.

Everyone tensed at the sound of heavy boots crunching on the dirt and gravel road. Ominous, those steps were. Everyone was completely awake now.

Prue's heart thudded loudly as she looked at her fellow passengers. All of them pleaded with their eyes for her to sacrifice herself.

"You can distract him," Cecil whispered quickly. "While we escape for help."

"Cecil, please . . . ," Prue begged, knowing it was useless. The very reasons she had assumed him safe doomed her now: he didn't care for her, he wouldn't touch her, he wanted only the distraction she offered.

"Go on, Prudence. Please," Cecil pleaded. He reached over her to unhitch the latch. The door swung open. He gave her a shove, then pulled the door shut.

Because she hadn't actually believed he would be so cruel as to physically shove her in harm's way, she hadn't braced herself. She went tumbling to the ground, landing on her bottom.

Immediately a bloodcurdling scream emerged from within the carriage.

As her eyes adjusted to the dark, she held her breath and peered under the conveyance. She saw moonlight reflecting off the highwayman's polished black leather boots *on the other side of the carriage.*

Chapter 2

PRUDENCE CLUTCHED HER valise to her chest and took one soft step backward, then another. And another and another. No one noticed, for Prudence had made an art of not being noticed.

She heard the vicar praying loudly. Prudence knew that wouldn't do any good—she knew first-hand that God didn't answer prayers. The stout matron wailed. Prue wanted to tell her there was no point in crying. Cecil loudly made promises to the highwayman. She wanted to tell the highway-man that Cecil would not keep his word.

She had just been jilted.

During a highway robbery.

Cecil ought to have protected her; instead he'd abandoned her. The vicar hadn't shown her any mercy. It proved to her, once again, that regretful truth: men never came to save the day.

No one ever came to save Prudence in her hours of need.

A girl was on her own.

She'd do well to remember that.

Thus, knowing better than to wait by the side of the road for a hero to come along, Prudence began to step quickly and quietly through the dark forest as she made her escape. Pine needles cushioned the steps of her thinly soled leather boots. The night air was cool against her skin and a welcome relief from the relentless heat of the preceding days. In her hands, she clutched her valise.

She ran as fast and far as she could, until her lungs were near to bursting. Then she slowed to a walk and carried on, speaking softly to herself.

"He won't come after you," she rationalized as she stepped through the forest, painfully aware of the shadows and strange night noises. "A highwayman has better things to do than chase after poor young ladies in a dark and, frankly, terrifying forest in the dead of the night."

Every so often she paused to listen for highwaymen, or Cecil, who perhaps had come to his senses and sought her forgiveness.

"I SUPPOSE MARRIAGE is utterly out of the question now," Prue sighed after she'd been walking for a few hours and hadn't encountered man or animal. "If anyone finds out that I attempted to elope and fled a highwayman alone, I'll be utterly ruined. As if I weren't already!"

She laughed softly, sarcastically.

"I must simply make other plans," she carried on. "I shall live with Emma. Or Olivia. It won't torture me at all to watch them in their wedded bliss with their revoltingly besotted husbands."

There was no one to hear the bitterness in her voice.

Not when she was alone. In the middle of Wiltshire. In the dead of the night.

"Perhaps I shall retire to a cottage by the sea. Or perhaps I shall spend the rest of my days with Lady Dare."

The glamorous Lady Dare had raised Prudence from the time she'd been in the cradle, a poor little orphan after her mother and father had perished from an outbreak of consumption. Prudence had been too young to have any memories of them, and instead she saw her aunt and her governess as her family. Lady Dare was currently in Bath with her friend Lady Palmerston, operating under the impression that Prudence was on her way back to London.

Which she was. Presumably. In a manner of speaking.

Finally the forest ended, giving way to a road. She followed it, hoping it would lead her to a small village where she might take a room, have a bath, and sort out what she might do for the rest of her life.

"Hint. Taken. No marriage for Prudence," she muttered. Marriage was all a girl was raised to do, so Prue was at a bit of a loss over how to proceed with her remaining days.

The obvious recourse was to return to London and pretend none of this had ever happened. She was very good at that. As far as anyone knew, she was Miss Payton, shy, retiring, wallflower. No one—not even Emma and Olivia—knew the dark, ugly truth about her.

Given that her last-ditch effort at procuring a husband had failed so spectacularly, there was no point in attending Lady Penelope's Ball; Prudence did not have the gumption to go alone, and it was inconceivable she'd find a husband now, which meant there was no point in hurrying back to town.

The sun began to rise. She kept walking.

THE SUN ROSE higher, beating her down with hot rays. She trudged along the dusty dirt road for hours and miles. Fields lined either side, making Prue wish for the shade of the forest, even with its dark, terrifying shadows.

Hours passed, with the sun climbing higher and higher in the sky.

Her reddish-brown hair had long ago worked its way out of the knot she'd styled it in and now was plastered to the back of her neck. Beads of sweat gathered between her breasts. The fabric of her dress clung to her, which was deuced uncomfortable in this heat. Her whalebone corset dug into her skin.

Prue switched the bag from one hand to the other. Both hurt. She debated leaving it on the side of the road, but she had faith that eventually she would reach shelter and would want the clean dress, hairbrush, and money contained within. So she held on until her hands were raw under her gloves.

Her pale skin was probably a furious shade of

red by now. Her freckles had probably darkened considerably. When she'd still been a student at Lady Penelope's, she had worried about her freckles, or forgetting the steps to the quadrille whilst dancing with a handsome young man, or other ridiculous things that had never been actual problems.

She carried on, walking another mile or two or twenty. It felt like twenty. The thick white clouds had begun to darken considerably. A rumble of thunder disturbed the birdsong. A storm. Perfect. Though the rain might be cooling, she didn't fancy walking when this dirt road turned to mud.

And then, oh happiness, the sweetest sound in the world reached her ears: the sound of a carriage approaching. The clip of the horses' hooves and the rumble of the wheels were unmistakable.

"Please let this be a lady and her maid," Prudence prayed, setting down her valise. "Or a nice family. Or an old dowager."

Prue turned to see if her prayers had been answered. An exceedingly fine—and fast—carriage rolled toward her, a cloud of dust behind it and two pure white stallions up front. Unfortunately, the carriage was driven by a man.

As the carriage came closer, she saw that he was a large man. A young man.

Then the carriage rolled to a gentle stop beside her.

She noticed his boots first: large, shiny black Hessians that reached his knees. His valet must have spent hours polishing them to such a high shine. Her gaze then traveled up, inevitably, to muscular thighs clad in very fitted kerseymere breeches. His waistcoat was a pale blue silk, the color of the sky approximately three hours earlier, before the sun had reached its peak in the sky.

His jacket was green, like the pine needles in the forest that had softened her steps as she'd made her escape. Of course his chest and shoulders were broad and, in her mind, imposing.

And when she lifted her gaze higher still, to his face?

To hell with you, God.

This man's face, with its blue eyes and easy smile, made her think of *Once upon a time*. Once upon a time, when she still believed in heroes that saved the day. Once upon a time, when she still believed that somewhere, out there, was a man who would love her. Once upon a time, when a young girl's dreams came true and happily ever after was just within reach. That was a long time ago. These days, Prudence knew better. She knew that wolves wore rogues' clothing and had a taste for young ladies.

"Good afternoon," he said with a tip of his hat and a smile that revealed a slight dimple in his left cheek. He was entirely handsome, from his slightly unruly brown hair down to the tips of his shiny black boots. And he was smiling at her in a way that made her feel like fireworks inside: hot, shimmering, sparkling explosions that left her breathless and entranced.

Prudence managed a tight smile, wanting to be polite but not encouraging.

She was quite aware of the fact that they were alone on a desolate country road.

"Would you care for a ride, miss? I'd be happy to oblige," he offered.

Of course she wanted a ride somewhere. At the moment, she wanted nothing more than to sit on the upholstered carriage bench, under the shade of the carriage top. She wanted to set down her bag and sigh with relief. She wanted to sit beside this impossibly handsome man and gaze up at his blue eyes and think about falling in love rather than being accosted and left for dead, or worse.

She knew about worse.

So even though this handsome man smiled at her kindly and had magically appeared during her hour of need to offer her a much-desired ride, Prudence said no.

To be more precise, she said, "No, thank you."

This was punctuated by another rumble of thunder.

The man, drat him, lifted one brow curiously and looked impossibly handsome whilst doing so.

"It's a hot day to be out walking," he remarked.

"I am well aware of that," she replied dryly, and he laughed. To her vast irritation, it was a warm, lovely sound that she might have enjoyed under other circumstances, or in another lifetime, or if she'd been another person entirely.

"It's also likely to rain," he said, gesturing toward the thick, dark clouds. There was another rumble of thunder so perfectly timed that she wondered if he had a way of commanding the weather.

"How refreshing." She glanced down the road. A plume of smoke was rising up, far off in the distance. Was that a town just ahead? Could she walk there before the rain started? Maybe. If this man would leave her to carry on.

"I beg your pardon, I haven't properly introduced myself. I'm Castleton," he said with the lordly authority that Prudence recognized from all the haughty peers she knew in London—and strenuously avoided.

She ought to introduce herself. Which name should she give him? *Prude Prudence*? Or perhaps *London's Least Likely to Be Caught in a Compromising Position*? Not being a complete ninny, she wasn't about to give her real name to a strange man encountered on the side of the road.

"I'm Miss Merryweather."

"Miss Merryweather, I'd be more than happy to drive you into town. It's just a mile or so ahead."

Oh, thank God.

"I'd prefer to walk, thank you," she told him. To prove her point, she started plodding toward town. Her feet throbbed. Her back ached. In her gloves, her hands were positively raw from carrying her bag. But there was no way she was going to put herself at the mercy of a man she didn't know.

"Would you like company?" he offered, oblivious to her lack of interest.

Correction: she was interested. But she had no intention of indulging in her interest and what he offered. Her life had made it plain that men were brutes not to be trusted, and God had made it abundantly clear that she was not to have love or marriage. There was no point in her furthering her acquaintance with this man. Nothing good could come of it.

"No, thank you," she said.

"Are you quite certain you don't wish for a ride, Miss Merryweather? I would feel like the worst sort of gentleman if I left you on your own by the side of a desolate country road with a rainstorm imminent. I'd be much obliged if you let me drive you into town."

"And I'd be much obliged if you left me to proceed in peace." She couldn't stand the temptation much longer, and she could. Not. Get. In. That. Carriage.

Not for the first time did she curse The Beast.

If it hadn't been for him, she could have climbed into that carriage and let herself fall in love. If it hadn't been for him, she'd probably have been happily married to a wonderful man with a baby in the nursery and another on the way. She wouldn't have been here—jilted and on the road with nowhere to go, refusing the offer of a handsome man.

She carried on, feeling his eyes on her. In London, she had made every effort to ensure men never looked twice at her. So it was deuced strange to have captured the attention of one here, now, when she was looking her worst and completely hopeless.

"As you wish, Miss Merryweather. Enjoy your walk. Good day," Castleton said with another tip of his hat and flash of his smile. He flicked the reins, the stallions picked up a trot, and Prudence was left behind in the dust.

Then, like all the others, he was gone.

Chapter 3

JOHN ROARK, FORMALLY known as Jonathan James William Roark Hathaway, Viscount Castleton, was on a winning streak of epic proportions. It had begun a few months earlier during a storm like this, in a place like this. Just when he'd hit the bitter end, his luck had turned and rocketed skyward, providing him with riches he'd never expected and opportunities he'd only dreamt of. He'd seized each and every opportunity, like a drowning man gasped for a breath of air.

But the thing with winning streaks was that they inevitably came to an end. What goes up, must come down. Eventually the other shoe would drop—a fact that was never far from his mind.

John accepted the inevitable—but not yet. He still had plans.

In the meantime, he waited by the window in the parlor of the Coach & Horses Inn, the first lodgings he'd found in whatever the hell town this was. Brandy in hand, he kept watch for Miss Merryweather, who did *not* seem to be on a lucky winning streak. Ladies in agreeable circumstances did not walk along desolate country roads in inclement weather without a chaperone.

As soon as he'd seen her, he'd been curious as to the whys and hows of her situation. She was too pretty and presumably too well born to be out there on her own, carrying her own bag. He'd taken one look in her brown eyes and seen trouble. He suspected she was on the run. He suspected that she was the kind of trouble he never could resist: a woman in need of protection, a woman he could care for, a woman he could give his heart to. The kind of trouble that was the downfall of many men.

John didn't want to push his luck. Not now, not when he was so close to success and painfully aware of the ticking of the clock indicating that time was running out.

His attention was captured once again by Miss Merryweather as she came into view: a drenched spot of girl on the horizon, trudging along with her valise in her arms.

He wanted to dash out into the summer rain, sweep her into his arms, and carry her back to the shelter of the inn. He never could resist a damsel in distress, his mother had always said. Most of the time the damsels didn't complain. Most of the damsels he encountered weren't as stubborn, determined, and captivating as Miss Merryweather.

It was unfortunate she had refused his offer of a ride, though he conceded that it was smart of her to refuse to put herself at the mercy of a strange man with whom she was not acquainted. But still, he would sooner cut off his arm than hurt a woman. And the longing had been so plain in her face. But what was he to do—pick her up, plunk her in the carriage, and abscond with her?

A gentleman honors a lady's wishes, even if they are mad. *They* being either the lady, her wishes, or both.

So he'd reluctantly left her on the side of the road.

John turned to have a word with the innkeeper, a small, older gentleman with a tuft of white hair and a deeply wrinkled face.

"Mr. Rutherford, a lady will be here shortly. Would you prepare a room with a hot bath to be ready upon her arrival?"

John reckoned Miss Merryweather would want both the minute she stepped inside.

"And the expense of a room and bath for a lady who may or may not appear, my lord?"

Oh, she would be here. She was determined, there was no mistaking that.

"I'll take care of it," he said quietly. While he needed to save for what awaited him in London, it was inconceivable that he wouldn't spend a little extra for a girl who was obviously having a rough time of it.

Besides, he'd won big at yesterday's horse race by betting on the filly everyone else had dismissed. Her bloodlines had been questionable, but he'd taken one look in her eyes and seen the toss of her head and laid down a few quid. When she'd crossed the finish line with a trail of weary colts eating her dust, John had taken one look at the darkened, angry expressions of all the gents that had gambled foolishly and lost big. He'd gotten the hell out.

Lord Dudley and Lord Fitz-Herbert, in particular, had looked ready to draw blood. It was a frequent occurrence. The winning. The angry lords. The quick, hasty escapes. Wondering if *this* was the moment his luck ran out.

Soon enough he'd be in London for the gamble of a lifetime. If he succeeded in this mad scheme, he'd be set for life. No more traveling from card game to card game, wondering if each hand dealt to him was the one that marked the end of his winning streak. He'd have enough to bring his mother and sister to town, where they could live in the fine style they deserved.

To that, he drank. The brandy warmed him up on the inside, but even that couldn't chase away his memories of a particular cold, wet night like this one . . . being soaked through to the skin, a chill settling into one's bones, hope getting washed away with the rain.

John turned back to the window. Miss Merryweather was closer now, slogging along the High Street with a furious, yet heartbroken, expression on her face. She crossed the road, which was up to her ankles in mud. She stomped wearily up the steps. The door burst open, letting in a sopping wet moppet of a girl, her rain-soaked valise, and a gust of wind and rain.

Her expression was one of both relief and triumph.

John felt his lips quirking into a smile. She was quite a sight—a wet, bedraggled lady, dropping a valise at her feet with a thud—and she stole his attention as well as that of the tradesman, his wife, and their three small children, who occupied a table in the main parlor. The barmaid, Annie, looked up from wiping down tables. The old drunk kept his face firmly planted on the long oak bar, where it had been since John's arrival earlier today.

The lot of them were curious about this woman traveling alone in adverse conditions.

The innkeeper bustled over.

"Your room and a bath are waiting, miss," Rutherford said.

She quirked her head in disbelief, as if she didn't have this kind of luck. As if she expected the inn to be full, including the stables and the manger, too. And then, as if she felt his presence, she turned and saw him.

You her gaze seemed to say accusatorily.

There was war blazing in her brown eyes. It was a battle between her desire for the comforts of a bath and a private room against her independent nature. Aye, he could already tell she had no wish to be indebted to him. But God, did she want that bath and the room.

"I simply alerted the innkeeper to your imminent arrival," he explained. She nodded and followed the innkeeper up the stairs to her room.

He turned back to the window, sipped his drink, and considered the odds that Miss Merryweather was another prize of his winning streak—or would this mysterious and captivating woman be his downfall?

The moment when a man starts to believe that his good fortune will go on forever is the moment the winning streak comes to an end. This, then, was his moment when everything crashed and burned.

John had donned his suit of evening clothes—a finely tailored coat, a silk waistcoat, a freshly laundered and pressed shirt and cravat, and all the other items befitting a gentleman perfectly turned out for a ball.

He whistled as he drove the carriage through London. That was the part that slayed him—he was whistling on his way to the woman he loved. He was happy.

John had, in spite of all his good luck, still dared to hope that his winning streak wouldn't come to an end just yet.

All he needed was one more night. . . .

That was the last thought he had before his luck ran out and his winning streak crashed and burned.

In the midst of everything falling apart, John looked up to a familiar face smirking. John saw all the moments leading up to this one, all the plans he had unwittingly put in motion. In an instant, it was clear that in saving her he had ruined himself.

They could stop him, maybe. They could try, certainly. But tonight, he was on a mission. He had made a promise to the woman he loved. John kept his promises.

Nothing, nothing *would stop him from making the journey from here to her.*

Chapter 4

Pᴿᴜᴅᴇɴᴄᴇ sᴛᴏᴏᴅ ʙᴇꜰᴏʀᴇ the window in the parlor of the inn, watching the rain fall steadily, as if it were on a mission and nothing, *nothing* would stop it from making the journey from cloud to earth in a direct and efficient fashion. Instead of dwelling on all of her misfortunes, or considering where she might go from here (wherever *here* was—she had no idea), she thought of happier times, a few years earlier, before she knew that bad things happened to good girls and that life didn't go according to plan.

Three of Lady Penelope's students were not in their French lesson, as they ought to have been. It was the sort of glorious day that begged one to be out of doors with the sunshine on one's skin and breathing in the scent of spring in full bloom. Three best friends, having had enough of lessons, skipped out and ensconced themselves at their spot: a lovely, hidden patch of grass near the river that ran through school grounds. Here they lolled in the grass or skipped stones on the water.

"Only one more month until we graduate," Emma said gleefully.

"Only one more month until our debut," Prudence said, feeling nervous but excited all at once. Lady P's was a wonderful school, with friendly students (except for Kate Abbott and her minions) and amiable instructors. But oh, they longed to be grown up and make their debut, for then life would truly begin.

But first—

"I hope my freckles fade before then," Prudence added. She had a smattering of them across the bridge of her nose and cheeks. Everyone knew they were not quite "the thing," and she diligently put lemon juice on them each night.

Emma and Olivia tossed aside their bonnets, but Prue kept hers firmly in place. She had only one more month for the freckles to fade and for her hair to darken from a less coppery shade of red. Along with choosing which gowns to order, these were her most vexing problems.

"I cannot wait. I've had enough of dancing lessons," Olivia declared. "I'm ready to be dancing with a tall, dark, and handsome rake instead of our Monsieur Dumas."

Monsieur Dumas was their dancing instructor. Occasionally, the girls read novels where gently bred ladies ran off with the dance master. If any woman ran off with Monsieur Dumas, Prudence would eat her bonnet . . . and then sit in the sun.

"I'm sure I'd forget the steps," Prudence said. "Even after all our hours of lessons, I bet I'd be too distracted by his smoldering gaze and thoughts of kissing."

It went without saying that a handsome man would waltz with her, holding her closer than was proper, and he would gaze at her smolderingly and she would think of kissing him. This was the stuff of her dreams, and as far as any of them knew, dreams did come true—especially to good girls like them.

"Oh, perhaps he'll be such a strong lead that you won't have to have a thought in your head at all," Emma said confidently.

"How do you know that?" Olivia asked.

"I read it in *Miss Minerva and the Malicious Marquis*," Emma answered, grinning.

"It's safe to assume that did not come from Lady Penelope's library," Prudence replied dryly.

"Of course not," Emma replied. "I gave a downstairs maid half of my pin money for it."

"So it's one of *Those Books*," Prudence said, grinning wickedly.

The school's library contained only those books determined suitable for young ladies. Thus there was a brisk black market of shocking novels and other scandalous texts amongst the students and servants of the school.

"I want to borrow it next," Olivia said, "as long as it's not like that Mad Baron book that got passed around. I couldn't sleep for weeks."

"We know," Prudence muttered. "Because you kept waking us up in the middle of the night seeking reassurance."

The entire population of the school had been riveted—in a ghastly, can't-look-from-the-carriage-accident sort of way—by a newly published broadside entitled *The Mad Baron: The Gruesome Story of an Innocent Maiden's Tragic Love And Untimely Death. A True Story.* It was about a lord who had murdered his wife.

"What if one of us has to marry the Mad Baron?" Olivia asked in a hushed, horrified whisper that made the hair on Prue's neck stand up. This was the greatest collective fear of Lady Penelope's class of 1820.

"Don't be absurd," Emma answered. "He never comes to town, and by the time he ever does, I'm sure we'll all be happily married to dashing rogues and charming reformed rakes."

"Which one of us will marry first, do you think?" Prudence asked. It went without saying they would all marry. As young ladies of the haute ton, they had one task in life: marry and marry well. It was unthinkable that they wouldn't.

"I think Olivia will marry first," Emma said.

"I think that is quite likely," Prue agreed. Olivia had beautiful blond hair and a pale complexion that begged for comparison with angels. She was the perfect lady, too, moving with grace and possessing perfect manners and a sweet disposition.

"Prue, I think you'll be next," Olivia said. "Some man will be enchanted by your dark eyes and your sly wit, especially compared to vapid creatures like Miss Dudley."

Miss Dudley, a year younger, couldn't hold a thought in her head for more than a minute—everything that crossed her mind was verbally expressed, whether it was her need to visit the necessary or her opinion of someone's "tragically unfortunate gown." Had she had interesting thoughts, it might have been forgivable.

Prue didn't say vapid things. She was too smart for that. Her governess, Miss Georgette, had said so before she'd retired to Stanbrook Abbey when Prue had gone off to school.

"The trick for you, Emma, will be finding someone who compares with all the heroes in your books," Olivia said.

"I'm sure he's out there," Emma replied dreamily. "I hope I find him soon."

"But not too soon," Olivia cautioned. "Remember our plan."

"The first season is for flirting," Prudence repeated. They all agreed they should have time to enjoy themselves, flirting and dancing with an assortment of gentlemen. It wouldn't do to go straight from the schoolroom to being wed.

"The second season is for settling down," Olivia finished. "After we've had some fun."

"One more month . . . ," Prudence said in a hushed and excited whisper.

The three girls smiled broadly, giddy for what awaited them once they arrived in London, made their debuts, and life truly began.

PRUDENCE OFTEN THOUGHT back to that day, pinpointing it as the moment when her entire life stretched ahead of her like a bright, warm ray of sunshine. With her best friends by her side, they would take London by storm. No more dull lessons on French, geography, or dancing. Their lives would be a whirlwind of balls, afternoon calls with their suitors, and shopping expeditions to Bond Street. They would all fall in love and live happily ever after.

Prudence had not expected to be married within her first season, but definitely by the end of her second. She had expected all sorts of things.

However, she had never expected this: finding herself stranded on her own in a small country inn. As a family dined noisily, she stood before the window in the parlor, watching the rain and wondering what had become of Cecil. Or her maid. Or the highwayman.

Prue was jolted from her thoughts by the arrival of Lord Castleton, whom she had not seen since her arrival yesterday. He stood beside her, looking out the window as well. He didn't have to utter a word for her to be agonizingly aware of him. Her nerves tensed, on high alert. There was a man. She was on her own, vulnerable. Discreetly she glanced about the room, searching for a way out. Having just survived a highway robbery and worse long ago, she wasn't about to break her habit of always noting a path of escape.

But really, where could she go? Out into the rain, on her own? Prue took a deep breath. There was no running today; she would have to face her fears.

She was just grateful that family was nearby, distracted as they were with their own business.

Prudence's gaze traitorously settled on Castleton. He was tall, lean, perhaps even lanky, but strong. He dressed informally, with just a waistcoat and the sleeves of his white linen shirt rolled up to the elbows, revealing bare forearms corded with muscle. She stared at his arms during a long moment in which her heart beat hard with a warning.

For once she tried to drown it out and imagine a man's arms around her affectionately.

But then her heart seized and her breath hitched in her throat. Beside her, Castleton loomed large. She didn't know him. She did know there were bad men in the world.

"Quite a rainy day," he remarked, now clasping his hands behind his back, standing at ease.

"Indeed," Prudence said. She didn't want to encourage conversation, but she also didn't want to be rude and make him angry.

"How is your room?" Castleton asked, still looking out the window.

"Dry," she quipped. She dared a sideways glance and saw him smiling.

"That's something, isn't it?"

"Thank you for alerting the innkeeper to my arrival," she said, and not just to be polite. Prudence was grateful for the consideration, even if it made her wary about what he might expect of her in return.

"Would you care to join me for luncheon, Miss Merryweather?" Before she could refuse, he carried on. "It seems absurd for both of us to dine alone in silence. Mr. and Mrs. Hammersmith are quite busy with their brood." She peered over her shoulder. A tradesman and his wife were obviously frustrated as they tried to dine with their six children. "And Buckley isn't talking."

She supposed Buckley was the one slumped on a rough-hewn stool, resting his head on the long wooden bar. Still.

Prudence opened her mouth to decline. She wasn't thinking about lunch with Lord Castleton; it was hard to think of anything, given the tremors of fear that rocketed through her at the prospect of being alone with a man. She hated that her instinct was to bolt when her heart maybe, might, perhaps wish to stay. She hated why she felt this way.

Over the years, Prudence had made an art of deflecting a gentleman's gaze and ensuring one never asked her for a waltz or a turn about the ballroom. She had let her slender figure grow round. Her gaze never connected with a man's. At balls, she found her fellow wallflowers and rooted herself in their corner.

BUT HERE WAS a man—a handsome one, with friendly blue-sky eyes and the sort of easy smile that suggested he did so often—and he was asking her to dine. Prudence had no good reason to refuse.

THOUGH IT WAS only midday, the overcast skies outside meant candles were necessary indoors. Rutherford was bustling about, lighting white tapers and stoking the fire in the grate. There was something electric in the air, enhanced by the moodiness of the weather and the strange circumstance by which Castleton found himself with this woman who raised more questions than she answered.

He pulled out the chair for her at the table for two the innkeeper had already set. There was no mistaking the suspicion in her large brown eyes as she took note of the cutlery and glasses already laid out. Waiting.

"Of course I had planned to invite you to dine with me," Castleton explained.

"And you presumed I would agree," she said, cheeks reddening with indignation.

"I did not anticipate much competition," he said with an easy smile meant to diffuse her nerves or temper or whatever had her bristling at the prospect of a gentleman arranging for lunch with a lady when they had no other company.

"There's Buckley," she said quite seriously, save for a spark in her velvety brown eyes. Her teasing took him by surprise.

"It'd be a sad day for me if I lost you to the likes of him," John quipped.

"Would that wound your ego?" Miss Merryweather asked.

"Tremendously."

"I know your kind," she said, with the faintest upturn of her lips.

"What, pray tell, is that?" His voice remained light, even though this line of conversation could be dangerous to him.

"The kind that expects women to fall at your feet and the whole world to fall in line and do your bidding."

She was so far off the mark that there was nothing to do but laugh and take a sip of wine. He offered her a glass, which she refused. What a pity; the girl was so tense, from her rigid spine to her slightly scrunched shoulders. Was it something about him in particular?

Some girls were just nervous about men. They were raised to be wary, to never speak with a gentleman with whom they had not been properly introduced. It was to be expected she would be nervous, especially when she was traveling without a protector. Judging by her dress, her accent, and her manners, she was not the sort of woman who should have been out roaming the countryside unaccompanied. In fact, girls like her did no such thing unless driven to desperate measures.

But then again, maybe the upper-class accent and refined manners were faked, and the fine gown was a castoff from her mistress. It had been known to happen.

Rutherford entered then, bearing a tray loaded with food—lamb stew, peas, roasted carrots slathered in butter, and thick crusty wheat bread. He served them. They began to eat.

"What brings you to Westbury?" John didn't know the town's name, but odds were that it wasn't Westbury, which he'd just made up.

After a moment's hesitation she told him, "I'm on my way to London."

John was more interested in the fact that she didn't correct him, which suggested that she didn't know the name of the town either. What was she doing alone in a town that she didn't know the name of? His sipped his wine and gazed at her curiously. Things did not add up with Miss Merryweather.

"I am also traveling to London," he told her. That he did not make up.

Great things awaited him in London. Everything he'd ever dreamt of was in London. Come hell or high water, he was going to London, and he was going to get there by Sunday, even if he had to swim, which seemed like an actual possibility given this relentless rain.

"Imagine that," she replied, treating him to another slight smile. It was quite ridiculous what those slight smiles of hers did to him. But like many a man before him, a pretty girl was his undoing.

"All roads lead to London," he quipped. "I'm curious. What awaits you there?"

As John watched her thinking of what to say, he had the distinct impression that she was hiding something. Of course that only made him more curious.

Prudence didn't answer with any of the immediate things that sprang to mind: *Mortification. Failure. Complete ruination if word of this encounter ever gets out. Nothing.*

Instead she replied, "My friends. And my family." Her friends were few and family fewer, but that didn't need to be said. She had Emma, Olivia, and Lady Dare, and they meant the world to her. For a second she felt a flash of guilt, since they were all ignorant of her whereabouts and she had deliberately misrepresented her travel plans. And then, eager to change the subject, she asked, "Why are you going to London?"

"It's a mad scheme, really," he confessed, grinning slightly, revealing his dimple and a spark of excitement in his blue eyes.

"Now I'm intrigued," she said, not untruthfully.

"Two gentlemen are working on a machine that will change everything," Castleton told her, leaning forward, his voice hushed. Prudence stilled.

"They're calling it the Difference Engine, and it will perform advanced mathematical equations correctly *every time*. This will change everything."

Prudence declined to mention that she was well aware of the Difference Engine and that she was acquainted with both inventors, the Duke of Ashbrooke and Baron Radcliffe.

She murmured, "How intriguing" rather than explain her connection. Prudence wasn't sure of this Lord Castleton yet, so she sipped her water rather than give this strange man too much information about herself. But she did tuck it away for possible use later. She asked, "Are you acquainted with them already?"

"Not yet," Castleton replied, after a sip of his wine. "They'll be at the Great Exhibition with the machine. I intend to get an introduction then."

One didn't just *get* an introduction to dukes, which everyone who was anyone knew. But then again, Ashbrooke was a friendly man who didn't stand on ceremony, especially when it came to talking about the beloved engine he had invented.

"What will you do once you have been introduced?" Prudence asked.

"The world will need more than one of these machines," John said. His voice was an excited whisper now, as if someone might overhear and steal his idea. She doubted the Hammersmith family or Buckley or Annie cared, but there was something in his enthusiasm that made her heart start beating a bit faster.

How lovely to be so certain of one's future ambitions. She envied him that. Castleton continued, "And I intend to build them. Or rather, my factory will build them."

"You have a factory?" Prudence inquired, a bit perplexed by this, for most peers concentrated their efforts on agriculture rather than the bustle of city commerce.

"Not yet," he admitted, leaving her to wonder how one just *got* a factory. Probably the same way one *just got* an introduction to one of the highest-ranking men in the country.

"I thought lords didn't dabble in trade," Prudence remarked. She eyed him carefully and compared him to the lords she knew. It was one thing for a peer to dabble with inventions, quite another to manufacture. But so much of Castleton said *peer of the realm*, from his accent to his manners and lordly way he had declared "I am Castleton" when they'd met on the road.

"This one will," John said confidently, though he had only a vague idea how to accomplish it. But he had this winning streak, which had already brought him more money and opportunities than he'd ever dreamt possible while back at Castlemore Court.

"I suppose ladies don't go traipsing around the countryside alone either," she mused. He grinned and laughed, because generally ladies did no such thing.

"I confess I'm intrigued, Miss Merryweather," he asked, resting his arms on the table and leaning forward. "Why were you trudging along that road, miserable and alone? Are you in trouble?"

"The mail coach I was traveling in had an unfortunate encounter with a highwayman," she told him. Her voice was light, as if she merely mentioned a broken axle or the horse throwing a shoe. However, she couldn't quite meet his eye.

"Are you all right?" His voice was rough with worry. "Did he hurt you?" His voice had deepened to a growl.

Highwaymen. Night. Young women. It was not a good combination. In fact, it was often deadly. Or worse.

He knew about worse. And even though he barely knew her, John was taken by an overwhelming desire to protect her, defend her, to bring to justice anyone who laid a hand on her. And by justice, he meant the sort of beating that left a man barely clinging to life.

He never could resist a damsel in distress. He always had to charge in and save the day. Under the table he flexed his fist, remembering the times he'd done it before.

Miss Merryweather blinked at him a few times. She seemed taken aback by the passion in his voice. He supposed he shocked her. Hell, he shocked himself by the surge of emotion he felt for a woman he barely knew. But, God, the thought of a woman hurt like that—it always made the bile rise in his throat. He'd seen it too many times.

"I'm fine," she said. John rolled his eyes. Women

were always "fine" even when they were a sobbing, incoherent mess, sprawled upon the furniture.

"But did he hurt you?"

"I'm fine. I escaped," she said evenly. She held his gaze for a moment: *drop the subject.* Then she looked away.

"You must have walked through the forest all night," he said as it occurred to him.

Prudence laughed. "What was the alternative, wait around for someone to rescue me?"

"A lot of women would have done just that," he said. "Sat right down on the roadside and cried. And waited. Someone would have come along eventually, thus sparing them the bother of walking for miles under a hot sun."

"Well, I know better," Miss Merryweather told him. "Prince Charming never comes. God doesn't answer. A girl is on her own."

"That is the saddest thing I've ever heard," John said softly. "You are too young to be so jaded."

"Would you like to borrow my handkerchief?" she asked. "Shall I excuse you whilst you have a bit of a cry?"

It was Castleton's turn to blink in surprise. There wasn't any malice in her voice, just the sort of impatience reserved for those in the throes of excessive emotion over trivial things. This girl was strong. This girl was something else.

And she didn't even seem to know it.

"I like you, Miss Merryweather."

"You don't even know me," she said with a girl-ish sigh.

"If this weather keeps up, we'll know each other very well," John said with a glance at the window.

"Whatever do you mean by that?" Her alarm was swift and obvious. He hastened to let her know he didn't mean it *that way*.

Not that he would turn down a kiss or more if she wanted it. Miss Merryweather had a lovely mouth. Her lips were plump and pink and smil-ing far too infrequently. Made him want to kiss her, cause her to laugh. She was so tense, her spine so rigid. Made him think about how a caress of his hands could send the tension fleeing. He imag-ined the feel of her softening under his touch.

From the moments he'd first seen her on the road, hips swaying, her figure had had him con-stantly at war with himself. *Look at those curves. Do not look. Just a glance. I can't look away.*

And then she just slayed him with her sharp wit and dry humor. He never did understand the appeal of simpering misses.

Of course he wanted her. But he could tell she didn't want him, and that was enough to keep his blood cool and flowing to his brain and not else-where.

"I don't expect to have many conversations with Buckley or that harried family," he explained. Buckley was still face down on the bar, and Mrs. Hammersmith was admonishing her brood to finish up already, for Lord's sake. "I doubt the innkeeper has time to sit back and chat over a brandy. That leaves you, Miss Merryweather, for all my conversational needs."

She was about to utter some scathing retort. He could tell by the flash in her eyes and the sudden part of her lips.

"That is," he added quickly, "if you are amenable."

Now what did she have to say about that? He waited, holding his breath, thinking how dangerous it was that he should care so much about her reply.

Chapter 5

The following morning
Six days before Lady Penelope's Ball

PRUE WOKE UP to the sound of raindrops drumming on the roof. She lay in bed, allowing her eyes to adjust to the soft gray morning light, remembering that she wasn't in London or Bath or any fashionable place for young ladies. She was alone, in God only knew where. With Lord Castleton.

She wasn't sure of him at all—like all London lords, he scared her. Yet he wasn't like the typical dissipated rake, and that intrigued her. She envied his ambition. And, dear God, she wanted to gaze into his blue eyes forever.

She wanted to gently smooth his unruly brown hair, feel the soft strands with her fingers. But that would never happen.

When he smiled at her, she wanted to revel in all the fireworks she felt. She wanted to have all the feelings a young woman did when a charming man bestowed kindness and attention on her.

Those feelings had been dead to her for some time now.

After waking, she quickly donned her dry dress, made of soft violet-colored muslin and edged in black ribbon. Emma and Olivia had insisted that the colors suited Prue's coloring. After pulling a brush through her auburn hair and tying it in a bun, she dared a glance in the mirror. She still looked so young, so wide-eyed.

She still had those cursed freckles, though the sunburn on the bridge of her nose and cheeks disguised them somewhat. If she was pretty or a beauty, she didn't know or care.

She descended the stairs, planning to dash through the corridor and into the main room. Hopefully she was early enough so that no one else was awake. By *no one else*, she meant Castleton.

Until she fortified herself with a pot of tea and toast, she feared she didn't have the nerves to battle her feelings for a handsome man who would seek her out for his "conversational needs."

She wanted to delight in his company. But she couldn't. What if he understood it as an invitation for more?

She wanted to feel the warmth of his smile, but she couldn't. What if she developed feelings for him—ones she couldn't fathom indulging?

She wanted to entertain thoughts of a kiss with anticipation and excited pleasure, but that would never happen.

Of course she ran right into him, given her luck lately. Her momentum on the stairs made it impossible for her to stop when he came around the corner suddenly.

"Oh!" The exclamation was wrenched from her lips.

She hit something hard. And wet. And warm. It was his chest, and he'd been out in the rain, yet she could feel the heat of his skin radiating through the wet shirt plastered against his chest.

Heat surged within her. It was a kind of heat she'd never experienced; it warmed her from the core. Then her nerves sparked, on high alert. The panic hit her swiftly, knocking her breathless. She hadn't felt a man's chest since—

Castleton's arms enclosed her. Logically, she knew he only acted on instinct. Logically, she knew this embrace was merely to prevent her from tumbling backward and possibly to the floor. She *knew* these things. But still her body stiffened and the warning bells in her head clanged loudly, drowning out the voices of logic and reason. They were alone, she was unguarded, and his hands were on her.

"No," she gasped. Air. She couldn't get air into her lungs. Her voice sounded strange and far-away. "No."

"It's all right, I got you," he said, holding her at arm's length now, away from his soaking shirt. But this reminded her too much of another man's hands gripping her. Prue's heart beat too hard and too quickly. *Danger.* The perimeters of her vision went black. She could only see his face—a man's face peering down at her. Like before. She had to get away. She had to *get away.*

"Let me go," she cried, twisting awkwardly in an attempt to get out of his grasp. His hands felt like iron bands holding her captive. "Please, let me go."

Castleton let her go instantly.

She stood away from him, gasping as she tried to catch her breath and will her heartbeat to return to normal. The whole exchange had lasted no more than ten or twenty seconds, but every one of them had felt like a lifetime. Each second had felt like *before*.

Eventually, she dragged her gaze up to Castleton's, afraid of the derision she would see there. *Silly female. Ridiculous, overreacting female.*

But she rather thought he looked concerned. In fact, she rather thought he was peering at her too intently, as if trying to unearth the reason why she had panicked from an accidental collision. It was almost as if he knew the truth.

Prudence felt the shame anew.

"Are you all right, Miss Merryweather?"

It took her a moment to remember that *she* was Miss Merryweather.

Her brain began to register where she was—rushing through the hallway of the Coach & Horses Inn on her way to breakfast. She was not in Lord and Lady Blackburn's corridor. The Beast was miles from here. The highwayman had presumably gotten his spoils and ridden off—along with her former fiancé.

"I'm fine," she said, anxiously smoothing her skirts.

"Women. Always saying they're fine when they're not." Though he kept his remarks light, there was an undercurrent of seriousness in his tone. He didn't believe her. "Care to tell me what just happened?"

Her heart kind of stopped, because he had noticed that she'd reacted strongly to what had essentially been nothing. No one ever really noticed how she rushed through corridors, avoided a gentleman's touch, or bristled at contact. No one except this blue-eyed stranger.

Castleton leaned against the wall, as if he didn't mind waiting around all day in soaking wet clothes just to hear her talk.

It wasn't really nothing, though, was it? Prudence was still painfully aware that she was alone in a corridor with a man whom she barely knew and who could overpower her in an instant. He was a handsome man that any other woman would have flirted with, especially without a chaperone looking on disapprovingly. But not her, oh no. She couldn't just be normal. She couldn't just have faith or believe in people's innate goodness. She had to be afraid all the bloody time, unless she was with Lady Dare or her friends. The bitterness that rose up in her throat caused her to bite her lip and look away.

It wasn't fair. That awful thing that had happened to her and all the quiet little devastations since . . . it wasn't fair. Not for the first time did she wish that once, just once, she didn't have to live so enveloped in fear. Not for the first time did she wrack her brain, wondering what she'd done to deserve this.

There was no going back, but she couldn't move forward either.

"Miss Merryweather?" Castleton stepped toward her.

"Excuse me," she whispered. Then she fled.

In the parlor

"He's a handsome one, isn't he?" Annie asked with a sassy grin, as she poured a desperately need cup of tea for Prudence, who wrapped her hands around the mug, savoring the slightly uncomfortable heat because it distracted her from other feelings.

"I see you had a little encounter with him," Annie ventured with a glance at Prue's bodice.

"Whatever do you mean?" Prue's instinct to keep such things private and make sure *no one knew* kicked in.

"Your dress is wet," Annie said with a pointed look at Prue's gown. "And he just returned soaking wet from checking on the horses in the stables. You could see right through his shirt, if you haven't noticed. And let me tell you—I noticed. But then I reckon you'd have to be dead not to notice."

Prudence had noticed.

In her mind's eye she recalled the sharply defined muscles and smattering of dark hair she'd seen beneath his shirt and matched them up with the firm feeling of his chest. Even though she'd only felt it for a second, it had been a potent, memorable second.

The Beast's chest had been soft, any definition of his muscles lost beneath the evidence of his debauched existence. She shifted her thoughts to Castleton's chest instead. Then she forced herself to think of something else.

"It's awfully upstanding of him to go out and tend to the horses," Annie carried on, now setting down a plate with thick slices of toast and a dish of cold salted butter. "Most lordly types would make Rutherford do it, as if he didn't have enough to do running the inn."

So Castleton was nice. Many men were nice. Her friend's husbands were kind men. That was another thing that she knew logically. But that knowledge didn't keep her from spiraling into a panic every time she found herself alone with a man.

Honestly, what had she been thinking, trying to elope with Cecil? They had never been alone, for they'd always been in the company of other ball guests or fellow travelers. At his estate, she was counting on the company of maids and the amiable and aged aunt he had mentioned. As for their marriage . . . she'd never thought about that. She'd just assumed he'd be off with Lord Fairbanks.

But if this morning's encounter had shown her anything, it was that she had no business marrying anyone. No, she needed to be alone or in the company of women she trusted. The sooner she returned to London, Lady Dare, and looming spinsterhood, the better.

It was just that . . .

No.

She no longer indulged in daydreams and fairy-tale thoughts.

Prudence sipped her tea and nibbled at toast positively slathered with butter. She knew that added a bit of padding to her petite frame. Once upon a time, she'd been a slender, willowy creature such as men preferred. But the curves she'd added to her figure kept men at bay.

Which was just how she liked it.

Wasn't it?

Chapter 6

MISS MERRYWEATHER REMAINED in her room all day long, leaving Castleton to wonder what the hell had happened on the stairs this morning as he spent a good portion of his day polishing his boots until he could see his face reflected in the leather. All the while, he thought about the girl.

The sheer terror in her eyes nearly made him fall to his knees. Again, he felt an overwhelming urge to soothe and console her, even though he hardly knew her. Castleton had seen that look in a woman's eyes before. Made him suspect that someone had hurt her. His throat constricted just thinking about it.

By evening he was going mad thinking about her, listening to the Hammersmith children play loudly in the parlor, and worrying that he wouldn't make it to London in time because of this cursed, relentless rain. The High Street was a veritable swamp.

He needed a distraction, and he reckoned Miss Merryweather did, too.

So he knocked on her door with one hand whilst easily balancing a tray of food in the other.

He heard a small voice from the other side of the door ask, "Who is it?"

John paused a moment before answering. "Castleton."

She unlocked the door and cracked it open.

"I have brought supper," he said.

"Thank you. That's very kind."

"For both of us," he added. Her eyes widened.

"And you brought it *here*? We cannot eat it in here. Together. Alone."

This he knew. He also knew that if he had simply asked for her company, she would have refused. He suspected she needed to come out of her bedchamber before she went mad. Thus, his scheme to secure her company for supper over a table in the parlor.

"I love to hear you say 'we,'" he said, grinning. She looked at him as if he were daft. "Come join me for supper downstairs, Miss Merryweather. I need someone to talk to about the weather."

There was nothing to say about the weather. It was still raining.

She cracked a smile.

It did things to him, that smile. It was just an upturn of her lips, nothing more. That's what he told himself, but he felt triumphant. She needed to smile more. He vowed to see to it.

"Dinner is getting cold," he said.

"I'll be right down," she told him.

She kept her word, appearing a few moments later in the parlor. She was tense again and glancing nervously around the room. Buckley had apparently woken at some point, resumed drinking, and was now sprawled on a bench, unconscious, snoring loudly. Annie mopped the tabletops.

"Would you care for some wine?"

"No, thank you."

"Just a sip?"

"My friend Olivia's mother says it makes a lady forget herself," she said.

"Is that such a bad thing?" Sometimes he wanted to forget himself. Wine helped. Whiskey reliably got the job done, too.

"Yes, it is a bad thing. At least for ladies," Miss Merryweather informed him. Then she pointedly took a sip of water.

"And what does wine do to gentlemen?"

"It makes them more foolish at a higher volume," she answered primly.

He laughed. "Spot on."

"Sometimes it makes them beasts," she added. There was something in the darkness of her voice that brought an end to his smile and laughter. He pushed his wineglass to the side.

"How was your day, darling?" he asked, changing the subject.

"Uneventful," she said, her lips quirking up into a faint smile. "And how was your day?"

"Wet." He explained about taking care of the animals in the stables because someone had to and he was desperate to get out of the inn. He mentioned his two white horses, named Snow and White.

"How imaginative of you," Miss Merryweather said dryly. "Why did you name them that?"

"I didn't. I won them in a game of cards," John told her. He'd managed an invitation to a bachelors-only house party at Lord Collins's country seat, where they'd drunk excessively, dined exquisitely, and, when they hadn't been winning and losing fortunes over cards, availing themselves of the prostitutes who'd been invited. Well, the others had. John had kept his drinking to a minimum and his eyes on his cards. That's why he'd left that party three hundred pounds richer and with two prize-winning stallions.

"A gambler, are you?" Miss Merryweather asked with the disapproving look of a temperance-minded matron, which oddly made him grin.

"You could say that," he answered. The extent of his gambling was possibly unparalleled. This was also not something he was prepared to let be known.

"You're one of those," she said. "I should have known."

"What do you mean?"

"There are the lords that tend to their estates," she explained. "And then the ones that gamble them away."

And then there were the ones, like him, that— John didn't even finish that thought on the off chance that Miss Merryweather possessed mind-reading capabilities. He didn't fit into her either/or view of lords, but he wasn't about to enlighten her.

So he just grinned and asked, "Can't a rogue have it all?"

"Where is your estate?"

"Yorkshire," he said automatically. "Castlemore Court."

"What's it like?" she asked.

"A stately redbrick home with large windows that make the interior rooms seem airy and light," John answered, seeing his old home in his mind's eye like he'd only been there yesterday. "The grounds are lovely, with extensive gardens. It's everything you would expect of a viscount's country home."

"That sounds lovely. I have always lived in London."

"I'm looking forward to London. If this damned rain ever stops," he said. "Care to wager how long until the sun comes out?"

They both laughed. She had such a lovely, lilting laugh.

"When the thunder started, I thought it would be just a quick summer storm," she said. "Knowing my luck, it'll carry on for days, possibly weeks, bringing great floods and extensive devastation."

"If that's your luck, it's a good thing you met me, Miss Merryweather."

"And why is that?" She tilted her head, curiously. It was adorable.

"I'm on a winning streak," he said, gazing into her eyes. They were a velvety, dark brown, fringed with dark, spiky lashes. There was so much emotion in her eyes, more than he could begin to comprehend. He could get lost in her eyes. "Perhaps my good luck will rub off on you."

She smiled ruefully and said, "Or I might end your winning streak. My apologies in advance."

AFTER SUPPER THEY retired to chairs before the fire. Castleton's conversational needs were apparently satisfied for the evening; he was absorbed by a thick book. She was curious about it but did not wish to disturb him.

Not wanting to be alone, Prudence took the chair beside Castleton and stared into the fire, basking in its warmth. So much had happened in just a few days, and her heart and mind had hardly settled from it all. There were so many questions that she frustratingly could not obtain answers to. What had happened to her maid? What about Cecil and the others in the mail coach? Had that highwayman been apprehended, or did he roam free in the countryside?

Her gaze fell on Castleton's boots. Shiny. She dared a sideways glance at him. Anything was possible, she supposed, including Castleton's being the highwayman. But something didn't quite add up to her, for Castleton had been nothing but kind and solicitous to her, which seemed at odds with the sort of man that robbed carriages in the dead of the night.

This was the sort of ridiculous notion that Emma would entertain, spurred on by her sentimental novels.

Instead, Prudence resumed fretting about her maid, and her fellow travelers, and Cecil, and if Cecil even deserved her worry. They had to be fine.

Just as she was *fine*.

She was a young lady alone in the world with no prospects for her future. There was a small part of Prudence that was quite content for it to never stop raining so she might stay here in this inn so she didn't have to return to London and face her failures on the marriage mart.

She could remain here. With Castleton.

Prudence glanced over at him again. He was still reading his book. There was something nice about a man who was absorbed by a good book. There was something pleasant about simply sitting quietly beside each other in a comfortable silence, as if they were an old married couple.

Is this what it felt like?

Prudence dared another glance his way.

No, if they were an old married couple she surely wouldn't feel these butterflies in her belly. She wouldn't be terrified and yet curious about kissing him. She wouldn't have memories of that bad thing smothering any lovely, sparkling feeling she might have when he looked at her and smiled.

The rain would stop eventually. At that time, she would have to do something—either beg Rutherford to take her on as an indefinite lodger with no hope of paying her bill or return to London.

Her gaze drifted away from the crackling fire

toward the bin of logs, kindling, and old sheets of newspaper. One sheet stuck above the rim, the masthead unmistakable: *The London Weekly.*

Suddenly Prudence felt a pang of homesickness. She missed the town house she shared with her aunt, Lady Dare, a fabulous woman in lovely gowns, strong perfume, exquisite jewelry, witty and amusing friends. Prudence missed her quiet bedroom overlooking the garden and being guarded by a bevy of reliable servants. Above all, she missed Emma and Olivia. With her friends, Prudence always felt some measure of happiness and peace, and was able, for hours at a time, to forget about The Beast.

That is, until her friends had fallen in love and married and now only wanted to do ridiculous things like complain about their handsome, attentive, besotted husbands. *Didn't they know?*

They didn't know. Prudence had never told them. What if they didn't believe her? What if they told someone? What if they looked at her with pity in their eyes? It would be unbearable. Which is why she'd never said a word.

With a sigh, Prudence picked up the old issue of *The London Weekly*, hoping for a distraction from her thoughts and news of her friends and acquaintances back home.

"Are you really going to read that rubbish?" Castleton asked, surprising her with how quickly he'd noticed her actions. She thought he'd been absorbed in his book.

"I haven't anything else to read."

"This book is excellent. You can have a turn with it."

"Oh, I couldn't possibly take it from you. Besides, I wish to catch up on town gossip. Perhaps there is news of my friends."

Castleton stared at her for a moment. Had she said something wrong? Then he nodded. She decided to ignore the odd moment and returned to the newssheet.

She skipped over the front page of parliamentary reports. As was her habit, she skimmed over the wedding column, "Miss Harlow's Marriage In High Life." It was too painful to read about everyone else's weddings, so she blocked it out as much as possible. Skipping ahead, she finally found what she sought:

"Fashionable Intelligence By A Lady of Distinction"

This is one of the duller seasons in memory (as I seem to write every season), however it is livened up by the arrival of the Mad Baron and his disastrous courtship of Lady Olivia, London's Least Likely to Cause a Scandal—who defied expectations by doing exactly that. Now married, they seem to be setting aside their former rivalry. By all accounts, they appeared most entranced with each other at the opera, and a lady's glove was even carelessly left behind in their box. This author dare not compose any more.

This newspaper wasn't too old, then. Three weeks, perhaps, or a month? After Emma and Olivia had found love and become utterly, revoltingly besotted with their perfect husbands, Prudence had become convinced she ought to join Lady Dare in Bath. Besides, she had no prospects in London.

And really, it would hurt too much to watch her friends move on without her.

She was happy for them. Truly. Honestly.

But she was also lonely. And she had counted on them to be lonely with her.

Prudence kept reading.

This author has learned that Mr. Benedict Chase has distinguished himself in the cavalry. And upon leave, he did not visit his wife, Lady Katherine, who is rumored to be pursuing an affair with the notorious rake Lord Gerard.

Wasn't that just delicious? Emma had almost married Benedict and . . . well, it was a long story. Lady Katherine had plagued the lot of them from their days at Lady Penelope's. Some say that she had married Benedict out of spite and desperation.

Prudence noted that she was at least married.

There is a dearth of dancing partners for the young ladies in London. It seems all the gents have fled London for the town of Pangbourne, where the boxing match of the century is taking place. Expect fortunes to be won—and lost.

Like most young ladies, Prudence had little to no interest in boxing matches. She kept reading.

Dear readers, I have saved the best for last. For the first time in an age, tongues are wagging about Lord Castleton. After his extended tour on the Continent and lands unknown, the handsome viscount—

The handsome viscount what?!

Prudence turned to the next page to learn more about the man beside her. She was confronted by a page with theater reviews, a "Dear Annabelle" advice column, and advertisements. The page containing the rest had vanished. Oh lud, she had the worst luck ever!

"What is the matter?" Castleton asked. "Why are you wrestling with the newspaper?"

Prudence looked at the fire. Glared at it, really. It had probably devoured the page she wished to read.

"I am not wrestling with it," she explained. "I am simply vexed because the page I seek is missing."

Castleton's expression darkened. "Oh? And which page is that?"

"The page that mentions *you*," she said pointedly, then held her breath awaiting his reaction. It was anticlimactic; he muttered something about gossip columns being rubbish and returned to his book.

"It says you are a handsome viscount. Do you think that is rubbish?" Prudence asked pertly. He frowned. Then reluctantly grinned. "I thought so," she replied smugly.

"What else does it say?"

Prudence read the Lady of Distinction's report to him.

"Where did you go on your tour?" she asked.

"The usual spots," he said with a shrug. "Paris, Italy . . ."

"I wish I had traveled more," she said with a sigh.

"Why didn't you?"

"It's not done for ladies to travel on their own," Prudence answered. "And my aunt doesn't care to travel very far."

"No wine, no travel to the Continent . . . poor deprived girl," Castleton remarked. Prudence pursed her lips. He had *no idea* how limited the options were for a young lady clinging desperately to her reputation, with nearly all hopes of matrimony vanished. A lack of wine and travel abroad was the least of it.

"What else does it say?" he asked.

"That is all. The next page is missing," Prudence said forlornly.

"Pity, that," Castleton said, then he returned to his book. She considered asking him more questions, but he seemed riveted by the volume in his hands and uninterested in further conversation on "rubbish gossip rags" with her. Besides, there was no point in becoming better acquainted with him. Nothing could come of it.

But what if something could happen? Honestly, she was going mad from staying indoors for so long. This endless rain was turning her wits and good sense to mush. Because it was absurd that something should happen between her and Lord Castleton.

Prudence took another sly glance at him. Then he caught her eye. Her heart thudded in her chest. Was it really so absurd? Or was something already developing between them?

She was aware that the hour was growing late, darkness had long since fallen, and she was alone with a gentleman. Her instinct was to flee. For once she considered staying.

Not for a moment did John consider staying. John was surprised to find himself here—he had expected Newgate. Make no mistake, the situation was grave. He had made a promise to the woman he loved.

Staying—voluntarily or otherwise—was not an option.

It was soon apparent that the jig was up, the party had concluded, the lucky streak was absolutely over. Unless . . .

Did he have one last trick up his sleeve?

He had to do something—SOMETHING. His plans were spectacularly, unsalvageably ruined. But what to do . . . he didn't know. He couldn't think now, with an angry peer of the realm giving him the haughty stare of disappointment and death. He didn't know what was worse. He didn't even care.

The clock was ticking and there was somewhere he had to be. At some point in their mad adventures, Prudence had become the most important thing in his life. He had to get to her now. She would be waiting, having a massive crisis of faith. He would not be the one to ruin that. He couldn't have her wondering what had become of him, the man to whom she'd opened her heart and who had then disappeared when he had promised to be there, holding her hand.

His attention shifted back to the demanding man before him.

John was forced to consider what would be worse: if she always wondered what had become of him, or if she knew the truth?

Chapter 7

Aɴᴏᴛʜᴇʀ ᴅᴀʏ ᴏꜰ rainfall. Another day spent fretting about Cecil and the rest of her passengers in the mail coach, wondering whatever became of the highwayman and trying to consider what she would do with her life once the rain inevitably stopped. Return to London—or roam the countryside indefinitely?

And if she did return, however would she explain her extended absence? These matters plagued her, and she had no good answer. It was almost a relief that the rain continued, providing more time to develop a plan.

She and Castleton dined together again. Afterward, in the corner of the parlor, the Hammersmith parents were having a devil of a time keeping their children from running laps around the room while hollering at top volume. To appease them, Annie blew the dust off the piano keys and began to play a lively tune.

The children started to dance. The elder ones seemed to know the steps; the younger ones just flailed about wildly, vaguely moving to the music.

Prudence found it to be adorable. She couldn't look away, though it pained her to remember what she would never have. A husband who, like Mr. Hammersmith, would bow before her, kiss her outstretched hand, and embrace her for a dance in a little country inn. A family of her own, like the Hammersmith boys and girls, who merrily danced in circles around their parents.

"Would you do me the honor of this dance, Miss Merryweather?" Castleton's voice was low, hinting at something more than mere friendship. She felt a tremor down her spine, and, oddly, it wasn't entirely unpleasant. In fact, she felt the mad urge to say *yes*. But then she imagined what would come next: his hand low on her back, her hand in his. She'd feel trapped and it would remind her of—

"Oh, no," she said in a rush. "I can't."

"You cannot dance?" He lifted one brow, obviously skeptical.

"Very well, I can dance. But I do not. Ever." She spoke firmly, which she found remarkable, given all the little tremors and quakes—not altogether terrible ones—she experienced at the thought of dancing with him. Any pleasure at the small triumph of feeling something other than fear at the prospect of a waltz was tinged by knowledge that she couldn't share it with anyone, because no one knew why she hadn't danced since her first season.

"I find it hard to believe that you do not dance,"

Castleton said. "You're obviously a well-bred girl, and everyone knows that well-bred girls have spent at least two-eighths of their lives learning how to dance."

"Two-eighths?"

"Two-eighths is spent fretting over fashions," he explained, and she smiled. "Another three-eighths are spent gossiping and talking about men. The rest are lessons, eating, sleeping."

Prue laughed out loud. He certainly had the right of it. And he knew it, judging by that grin of his.

"Tell me I'm wrong," he said charmingly. His blue eyes sparkled at her, and for a moment, her heart did skip a beat. When her breath caught, it wasn't because she was scared but because of the way he looked at her with a happy affection.

"You're mad," she whispered. Was she talking to him or herself?

"Dance with me, Miss Merryweather," he murmured in the devastating way of charming rakes the world over.

God, she wanted to. More than anything, Prudence wanted to be a girl who slipped her hand in his and allowed herself to be whirled around the drawing room. She longed to be the girl she was *before*. But her body had a memory of its own, and that held her back.

Stupid, stupid, stupid Beast. Would he ever ease his control over her?

"Just one dance. That is all. It won't mean anything," Castleton said. "Look, our companions are children. Mrs. and Mr. Hammersmith will act as chaperones. I promise I won't get any ideas."

She gazed up at him. Too bad she couldn't explain why she was so hesitant.

"I can see you tapping your foot in time to the music, Miss Merryweather. I beg you, don't waste two-eighths of your life."

Don't waste two-eighths of your life.

The words, casually uttered just to cajole her, struck hard and struck suddenly. Prue felt the impact of it ricochet around her body, from her head to toes curling in her boots and everywhere else in between.

She was wasting her life, letting this fear hold her back.

It had been easy to pretend before that she hadn't, but there was no denying it now. There was a handsome man before her who had shown her nothing but kindness, and all he wanted was a dance.

The truth was: she yearned in her heart of hearts to dance with him.

But The Beast—

She'd had enough of The Beast. He had taken her innocence and stripped her future of possibilities. But perhaps she could just claim this one dance, once. It was just a waltz, nothing more.

"All right," she said softly.

The last time she'd placed her hand in another man's it had been the beginning of the end. But

Castleton was not The Beast. He clasped her hand lightly. She hardly even felt his hand on her lower back, though she was aware of it. If she needed to, she could break free.

They began to dance.

She did not, as she feared, forget the steps. She'd spent hours and hours of her life practicing them so that when this moment came—waltzing in the arms of a handsome man—she could move in time to the music without counting to three and look into his smoldering gaze instead of at her feet.

Two-eighths of her life. For *this* moment.

Prue forced her breath to be even. In. Out. In. Out. She willed her heart to beat in a steady rhythm as she tried to reclaim power over her emotions and fears.

Castleton's gaze settled on her face. She peered up at him. This time she really looked at him, focusing on his mouth, which was firm, sensual, and smiling encouragingly. It wasn't like The Beast's tight and cruel smile. The memory of that made her stomach ache and her palms dampen.

Everything about Castleton was different. His blue eyes had darkened in the candlelight. That friendly sparkle had been replaced with something darker. In spite of her efforts, her heart began to race. This was a mistake. She wasn't ready for this. Her limbs tensed. Her lungs started to tighten and she couldn't quite breathe.

"Are you having fun yet?" Castleton asked her affectionately.

Her gaze flew up to his. Ah, those eyes. Knowing. Dark.

"It'd be rude to say no, wouldn't it?" he murmured. "So you won't say anything. How about now?"

"I can't explain what this is making me feel," she said, her voice breathless. But, for two-eighths of life, she wanted to make it through one dance.

"Tell me," he urged.

"I hardly know you," she said. She couldn't even explain it to her best friends, because she hadn't even told them what had happened to traumatize her.

"I was born and raised at Castlemore Court in Yorkshire. I've read over three hundred books. My sister's name is Martha. I spend an inordinate amount of time traveling around the countryside, playing cards and wagering. I'm on a winning streak. And I hate turnips."

She let out the breath she'd been holding and smiled faintly.

"Everyone hates turnips," she said.

"See, we have something in common," Castleton murmured with a smile that made her feel warm on the inside.

"What about you, Miss Merryweather?"

What could she tell him? That she was so nervous right now, she might be sick? That she wanted to lose herself in the pleasure of his touch and just enjoy this moment of being a young woman dancing in the arms of a handsome man, but she couldn't because of The Beast? That she'd done everything she could to make sure men never looked at her, yet here he was gazing down at her with those ridiculously lovely blue eyes of his? God, he positively sparkled when he looked at her.

"I also hate turnips. I look terrible in yellow. My best friends are Emma and Olivia, and they just got married. I haven't danced since my first season."

"What season are you on now?"

"My fourth."

"You're dancing now. And with the most handsome man in the room, too."

That made her laugh aloud and smile broadly. In spite of everything, she couldn't fight the upturn of her lips and the crinkling around the corner of her eyes. Lady Dare always warned about wrinkles around the eyes. She'd just never warned Prue about men.

"You haven't much competition," Prudence couldn't help but point out.

"Shhh. Don't let Buckley hear you," Castleton replied.

"Or Mr. Rutherford."

"Miss Merryweather . . ." His voice was soft and low and a question. Prue looked up at him. He took that as a yes and pulled her just a bit closer.

She tried to breathe. She closed her eyes, hoping to shut out the memories of the last time a man had held her close during a waltz—and what had come after. Instead of Castleton's touch, she felt the pressure of The Beast's hand on hers and how firmly he had pressed her against him. The scent of stale cigar smoke and wine assaulted her senses—it wasn't Castleton but her memory coming on strong.

Other things she wished she could tell him: how she wanted to enjoy this but could not.

What she never wanted him to know: why this was torture for her.

The instant he knew would be the instant that his eyes stopped sparkling when he looked at her. The feeling was too new, too fragile, too wonderful for her to lose already. The instant he knew would be the instant he turned away because she was damaged goods. Or worse, the instant he knew would be the instant he thought he could have her without tenderness or promises.

Breathing. It was difficult at the moment.

Prudence had always wondered what it would be like to have a man look at her as Castleton did now—with affection and perhaps lust, with kindness and curiosity. With all sorts of good things. Now she knew.

But The Beast was still present, his memory hovering over her shoulder, ruining everything by reminding her of the last time she had waltzed with a man. . . .

The Beast's hands had been firm on the small of her back. He had gazed down at her. She'd thought it had been with adoration—what a fool she'd been! She'd been just out of the schoolroom and utterly ignorant in the ways of rogues disguised as gentlemen. She hadn't known it had been the smile of a lion before devouring a weak baby gazelle.

It had been like this. A man, holding her. A man, looking down at her. A man, clutching her close.

Her vision darkened at the periphery. In her mind, Castleton's features seemed to merge with The Beast's. She remembered the sick feeling in the pit of her stomach she had felt that night, as if on some level she had known that something awful was about to happen. She felt it now.

"Let me go," she rasped. Her lungs seemed to clench in her chest.

"Miss Merryweather—"

"I have to go. You need to let me go. I must go." It was such a struggle to get the words from her heart to her tongue and then to say them aloud.

What had she been thinking? She was ruined, deep down in her soul and in her head. One waltz wasn't going to cure her or reclaim two-eighths of her life. She was done. Done. Forever.

She ran, as she should have done those years ago. She dashed up the stairs, tears stinging at her eyes. She threw open the door to her bedchamber, slammed it shut, and locked it.

Back against the door, she slid down to sit on the floor and pulled her knees against her chest.

Chapter 8

London, 1820
Four years earlier
Prudence's first season

WITH HER BACK against the wall where that hurtful thing had just happened, Prue finally let her knees give out. She slid down to sit on the floor, knees up against her chest.

Sobs were stuck in her throat. What had just happened? Snatches of it flashed across her brain, hurting her anew. She thought she might be sick. Then she felt the stickiness between her legs and remembered and then she was sick, right on the floor in Lord and Lady Blackburn's corridor.

Faintly, she heard the sounds of the orchestra and the voices of hundreds of the haute ton chattering and laughing as if Prudence's innocence hadn't just been stolen from her. She did her best to stitch together the events of the evening, trying to understand how this bad thing had happened. To her.

How could this have happened to her?

Ladies did not refuse invitations to dance, and Prudence had been raised to be a proper lady. When Lord Dudley had invited her to waltz, she'd had no choice but to accept. It was the height of bad manners to refuse a man. People would talk and say cruel things about her if she did (*who does that Miss Payton think she is*). Dudley would be angry and embarrassed, and might spread vicious rumors about her, which would devastate her marital prospects. Rumors alone could wreck a girl's reputation. Then *no one* would ask her to dance and she would become a dried-up old spinster, which, up until an hour ago, was the worst fate she could imagine.

Besides, it was a few weeks into their first season and it was swiftly becoming apparent that she, Emma, and Olivia would not be taking the ton by storm as planned. Instead, they languished with the other wallflowers. The romances they had hoped for did not materialize. She was in no position to refuse an invitation to dance.

She tried to tell herself that Lord Dudley wasn't the worst. He wasn't geriatric or decrepit or odious. He had all of his teeth. In fact, some considered him handsome. He was young, his blond hair was slicked back with pomade, and his eyes were a clear, icy blue. There was just something about him—something hard around the edges, even when he smiled. He made her stomach hurt.

Nevertheless, Prudence accepted.

Down on the floor, after, Prudence closed her eyes and moaned. God, she felt dirty. His hands had been on her in places she'd never even touched herself. His mouth. She felt another wave of nausea remembering the taste of him. He'd been inside of her.

This Beast had been inside of her.

She wanted to cry. She wanted to be clean. But shock had stricken her numb, and she couldn't quite move from the floor.

Did she deserve this? Was it her fault? She had agreed to dance with him—nothing else. Or had she misunderstood things? She could hardly make sense of it all.

The pressure of his hand on her back—she remembered that. He grasped her hand, hard. Trapped, she had felt trapped. But it was just a waltz, and ladies were supposed to smile and dance with whoever asked, and it would be over in a minute or so. She counted the seconds.

She had been raised to be A Lady. She'd had a governess, the chaperonage of her guardian and aunt, and four years at Lady Penelope's Finishing School for Young Ladies of Fine Families. Her entire education had been devoted to making herself agreeable to gentlemen.

His arm linked with hers when it was over. "I shall walk you back to your friends," he said, and the relief she felt was palpable—until he started leading her away from her friends. She felt her heart thumping in her throat. Panic.

"They're on the opposite side of the ballroom," Prudence said, head turning back to look longingly at the wallflower corner.

"We're going this way first," he said firmly.

His grasp on her tightened. None of the lords and ladies they passed seemed to notice the tears stinging in her eyes or the way she tried to drop her weight in the manner toddlers did when they didn't wish to be picked up. Prue's desperate, pleading gaze locked with that of her tormenter from school; Lady Katherine turned away.

Dudley just laughed and forced her along, her feet stumbling around her skirts.

Why hadn't she just screamed? Another sob lodged in her throat. God, she was so ashamed. Another wave of bile surged up her throat. She was so stupid. She ought to have screamed.

Young ladies don't cause scenes.

She'd been raised to be a lady.

What a cruel twist that in an effort to be what was expected of her, she found herself awash in shame, a spoilt, pitiful creature, unfit for polite company.

Another sharp stab of a memory pierced her again.

Dudley had pushed her up against a wall in the corridor—a dark one, far from the public rooms and bustle of servants. She had struggled and pleaded every step of the way. He just pinned her against the wall with the weight of his hips pressed into hers. His hands snaked around her wrists and gripped them tight, pinning them behind her back. With his hips pressing hard against hers, it was impossible for her to escape. She thought she had been scared a moment ago. That was nothing.

What would he do to her? She feared the worst.

Squirming and trying to get away only made him laugh softly.

"When you move like that, it makes me harder," he whispered in her ear. She felt his hot breath on her neck and she retched. "Can you feel it?"

She did feel it, hard, thrusting against her belly. She felt his body smothering hers. She didn't have the physical strength to push him away, and the realization that he could overpower her was soul crushing. She didn't want this, but what could she do to stop it?

"Let me go," she whispered. "Please let me go." *Please God, let me go.* She prayed. She pleaded.

"Not quite yet," he murmured. And when she tried to scream, he said, "Just a little kiss first."

His mouth closed over hers, cutting off the scream she finally decided to allow. She tasted the wine he had been drinking. She felt his slug of a tongue in and out, plumbing the depths of her mouth. It made her heave. She turned her head. One small act of rebellion.

"Don't be like that, *Prude Prudence*," he said mockingly. Later, she would be glad of the name, for it seemed to scare off other men. In the moment, she hated every word he uttered.

She kept her head turned. Lips shut tight. His mouth found hers anyway. His tongue forced its way inside her mouth.

This was not how she imagined her first kiss. Another little devastation.

"Kiss me back," he growled.

She bit his tongue. Metallic taste.

"Bitch," he swore, his eyes hard and inches from hers. She tried to break away. He shifted, pinning her wrists with one large hand, and lifting her skirts with the other.

This couldn't be happening. It became too much for her to bear. Vaguely she was aware of his fingers, rubbing against her legs where *no one* had ever touched her. That couldn't be a real sensation. Her knees buckled. His grip on her wrists tightened. There would be bruises in the morning—bruises which no one would ever see because Ladies wore long sleeves and gloves to preserve their modesty. Even if their modesty was ripped away from them.

Something salty hit her tongue, mixing with the metallic taste of blood. Tears.

"No," she moaned. "Please no," she moaned again when she felt him pressing hard against her entrance.

Prudence struggled against him. It only made him angrier, which made him more forceful. Fear took over, rendering her mute. She didn't know what this was. She didn't know what was happening. All she knew was that ladies took care not to show their ankles. And here she was, with her skirts hitched up to her waist in a corridor where anyone might happen upon them.

God, why didn't someone happen upon them and put a stop to this?

Ladies didn't allow gentlemen liberties, but this one was taking and taking and taking and taking.

He forced himself inside her. It hurt, God, it hurt. The pain was unreal. She felt it *there*. She felt it in her wrists, where he held her fiercely. She felt it in her lungs, which burned with the scent of him, like stale smoke. She felt it in her soul.

This could not be happening. Someone would surely come and put a stop to this. Someone would come and save her. Wouldn't they?

Wouldn't someone come?

Please?

Prudence felt herself go away . . . outside herself. . . . It wasn't enough.

With every thrust, she died a little inside. There were so many thrusts over and over and over and over and over. Finally, it was over.

He spent himself inside her. Released her wrists. Her skirts fell down, covering her. He stepped back and buttoned his breeches.

"Don't tell anyone," he said. "Or I'll say that you asked for it."

As if she would ever breathe a word of this.

Then he sauntered off as if her life hadn't suddenly ended. Her knees gave way. She sank to the floor.

She was no longer a lady. She was no longer a girl.

She was no longer. She wanted to scrub her skin with scalding water and soap until it was gone. She wanted to disappear—or what was left of her, anyway.

Prudence understood that her virginity had been taken from her. She knew that without her virginity, a woman was nothing. *Nothing.* She spit on the floor, trying to get the taste of him out of her mouth. No man would ever marry her—not that she ever wanted a man to touch her again so long as she lived. If anyone ever found out about this, she would be shamed and ruined. The ton would label her *bad* and *damaged* and shut her out. And as they should—she was bad and damaged now.

She would never marry.

Everything in her life had been about getting married. What was left?

The Beast hadn't just taken her innocence; he had stolen her future.

Somehow she got through the rest of the night, and the rest of the season, and all the seasons that followed. She kept her gaze down, she took care never to be alone, and she found the wall-flower patch at every ball and stayed there. She stuck with her two best friends and pretended that awful thing had never happened. No one ever asked her to dance, and she never once complained about it. All she did was get by, get through the day. Occasionally panic would seize her—in corridors, when she caught a glimpse of The Beast, or when she thought about what would happen to her when everyone else married and she still couldn't even bear a man's touch upon her hand.

Somehow, she ended up here, on the floor of her room at the Coach & Horses Inn with a past she wanted to forget and no future to speak of.

Chapter 9

THE HOUR HAD grown late and the music and dancing had long since ceased when two more guests stumbled up the stairs to the inn and pushed open the door.

"God, that rain!" Lord Fitz-Herbert exclaimed, trying to dry his hair and brush the water off his jacket. They'd gotten soaked just from the mad dash from their carriage to the parlor. Their valets had been sent around to the stables to see to the horses.

"How bloody inconvenient that the road to London should be practically washed away," his companion grumbled. In an effort to reach Pangbourne for the boxing match in time, they had planned to travel through the night, only to find the roads a mess and a bridge washed away. They'd turned back and sought refuge here.

"I told you we should ford the river."

"Yes, if we wanted to drown."

"Like we're not practically drowned now."

Fitz-Herbert snorted. "Just because you're so

desperate to get to London on your daddy's orders doesn't mean the rest of us are."

Fitz's friend gave him a withering stare in the dim light.

"Do shut up, Fitz," Dudley snapped. His father controlled the purse strings and used them to manipulate his son like he was a bloody puppet. Not fancying himself penniless, Dudley tended to obey orders. But he didn't like it. Especially when it meant he was *wet.* "Might I remind you that on our way to London is the boxing match. And I know you want to see that as much as I do."

"Hello!" Fitz hollered out into the recesses of the darkened inn. "Is anybody home?"

"The service here is terrible," Dudley complained. "We've been standing here for ten minutes already."

It might have only been five. But it felt like ten, especially when they were soaking wet. And hungry. And, worst of all, sober. He needed a servant, immediately.

That it was the middle of the night and people were sleeping did not factor into his consideration. That only madmen and fools ventured out into rainstorms like this—and thus the innkeeper was likely not expecting anyone—was irrelevant. He was the heir to the Marquis of Scarbrough, one of the most powerful men in England; the world existed to please him.

Dudley was cross because his current options were to tolerate this slow service or venture out into the rain again. Really, he had no option at all.

That made him feel powerless.

There was no feeling he hated more than being powerless.

And wet, tired, and hungry.

Finally the glow of a taper appeared, illuminating a little old man in a cotton nightshirt and cap descending the stairs at the speed of an old donkey on his last legs.

"We'll need two rooms," Fitz-Herbert said before the man had placed a bare foot on the parlor floor. "And space for our valets, who are seeing to the horses."

"And a hot bath," Dudley added with a shiver. He felt better just issuing the order, knowing his wish would be fulfilled.

"Make that two," Fitz-Herbert said. And then, turning to Dudley, he asked, "Are you hungry? I'm a bit peckish."

"Let's have some food as well," Dudley told the innkeeper, who looked a bit peevish. He might have been woken in the middle of the night, but at least he wasn't wet. Besides, he should be honored to have two well-known lords under his roof, especially ones with the blunt to make it worth his while to attend to their every whim.

"And wine," Fitz-Herbert added.

"God yes, wine," Dudley said enthusiastically, rubbing his palms together. "A good red would be grand on a night like this."

The innkeeper didn't say anything; he just sighed and reached for his coat and boots. As if he weren't glad for the paying customers.

Dudley ignored him and crossed the room to stand before the dwindling embers of the fire.

"It feels so good to be warm again," Fitz-Herbert said. The innkeeper gave them a hard, cold look over his shoulder before stepping out into the cold, rainy night and slamming the door behind him.

Chapter 10

PRUDENCE SAT AT a table in the parlor and wrapped her hands around the hot mug of tea, savoring the warmth. The chill from the rain was starting to sink into her bones. Or perhaps that cold, heavy feeling was just the memories she couldn't seem to shake.

What a fool she had made of herself last night. It was ridiculous of her to think she was *fine*. As if the memories would fade until eventually enough time passed for them to disappear. Perhaps that was possible. But last night proved that The Beast still had her firmly in his grasp.

Prue sipped the tea and tried to focus on the lovely moments instead, as if they could crowd out the bad memories if she only accumulated enough of them. One of the loveliest moments had come when Castleton had gazed at her with the sort of adoration she had long dreamt of. She started to warm up from the inside.

Prudence took another sip of her tea and recalled how her hand had felt in his and the warmth of his touch. Just the memory chased the chill away. Or it might have been the tea.

Perhaps one day she would be able to enjoy such looks and affection. She ought to be considering more pressing matters, like what had happened to Cecil. Had he survived? She was certain he must have done; the alternative was too horrid to contemplate. If he lived, were they still betrothed?

And if so, did she still wish to marry him, especially if this rain prevented her from returning to London before Lady Penelope's Ball? Her heart said no, which begged the question: had she given up on love entirely, or had she only just started to believe?

Teapot in hand, Annie slowly approached the table where Prudence sat.

"Would you care for more tea?"

"It looks like you need this tea more than I do," Prudence remarked. Annie didn't seem quite as cheerful as usual. Her eyes were heavy lidded and her hair a bit disheveled.

"I just might," she replied with a sigh. "Two gents arrived late last night. Very late."

"So I did hear a commotion," Prudence said. "I thought I had dreamt it."

"I wish I had," Annie said darkly. "They wanted hot baths, something to eat, and wine in the middle of the night! But that's London gentlemen for you."

Prudence concentrated on remaining very still. What an intrusion! She had come to think of this inn as a refuge, and this time away from town life as a respite she had very badly needed. But now there were London gentlemen here. It left a bad taste in her mouth. She would have to avoid them—a tricky endeavor, given the confines of the inn—for if it was discovered that she was here alone, they would certainly take the news back to town with them. The ton would assume the worst, and Prudence didn't exactly have the reputation strong enough to weather such tarnishing gossip.

Poor Annie yawned.

"You must have been up late," Prue said.

"Slept in, too. Now I'm behind on the baking for the day," Annie sighed. "But what am I complaining to you for? It's nothing you need to worry about."

"Can I help?"

"Oh no, miss."

"Please? I am beginning to go mad just sitting around doing nothing," Prudence said. It was the truth. Furthermore, if she was to avoid the London gentlemen, there was no better place to hide than the kitchens.

"What about flirting with Lord Castleton?" Annie asked with a grin.

Prue was so surprised by the notion that it took her a moment before she replied, "We're not flirting."

"He's sweet on you, Miss Merryweather," Annie said. "Anyone can see it."

"That's ridiculous," Prue muttered, smiling down into her mug of tea.

"Is it? You're a lovely and kind young lady."

"I am now even more inclined to help you, Annie. What needs to be done?"

"Can you bake bread?" Annie asked with a skeptical lift of her brow.

"I haven't before," Prue admitted. "But how hard can it be?"

AN HOUR LATER, Prudence found that baking bread wasn't complicated, but it was challenging. After Annie's instruction, she found herself kneading a large ball of dough. While Annie kept up a steady stream of chatter about Rutherford (her uncle), the village (the dullest place imaginable), Buckley (the beloved town drunk), and all the town gossip (Mrs. Walpole was having an affair with the magistrate, who had been bribed by the local gentry's son to turn a blind eye to his curricle racing), Prue pushed and pulled on the dough, giving it all of her strength, but it was tough and unmalleable in her hands. This kneading business was tougher than she'd assumed—but then again, what would she know about baking? Kitchens were foreign lands to her.

"Is it done yet?" Prudence asked. In other words, how much longer? Her arms were starting to ache. However, she refused to complain.

"A bit longer, Miss Merryweather. Suddenly, it'll just transform right under your hands. You'll just know when it's ready."

Annie kept chattering while she prepared the

meals for the day. Prudence kept fighting with the dough. And then Castleton interrupted them.

He stood in the doorway to the kitchen. From the relative safety of the far side of the room, the first thing Prudence noticed was his shirt. After being soaked in the rain, the white linen was transparent. It clung to the broad planes of his chest. The other day she had been too overwhelmed to pay much attention.

This morning, she really noticed. Castleton had the sort of chest that was just pure manliness, strength, and power. Prue was curious how it would feel under her palms. Then she sighed, knowing she would probably have to live with the mystery. After all, she had panicked at just the touch of his hand.

"Well, isn't this a sight for sore eyes," he murmured, leaning against the door frame and gazing at the two women in the kitchen. Prue glanced at Annie and saw a blush stealing across her cheeks.

"Good morning, Lord Castleton," Annie replied cheerily. "How are the horses?"

"There are more in the stables this morning than when I went to sleep last night."

"Two gentlemen arrived after midnight," Annie explained.

"That explains the extra horses," Castleton said. "And the noise that woke me."

"After they stayed up drinking until long past midnight, I reckon they'll be asleep for most of the day," Annie said. "At least, one hopes."

"In the meantime, I see you have pressed Miss Merryweather into service."

"I begged for her to give me something to do," Prue answered.

"Are you bored with staring out the window at the rain, Miss Merryweather?"

"This might surprise you, but *yes*," she replied, smiling.

"What would you do if you were in London?"

"Yes, tell me about the life of a fancy lady in London," Annie exclaimed. Prue glanced from one to the other, both of them watching her, waiting to hear how she spent her days when she wasn't helping bake bread in a small country inn.

"My aunt and I began each day reading the newspapers and drinking chocolate in her room." It was a lovely ritual. Lady Dare sat up in bed, whilst Prue sat comfortably on the settee. "We trade pages of *The London Weekly* and discuss the news and gossip."

"Already I am jealous!" Annie said with a sigh. "I'd love to have just one day to sit abed, drinking chocolate. Tell me it gets even better after that."

"Then we dress," Prudence said. "And pay calls. Or remain in our drawing room if it is our day to entertain visitors." She neglected to mention that those visitors were usually for Lady Dare, never suitors for Prue. "Often I spend time with my friends at the shops, or museums, or we walk in the park."

"Do you go to fancy balls each night?"

"Most evenings, yes," Prudence said.

"How fabulous," Annie sighed. She had a sparkle in her eyes and a dreamy smile. Prue didn't have the heart to tell her she spent each ball rooted in the corner with the other misfit girls. She didn't waltz with handsome gentlemen, or sip champagne, or get swept up in the romance of it all.

"I suppose," Prudence said with a sigh of her own. Four seasons, wasted. Another two-eighths of her life spent cowering in fear rather than celebrating the fact that she was a young woman of good reputation, connections, and money. She was a proper young lady.

Was.

The Beast, the failed elopement, highway robbery, and now days spent without a chaperone in a country inn had put an end to calling herself a proper young lady.

But was that really the worst thing? Or did she dare to confess it felt the slightest bit freeing, like a loosening of her corset strings?

"What brings you this way?" Castleton asked. There was something in the way he looked at her that was unnerving. As if he really saw her. As if he read between her lines. As if he knew all of her secrets.

"Oh, it's a long story," Prue said.

"We're not going anywhere."

"Perhaps you might like to don dry clothes," she suggested. "Or else you'll catch your death of a cold."

"Are you concerned about my welfare, Miss Merryweather?"

"No, just the horses," she replied, half smiling. "Someone has to tend to them, and I fear I would do a terrible job of it."

"Perhaps if the rain lets up, I'll show you this afternoon."

She turned her attentions back to the thick mass of dough under her hand. As she kneaded, she thought of all the reasons she could not go out into the stables with him alone. Or rather, she grasped at reasons.

What of her reputation? A lady oughtn't be alone with a man. But that ship had long since sailed for her, and it was quite silly to insist on such propriety now. Besides, if she was determined to avoid the London gentlemen, the stables were another place they'd never find her.

But she was afraid to be alone with Castleton. Why, he could be the highwayman who had robbed her mail coach, for all she knew! She doubted it, but with her luck, it was prudent to consider it.

And yet . . . how would things have been different if The Beast and the highwayman had never appeared? She certainly would have danced more, especially with Castleton.

Perhaps when a gentleman smiled at her she would have had the strength to return his gaze rather than fix her attention upon the floor. She would have gotten in Castleton's carriage and

allowed him to sweep her off her feet. That per-
fectly timed rescue would have convinced her that
Prince Charming existed and he had come for her.
Then again, if she still believed in true love and
happily ever after, she wouldn't have eloped with
Cecil in the first place.

If it weren't for this fear grasping her by the
throat, who knows what her life would be like?
Who knows what happiness awaited her if she
could just shake it off?

And then she felt it: the moment when everything changed and the dough became soft, pliant,
and wonderful under her palms. The moment
when all that hard work delivered its reward.
The moment when there was a phase change. The
moment when the dough was ready to rise.

DUDLEY GLANCED AT the time and rolled back
under the covers with a groan. Noon had come
and gone. But the rain—that was still pounding
on the roof and lashing at the windows. He'd
care less if he didn't have places to get to, like the
boxing match. He'd been looking forward to it
for weeks. One bright spot in the insipid round
of parties. One spot where his father wouldn't
be nagging him about duties in London, how he
ought to marry, how he ought to behave. He was a
man, not a boy, for Chrissakes. Men did what they
damned well pleased.

Such thoughts always made him cross and
were unbearable before he had coffee and some-

thing to eat. When his valet didn't come quickly enough after ringing, Dudley dressed hastily and went out in the corridor.

He took a guess which door belonged to Fitz-Herbert.

Then he knocked.

PRUDENCE WAS STARTLED by the knock on her door. She hadn't requested anything. The beating of her heart started to echo the knocking at her door. Who could it be? What if it was one of the London gentlemen?

This was the fear again, taking hold and refusing to let go.

She took a deep breath, willed her heart to slow down, and asked, "Who is it?"

FITZ-HERBERT STUMBLED AROUND his room, pulling on his shirt, swearing when he stubbed his toe on the foot of the bed. What bloody arse was pounding on his door at this ungodly hour? What was the hour, anyway? He glanced at the window and saw more gray, more rain. If this kept up, they could kiss away their plans to attend the boxing match.

At least they weren't drowned at the bottom of that river. Dudley was his friend, but he was also an idiot.

Knock knock knock

"Bloody hell, give a man a minute," Fitz-Herbert shouted at whoever had the audacity to interrupt his much-needed sleep with their persistent pounding.

He opened the door.

"WHO IS IT?" Prudence asked.

"It's me," a male voice answered. She recognized that voice. It brought a nervous smile to her lips.

Prudence opened the door.

John stood before her. He wore a clean, dry shirt (alas), buff breeches, a waistcoat, and jacket.

And, oh, that smile of his: shy and warm, with that dimple and the sparkle in his blue eyes. If she weren't so afraid, she would let herself fall in love just for his smile alone. She was more and more determined to conquer her fear . . . which meant she might fall in love with him. Which terrified her anew.

"I was wondering if you'd like to join me in the stables. That is, if you're not busy."

Prudence gave a happy, nervous little laugh. The circumstances were strange, but this felt like a suitor asking if he might call upon her one afternoon or take her for a turn around a ballroom.

In London, a proper gentleman would never ask a proper Lady to join him in the stables. But they were not in London. And she couldn't really claim to be a proper lady anymore, anyway. She decided the rules did not apply.

Nevertheless, she murmured, "I don't know."

The question wasn't whether she wanted to go

to the stables with him (she did) but whether she trusted him enough.

"Of course. Ladies don't go to the stables," he said, and though he smiled, this one didn't reach his eyes. She was aware, immediately, of someone offending him or perhaps disappointing him. How or why she could not fathom. But there was a sudden, almost imperceptible change in his demeanor because of her hesitancy. Did he think her a snob? Why did his altered opinion of her make her sad and immediately determined to win back his favor? She could explain her trepidation . . . or she could just say yes and have faith.

"I will," she said with more confidence than she felt. "I just need a moment, and then I will meet you there."

ONE DOOR SHUT and another opened.

Dudley and Fitz-Herbert lumbered down the stairs into the parlor, talking loudly of being starving and in desperate need of food, coffee, and dry weather.

Meanwhile, Prudence waited behind her closed door.

She thought she'd heard The Beast's voice, but that was ridiculous. That was just her fear talking, and she was tired of listening.

That racing heart of hers? Perhaps, just once, it wasn't fear but anticipation. Thus she grabbed her shawl and hurried down the back stairs, through the back door, and out into the rain.

She started to run, as if she'd be so fast the raindrops couldn't touch her. But then she took a moment to stand still and turn her face up to the sky. The air was surprisingly warm. The sky was a light gray. The earth smelled fresh and wonderful. It felt *lovely* to be outside, breathing in fresh air and the scent of warm rain and wet earth.

And then she dashed toward the shelter. And Castleton.

After wrenching open the thick wooden door, Prudence slipped inside. The stables were dimly lit; just a little of the gray light from outside filtered in from the new windows. The floor was hard-packed dirt under her boots. And the air was thick with the scent of horses and hay and rain.

She heard the rain drumming on the roof and the soft breathing of the horses and their shuffling in the stalls.

And then there was Castleton: tall, strong, and impossibly handsome. He seemed perfectly at ease here, yet she could easily picture him in a ballroom, with all the women giving him coy smiles and flirtatious glances. She wondered why she hadn't seen him in London.

"Fancy meeting you here," Castleton said, strolling toward her. As he passed the horses, they stuck their heads out of the stalls and followed him with their eyes.

"No one is more surprised than I to be out here," she said.

"Indeed, for a fancy London lady—"

"No, it's not that," she said, cutting him off. "It's just . . . we're alone."

"Under the watchful supervision of these horses," he said, with a gesture to all the animals that were, indeed, watching them. That made her smile.

ONCE AGAIN, HER smile did things to him. Castleton watched her glance around nervously with those brown eyes of hers, like the chocolate she drank in bed every morning. In these stables, she was worlds away from home.

Why was she traveling alone, anyway? The question nagged at him.

The more he knew about her, the more he was sure that something had sent her running from the world where she belonged, and the more he wanted to know her story, to know *her*.

What was he to do about it? A gentleman always honored a lady's wishes. . . .

There was nothing to do, really, but introduce her to the animals.

"Would you like to say hello to the horses?"

"Yes," she said, with the sort of determined tip of her chin that revealed she was intent on overriding her hesitations. It was those little things that made him want to hold her, to know her, and to strip away layer after layer until he knew, intimately, the real woman beneath.

But some creatures were more skittish than

others. They needed patience and restraint and a gentle touch. But first, the horses and keeping Miss Merryweather so entertained that she forgot to be scared for just a moment.

Castleton led her to the first stall.

"This is Penny," he said. "Rutherford's mare."

"She's beautiful," Miss Merryweather murmured. The mare was a dark copper-colored horse with a darker mane and tail. There was a white streak along the bridge of her nose that was her most defining mark.

"What do I do?" Miss Merryweather asked, staring up into the large, dark eyes of the horse.

"Hold out your hand as you would to a gentleman at a ball."

Miss Merryweather burst out laughing.

"I'm not jesting," Castleton said. "You cannot just jump on a horse and have a ride. You have to make their acquaintance first. Then assure them your intentions are good and earn their trust. Go on, I promise this will be fine. Hold out your hand."

Miss Merryweather extended her arm, palm down. Penny tentatively took a sniff, blowing hot, damp air across Prue's hand. She gasped and yanked it away, and the horse lifted her head and took a few steps back.

"She knows you're afraid."

"How?"

"Many animals can sense a person's emotions. Like fear." He leaned against the stall, watching

Miss Merryweather approach once more. Penny
looked at her warily, then at him, as if seeking his
opinion of this nervous girl. "It makes them skittish, too. Some horses, like Penny, have a strong
mind, and if the human isn't in control and assured, they'll try to take advantage to do what
they want. They know they don't have to listen."

"Oh," Miss Merryweather sighed, lost in her
thoughts. Everything Castleton said had struck a
chord with her. She was skittish and nervous and
never forceful enough to ensure people respected
her.

Then again—she had been raised to be demure,
obliging, and deferential. All girls were.

"Try again. She won't bite," Castleton urged.
Prue looked up at him, half wary, half smiling.

"Are you sure?"

"Nope," he said with a grin. "But I doubt it."

He watched, kind of enchanted, as she drew a
deep breath and tried again. She stretched out her
arm and waited for Penny to become aware, then
curious enough to take a few steps over and sniff.
This time Miss Merryweather remained still.

"Here, now give her this," he said, reaching
into his jacket pocket for an apple he'd plucked
from the tree in the garden. "She'll love you forever once you feed her."

"Is it that simple?"

"For men, animals . . . yes. For women, it's a
little more complicated."

More assured now, Prudence took the apple and

held it out to Penny. But once the horse's mouth opened up, revealing giant teeth, Prue shrieked and dropped the apple.

"Hold it like this," he said, demonstrating a flat palm. "That way she can't bite you."

It took a few more tries, but eventually the horse was eating from her hand. It wasn't much longer after that before Miss Merryweather was resting her cheek against the horse's neck and breathing in deeply. She turned to Castleton with one of those smiles that could take a man's breath away. In this moment, she was happy. When she was happy, she was radiantly beautiful. She reminded him of a bird just learning to fly again after a broken wing.

What happened to her? he wondered.

Who knows what would happen when the rain stopped? They would go their separate ways. But . . . even though he was desperate to get to London in time for the Great Exhibition, he was glad for the rain, because he wasn't quite ready to part ways with her yet.

Did she feel the same? From the look in her dark, velvety brown eyes, he thought yes.

Hesitantly he took a step closer to her. The world, save for their immediate surroundings, ceased to exist. There was only the sound of the rain, the scent of earth, Prudence's plump, pink mouth that he wanted to taste.

He peered closer, noting thick black lashes and a smattering of freckles across her nose and cheeks.

There was the slightest part in her lips. Her hands anxiously gripped the folds of her skirt.

And then there was his desire. There was the driving need to kiss her and the ache to enfold her in his arms. There was just plain wanting.

He stepped in closer. She took a deep breath, tilted her head up, and lifted her lips to his. And then she closed her eyes. Before his gaze was riveted to her lips, he noticed, for a second, those dark lashes resting against her cheeks.

His mouth touched hers. It just had to happen.

For one fleeting second, everything was right in the world. All the things that could keep them apart were kept at bay. For one fleeting second, there was bliss and there was happiness. There was just enough that he wouldn't be able to let go of the sensation or the memory when it was over, but not enough that he was satisfied.

Too soon, it was over. Penny whinnied and pawed the ground, wanting more apples. That jolted them both back to reality: two strangers with secrets, in the stables, in the rain, in this town no one knew the name of.

When Miss Merryweather whispered, "I have to go" and ran off, he wasn't surprised in the slightest.

Prudence ran across the garden, through the back door, and up the back staircase. She didn't stop until she reached her bedchamber, shut the door, and locked it. Then, back against the wooden boards, she slid down to the floor, touching her lips all the while.

It was just one little kiss, just the merest caress of his lips against hers. It was brief—it only felt like an eternity. It certainly wasn't enough to ruin a girl or to constitute grounds for marriage. The kiss wasn't even very passionate, or deep, or intense. The kiss was sweet and innocent, and it was exactly what she needed.

She felt a surge of triumph, for she had done something that scared her. She had faced her fears and was rewarded with a sweet kiss from a handsome man. Alone in her room, Prudence was quite nearly ecstatic.

If only those London gents weren't downstairs in the parlor! She would have to stay in her bedchamber all evening. Especially since she overheard one of their voices and oh lud, if it didn't sound uncannily like The Beast.

She banished the thought of *him* and touched her lips, remembering Castleton's kiss.

Later that night

"Ugh, this rain! I feel like a caged beast, trapped in this inn," Dudley grumbled as he paced across the worn floorboards of the parlor. His blond hair bore evidence of his frustration, for he had taken to pushing it back and even grasping handfuls. Every so often he caught a glimpse of his reflection in the window—he looked like a madman.

He *felt* like a madman.

Fitz-Herbert lounged in a rickety wooden chair, pushed back from the table. The remnants of a humble, but admittedly delicious, feast spread out before them: savory meat pies, roasted squab, boiled potatoes, and thick slices of freshly baked bread with salted butter. Their wineglasses were, tragically, nearly empty.

"Whilst you're up, do ring for more wine, will you?"

Dudley stalked across the room and pulled the cord.

"Cards?" Fitz-Herbert suggested.

"All we ever do is play cards," Dudley complained. "I'm bored of cards. I'm bored of this rain."

"Sometimes we wager."

"Yes, on cards," Dudley said witheringly. "Or stupid things like who can piss the farthest."

"I wager you five pounds that I can."

"I'm not in the mood for a pissing contest. Not when it's pissing rain like this. At this rate, we'll never make the boxing match."

"We should build an ark."

Dudley looked at Fitz-Herbert like he was an utter moron, which he was. Being an utter moron, Fitz-Herbert thought he'd been misunderstood and endeavored to explain himself.

"It's biblical. Forty days and forty nights of flooding, remember? I know it's been a while since you darkened a church door, but everyone knows the flood and the ark that Noah built. So we should do that. And *then* we'll be able to cross that river and get to London."

Dudley was spared from replying by the arrival of the barmaid, who had anticipated their desires and brought another bottle of wine. As he took it from her, he wondered if she might satiate some other desires of his. He allowed his gaze to slide down to her ample bosom and flared hips. Then he looked up to her face. She gave him the sort of hardened look that let him know, plainly, that she'd be more trouble than she'd be worth. As if the maid could read his mind, the old innkeeper, Rutherford, attended to them for the rest of the night.

Thus he spent the rest of the night drinking red wine and pacing across the floorboards whilst Fitz-Herbert rambled about gossip from town. It was just that he felt so *powerless*. He couldn't travel in this rain, so he was forced against his will to stay here. And that was just today's injustice. His father, older and older each day, clung to control of the estates right down to the unfairly ungenerous allowance deposited in Dudley's accounts—provided Dudley did as he was told. He was a man with nothing to do, no control over his fate, no control over anything. It rankled, that. No, it burned. He was a man. He could prove it. He *would* prove it. At the next opportunity he would show them all he didn't take orders from anyone and that no one ever said no to him.

Chapter 11

JOHN FOUND IT amusing that he should be standing next to Miss *Merryweather* while the rain poured down for yet another day. Even though he was increasingly anxious about returning to London in time, the thought made him laugh softly to himself as he stared out the window.

"What is so amusing?"

"I am standing with a girl named Merryweather during an epic rainstorm," he told her. "Whilst I am curious as to your Christian name, I'm afraid to ask. What if it's Hellfire or Plague of Locusts? Or Peace on Earth?"

She laughed in spite of herself, a lovely, lilting sound. Some of the tension in her shoulders eased. He really shouldn't be so attuned to the tension in her shoulders or anything else so intimate about her. But John couldn't help it; he was just aware of her.

The little trembles that shook her, her haunted expression and wry smiles, the occasional bursts of laughter—he noticed it all. There was something about her that put him in mind of a baby deer. Those eyes, big and brown and full of fear. The way she startled at the slightest thing and ran.

He was not a hunter.

In fact, he was the sort that had brought home every wounded animal he'd come across. His mother had always sighed and said, "I don't know about this" fretfully as he had nursed back to health birds with broken wings and rabbits with broken legs. Letting them go had always been difficult.

"Prudence," she said, apropos of nothing.

"I beg your pardon?"

"My name is Prudence." She turned her head and looked up at him. "My name is Miss Prudence Merryweather."

"Mine is John Roark." He punctuated it with a lordly, rakish bow that drew a smile to her lips.

"Shouldn't you have at least seven middle names, which consist of some combination of William, George, Peregrine, Edward, and Henry?"

"Well, my full name is Jonathan James William Roark Hathaway, Viscount Castleton."

"I knew it. Most peers have names longer than they are tall. And you're rather tall."

"You noticed," he said. Not that it was a detail easily overlooked.

"I noticed," she confirmed with a slight blush.

"What else have you noticed?"

"You didn't follow me the other night. Or yesterday afternoon," she said softly. "Thank you. I wanted to be alone."

Something bad had happened to Prudence; he

was sure of it. Even the most propriety-minded miss relaxed a bit more around a man during a chaperoned waltz. Their brief kiss yesterday was not the stuff that ruined a maiden. But it was the haunted look in her eyes and her skittishness that made him sure.

What he wasn't sure of: why this broke his heart as much as it did and why he ached to make her better. As if that was even in his power. As if she even wanted his help.

"Do you want to talk about it?" he asked.

"Of course not. I'm *fine,*" she said with a determined squaring of her shoulders. It was for the best. Who was *he* to help her? He wasn't the man she thought he was, and he had already revealed too much. Besides, he had to get to London as soon as possible. There was no time to care for a wounded creature he'd just have to let go of eventually.

Midday

A few hours later the rain still continued to fall, as if there were an endless supply. It was beginning to get to the point where one could believe in the wrath of God. John knew what sins he had committed, but he was hard-pressed to imagine what Prudence or even Buckley could be guilty of. The gents he'd briefly glimpsed in the dimly lit parlor last night were clearly the sort of men who were riddled with sins. But that was neither here nor there, and they were upstairs sleeping off their late night and the excessive amounts of wine they'd consumed.

They were not worth his attention. He had to remain focused on what really mattered. His thoughts drifted to the Great Exhibition, which was just five days hence. He imagined scenes of England's finest investors and craftsmen setting up displays of their new innovations. What excitement and energy must be in that grand room! His blood rushed faster through his veins just thinking about it.

He grew anxious considering the very real possibility that he might miss this opportunity as he stood in this parlor, watching the rain. God, he feared he might grow old and die just waiting for the weather to turn.

But this rain! His carriage, a fashionable and highly impractical town conveyance, did not have suitable coverage for this kind of downpour. Perhaps he could just be wet. According to the "gentlemen" in the inn, the bridge on the road to London had been washed away. But surely there was another, more circuitous route he could take. If he left now, he might just make it.

John turned away from the window to glance at Prudence. The name suited her. A cautious, reserved girl. And yet she was out in the world, dangerously alone. She didn't make sense. He wanted, so badly, to know her.

She sat near the fireplace with a book she pretended to read—he knew, because after watching her for a few minutes, he realized that she didn't turn the pages. On a small table nearby was a cup of tea that she occasionally sipped. In the silence and the relentless rain, he became acutely aware of the hours and days slipping away.

A lucky streak only lasted so long, and he was spending it—wasting it?—here. He didn't even know where here was.

But Miss Merryweather was as content as could be here. Why? Where was she coming from? Why wasn't she in a rush to go anywhere? Surely something or someone awaited her. And why wouldn't she confide in him? Why was he so bothered that she didn't?

John paced before the window. It. Was. Still. Raining.

"Something is bothering you. What is it?" she asked, glancing up from the book.

"I'm worried about making it to London in time for the exhibition," he confessed, pushing his fingers through his hair. "I may not have another chance to meet the inventors of the engine otherwise."

She paused, with pursed lips and lowered eyes, before answering.

"I'm sure they would want to talk about their machine with anyone interested."

"That's what I'm afraid of," he admitted. "I want to be the first. There's money to be made here, and I intend to be the one making it."

He had to have every advantage and get as much done as soon as possible. Because once his past got out, they wouldn't be doing business with him and he'd be worse off than when he'd started. If such a thing was even possible.

"It's just a little rain," said Miss Merryweather.

"I'm told the direct road to London is impassable, due to flooding. The gents that arrived the other night said so. I could go around it, I suppose," John said. He sighed. "If I left this afternoon."

"The rain does seem to have lightened," she said. "You could probably get through."

In an instant he knew that he felt something powerful for Miss Prudence Merryweather. The thought of leaving her caused an actual physical ache in the region of his heart. The thought of never seeing her again was gutting. She was a wounded creature alone in the world. He couldn't leave her and call himself a gentleman. He couldn't leave her, because he would miss her.

He wasn't done with Miss Merryweather. Not that he had plans or designs, just that there was more there to explore; he knew it with a bone-deep certainty. He could not go, not yet, and that is why he was vexed. He was tugged in two directions.

Those eyes. That rare smile that made him forget everything else. The hint of what she would feel like in his arms. He wanted to lose himself in her curves, taste her, know her, soothe her, protect her. In more ways than she would ever, *ever* know, he wanted to be the man for her.

He felt all that for a woman he'd known just a few days.

John pushed his fingers through his hair again. He was ridiculous. His mother had warned him that his tendency to throw caution to the wind and care for wounded creatures would do him in.

But really, what was he going to do—stay here with her? Would he really risk missing his chance to connect with the inventors of the Difference Engine for a lovely, curious young girl all alone in the world?

Yes. If she wanted.

His breath hitched in his throat as that thought struck. There was too much at stake for him to lose himself to a woman. If he failed to make this scheme work, he wouldn't be able to rescue his mother and his sister. Prudence wasn't the only distressed damsel in his life.

He glanced again at her. Lips parted slightly. The rise and fall of her breasts covered up in a modest dress. Auburn hair pulled back in a bun at the nape of her neck. She was so prim. He wanted to see her in the throes of pleasure, wild with abandon. He wanted her laughter, her smile.

John wanted to know that she was experiencing these feelings for him. But she was always so reserved and restrained, as if she couldn't possibly wish to let go.

His voice sounded weary when he spoke: "What should I do, Miss Merryweather?"

He wasn't asking about his travel plans, but the innermost depths of her heart.

To which she replied, "I couldn't say."

Suddenly, he was irritated—no, furious—that this slip of a girl had captivated him so completely as to forget his plans. Because of her, he was considering waiting out this storm that could last for God only knew how long, in this inn which was in God only knew what town. Because of this girl, who fled after the briefest kiss, he was considering missing his chance to have the advantage of being the first manufacturer of the Difference Engine. It wasn't just a deal; it was everything to him.

His temper flared, but he gritted his jaw, containing himself.

It was a way to save his mum and sister from a cruel fate they didn't deserve. It was a way for him to be the man he yearned to be, even though society made it nearly impossible. Didn't she realize that? Didn't she *know* what she did to him?

"What do you intend to do?" he asked. "Will you wait here for the rain to cease? And then where will you go?"

What did she want? Why did he care so much?

"I am not certain of my plans yet," she replied.

She gave the impression that she wasn't speaking only of when to leave for London; it seemed as if she was also speaking about what she would do with the rest of her life, which was absurd. She was lovely. She'd find a husband and have a passel of auburn-haired babies with doe eyes.

He could so easily imagine himself marrying her. Loving her. Making a family with her. God help him, he ached with wanting at the thought.

A wife was out of the question, though. He'd laid that possibility to rest the night his luck had changed. He had no future with any woman, least of all a fancy London Lady like Prudence.

Pushing his fingers through his hair, he reminded himself to think of the Difference Engine instead of the girl. A girl! This was his *one* chance. He'd gambled and won enough to own a significant chunk of a factory—and the profits from its products. Enough to provide for his sister and mother.

Enough to provide for Miss Merryweather. If she wanted. But he doubted she would.

Her head was bowed, attention focused on her book. She didn't want him.

The truth of it affected him more than he cared to admit. But there was no denying the tightness in his chest.

"I think I'll go pack my things," he said, carefully watching her reaction with bated breath. He wanted her to want him to stay. He couldn't breathe as he waited for her response. John had played games where thousands of pounds had depended upon the flip of a card—a sum that could have saved him or ruined him. He'd never felt such anticipation then as he did now.

He counted the silences where his heartbeat should be: *One. Two. Three. Four.* His whole life, suddenly, depended upon the words she uttered next.

Prudence just nodded. That was all. A little nod of her head, which put into perspective the rash things he'd been considering. He turned to go.

PRUDENCE NODDED, BECAUSE she didn't trust herself to speak. There were a million words on her tongue and caught in her throat. She wanted him to stay with an intensity that rendered her breathless and mute. If only she could say the word "Stay" without fearing that he would interpret it to mean she'd welcome liberties she could not grant him.

She'd felt a yearning deep inside ever since she'd first laid eyes on him. She, who had long been dead on the inside, was stirring to life with his every smile and kindness. With that oh-so-brief kiss, he awakened even more senses in her that she wanted to explore.

She thought she had died and he was bringing her back to life. Didn't he *see* that? How could he not see?

She did not want to be left alone, but that was her fate, wasn't it? How many tragedies must she endure—like Dudley violently compromising her or Cecil ruthlessly sacrificing her—before she stopped holding out hope?

She had survived all that, as well as ballrooms and dark forests, on her own.

She was *fine*. FINE.

It was torture, this. For the first time she yearned for a man's touch, yet she was still terrified of finding herself in a vulnerable position. If only she could be a normal young lady, even in these abnormal circumstances.

Prudence thought all these things whilst Castleton was upstairs packing his bags and preparing to leave her. Perhaps they would reconnect in London, when he finally met the duke about the engine. It was likely that they would; this, then, was not the end. She felt an undeniable happiness at the prospect, which told her all she needed to know about her feelings for him.

But . . .

Would he be angry at her for not telling him about her connection? Possibly. But she couldn't share that information without revealing herself as Miss Payton, not Miss Merryweather. Oh, did she sigh in frustration, a sad little exhalation.

She just couldn't win, could she?

Prudence was just a bundle of secrets and lies. No man in his right mind would want her once he knew the truth. She ought to really give up all hope. She ought to just stay in this chair, in this parlor, for the rest of her days.

The sound of gentlemen's voices made her immediately reconsider her plans to stay before the fire bemoaning her fate. The voices came closer, accompanied by the sound of boots thudding down the stairs.

Ba bump. Ba bump. Ba bump.

Was that the sound of their steps, or was that the sound of her heart, pounding hard and loud? Because Prudence recognized that voice. When he stepped into the parlor and glanced her way, she recognized that face. That smile. The way it made her lungs constrict and ice pulse through her veins.

The Beast.

Lord Dudley.

Here.

Why was he here? *She* didn't even know where she was, and yet he had found her. It must be some coincidence. Some sick twist of fate. Had she not suffered enough?

To hell with you, God.

Dudley's cold, hard eyes fixated on her. This knot in her belly was cold, hard fear, and its icy tentacles were stealing throughout her limbs. She was frozen.

This was a young wounded lamb looking into the eyes of a wolf. So pathetically vulnerable.

Are you there, God? No, obviously not.

When The Beast's lips curved into a smile—she knew that smile—Prudence thought she might be sick. What. Was. He. Doing. Here?

What did it even matter? He was here, ruining everything, again. Just when she had started to snatch back something like happiness! John had gone upstairs to pack, leaving her alone to face her worst nightmare in the flesh.

"Well, well, well . . . ," The Beast murmured. Even his eyes upon her felt like a violation.

Because Prudence was no longer A Lady, she did not feel bound to uphold modes of proper behavior. This time she fled, pushing past him (ah, the advantage of surprise!) to run up the stairs, where she might barricade herself safely in her room and never, ever leave again.

On the top step she tripped. Her toe caught on the stair and she hit the wooden floorboards with a thud.

Dudley, just a short step behind her, hauled her up, twisting the fabric of her dress as he did.

Ladies did not scream. Prudence did. The wretched, fearful, mournful sound was rent from her soul, and it scared her. It must have scared Dudley, too, for he froze for a moment. She tried to seize the moment and scramble away, but then his grasp on her arm tightened. There would be bruises. She could survive bruises. It was what came next that she didn't think she would survive a second time.

"Hello, Prude Prudence," he said amiably, as if they'd met under polite circumstances. Say, over tea, during calling hours. As if he didn't have an iron grasp on her arm, holding her against her will. "Fancy meeting you here."

She spat in his face, her act of defiance surprising her as much as it did him.

He didn't like it, no.

Then Dudley pushed her against a door. Her head smacked against the wood.

Dudley, The Beast, ground his hips against hers. Prudence felt him prodding her. She felt the nausea and the bile rising.

She also felt adamant. Not this. Not again. *Where was Castleton?*

Where was Castleton? John knew the question on her lips, in her heart, uttered uselessly to an empty drawing room. And he was stuck here, in this damned interview that could lead to nothing good. John glanced at the clock. He had somewhere to be. He had made a promise.

Some believe that luck was bestowed upon them. John knew that luck was something to be seized and held onto with both hands. Luck was something a man couldn't think twice about.

John knew he had to act now. To hell with the consequences.

There would be consequences. But all that mattered was getting to Prudence before it was too late.

He seized one opportunity, then another, until he was on his way to her, galloping on a massive beast of a stallion. Hooves thundering. Breath heaving. Heart threatening to explode with each and every beat. John whispered her name into the wind. There was no stopping—until the screaming began.

Chapter 12

WHEN HE HEARD the scream, John was carefully folding his linen shirts and placing them in his valise, along with his one suit of evening clothes and a thin packet of letters from his mother and sister. He had been mentally calculating how much longer it would take to arrive in London in these conditions, and by a more circuitous route and if he might still make it in time.

First he heard the voices of those two London gents as they emerged from their bedchambers and stumbled down to the parlor in search of breakfast, even though it was late in the afternoon. He ignored them.

Next, he heard little footsteps racing up the stairs, followed by a thud. It was probably nothing more than one of the Hammersmith children racing around and running into things. Unsurprisingly, they were becoming rambunctious after being confined indoors for so long. Heavy boot steps followed. It was probably Mr. Hammersmith, chasing after one of his wayward brood.

John carefully folded a linen shirt and placed it in his valise.

And then he heard the scream, the kind that was not something in a child's playful game or a shriek at a mouse. This was the sort of scream that was pure terror.

John threw his door open immediately. He felt nothing, only acted on instinct to stop anything that made a woman scream like that.

Then he saw Prudence. Then he felt everything.

She was pinned up against a door, her face ashen as she pressed her cheek against the wood, angling her face away from the man who was forcing his weight against her.

John recognized the man in an instant. Dudley, a sore loser he had encountered at the Kingswood Race and other house parties attended by bachelor gamblers and prostitutes. He was an ass. That was the last coherent thought John had before he sprang into action.

John roared. He lunged, throwing his not inconsiderable bulk onto Dudley. They hit the floorboards with a brutish thud, in a tangle of limbs. John pulled his arm back before slamming his fist into Dudley's face. Something cracked. Something bled. He did it again.

Then Dudley heaved himself up and forward, launching them both down the stairs in a series of sickening thuds and sharp jabs of stair edges into spines. Dudley swung on the way down, a few of his punches landing on John's jaw, the side of his head, his shoulder.

Dudley's friend stepped out from the parlor, took one look at the situation, and dropped his weight onto John's back, drawing a roar from deep down inside because of the pain that started at his spine and radiated through his limbs. John was vaguely aware of the sound of others screaming to stop. But they sounded so far away, and as long as Dudley was fighting back, John would not stop.

He heard the smack of his fists connecting with someone's face. The grunts of a man taking a hit. The sounds of heavy, labored breaths. Then there was the dull rumble constantly ringing in his ears. Were they ringing from a hit? Or was he yelling? He might be yelling.

And then they were limp beneath him. John stood and looked down at the two bruised and bloodied *gentlemen*—ha!—sprawled on the floor at his feet.

"There's no room here for them," John informed the innkeeper between deep, heaving breaths.

"With all due respect, my lord, I have spare rooms and mouths to feed," Rutherford said apologetically.

"I'll pay for them. All of them. Double the regular rate. You're fully booked. There are no rooms."

"There are no rooms," Rutherford informed the two lords who lay in a bruised and bloody heap on the foyer floor.

One of the jackasses on the floor shuffled up, balancing his weight on his elbows. His black eyes narrowed as he focused on John.

"Who the fuck are you?"

"Castleton." He pronounced this with more

authority than God did when declaring, "It was good" on the seventh day.

Jackass's lips twitched.

"Castleton? Really?"

He stopped smirking when Castleton delivered a boot to his gut. But something about his mockery struck him badly. Had Prudence heard it? He turned to look.

Prudence stood trembling at the top of the stairs, her hands anxiously twisting the fabric of her skirts. Her gaze locked with his. There was nothing else in that moment but her. And him.

She didn't avert her eyes, even though he must have been a frightful sight. His white shirt was damp with sweat and blood. His jaw hurt like something else. He reached up, tentatively touching the painful spot near his eye. Blood. And his hands—they were a bruised, red, and swollen mess.

He placed one foot on the stair, as if to make his way up to her. She flinched. But she stood her ground.

He took the step. Then one more. She held his gaze. His heart started to pound. His feelings for her were written all over his face and hands; the cuts and bruises confessed what he hadn't even expressed to himself.

When he reached the top of the stairs, she whispered, "Thank you."

"Of course," he said, voice rough.

Of course he was going to fight for her, protect

her, care for her. John would do so for any woman,
but this time he had been scared. This time he'd
felt so damned much he was lucky he hadn't
fought to the death.

She shook her head and led him into her
bedchamber—careful to leave the door wide
open. At her bidding, he sat down on the chair as
she dipped a cloth in a basin of cool water.

Quietly she worked, dabbing the cloth against
his face. He closed his eyes, savoring the pleasant
feeling of the cool water against his hot, sweaty
skin. Gently, she smoothed the cloth across his
brow, his cheeks, his neck. She wrapped the cold,
wet cloth around his hands one by one, holding it
in place for a moment to soothe the burning.

Prudence's thoughts were a jumbled mess as
she worked to clean up Castleton. He had saved
her. He had come, when no one ever came. He
looked hurt, raw, ragged. Nothing like the dapper,
charming gentleman she had met on the side of
the road. This was another side of him—raw,
powerful, uncivilized.

The sound of Dudley and Fitz-Herbert arguing
with the innkeeper reached them. Judging from
their shouted conversation, the two devils would
be packing up soon. Prudence was inspired to do
the unthinkable: shutting and locking the door,
leaving herself barricaded in a room alone with
a man.

Before the panic could overwhelm her, Prue
dipped the cloth in the basin to rinse it before

smoothing it across his brow. She was touching a man—with a cloth, but it was something. It was the least she could do after what he had done for her. And she wanted to soothe him and offer some comfort. As she did, she found it soothed herself, too.

She felt his blue eyes on her, watching attentively.

"Was he after you? Are you running from him?" His voice was rough, and from that alone she knew that he ached for answers only to protect her. Castleton wouldn't gossip.

"I think it was a coincidence," she told him. No one knew where she was or where she was going.

"But you know him."

"From London. I hate him." Her voice cracked. It was the first time she'd said it aloud. Because of him, her heart was filled with hate when it should have been bursting with love. She hated him all the more for it.

John's eyes were still fixed on her. She could feel him seeing her secrets. It felt agonizing and wonderful all at once.

"He hurt you before."

It took every ounce of strength Prudence possessed to look Castleton in the eye. She'd told no one what Dudley had done to her—not Emma, not Olivia, not Miss Georgette, not even Lady Dare. She had never even whispered the words in the dark of night or even thought them in her head.

The word "yes" refused to form on her tongue,

wouldn't dare cross her lips. He had hurt her so profoundly that she might never be healed, unlike the bruises on Castleton's hands, which would fade in a few days' time. But the answer was plain to him anyway. She managed a slight nod to confirm it.

"I wondered," he admitted.

"You can tell? Can everyone tell?" Prue's eyes widened. The only saving grace was that no one knew. She could pretend to be fine and to be whole. But if everyone knew . . .

. . . and they hadn't done anything?

Her heart stopped. She quickly looked away. She bit her lip, holding back the word *betrayal*.

"My sister . . . it happened to her, too," Castleton said. The anguish in his voice broke Prue's heart. She understood why he wasn't the slightest bit affected by all the cuts and bruises on his body: they were nothing in comparison to the agonies that she and his sister had experienced. There was no comparison, and he knew it. "She wasn't quite herself after. Never wanted to be touched. Anything that reminded her of it set her off. Don't blame her."

It had never occurred to Prudence that she wasn't the only one who had suffered this way. After all, what Dudley did to her wasn't exactly discussed in polite company. In fact, it wasn't discussed at all, ever, except in vague warnings to young ladies. The risks, the dangers, the pain were never talked about. Knowing she wasn't the only one was a bittersweet knowledge. Prue wouldn't wish this upon anyone, yet for the first time since it had happened, she didn't feel so alone.

"No one knows," Prudence whispered. "No one can know."

"I won't tell," he promised, his gaze locked with hers.

"It has been so hard keeping this secret," she confessed. "It is exhausting."

It was terrifying that he knew, but there was also a welcome sensation of relief. There were so many things she wanted to say to him about it now that she had admitted it. How it had hurt. How scared she'd been and how she hadn't stopped being scared. How badly she had wanted that carriage ride with him but just . . . couldn't.

Castleton didn't say anything to that. He looked away. Gritted his jaw, and winced. Flexed his hands, and grimaced.

"Prudence?"

"Yes?"

There was a moment, a long moment. Gazes locked. Then he blinked.

"I taught my sister how to defend herself. In case I wasn't there for her," he said, and she had the impression that it wasn't what he planned to say. "I want to be there for you, Prudence," he exclaimed as he reached out and impulsively clasped her hand. Instinctively she withdrew.

With a fierce determination she didn't think she possessed, Prudence placed her hand over his. She was so tired of living under Dudley's spell. If she couldn't escape him, she would have to fight him. If she could just override her fear long enough, Castleton could instruct her on how to defend herself so she needn't be so terrified all the time. The promise of that was like the promise of sunshine after this endless rainstorm.

Prudence looked into Castleton's eyes. "Show me."

Chapter 13

THOUGH IT PAINED him to do so, Castleton stood and pushed the chair and basin aside. Prudence stood, too, and her head just reached his shoulder, reminding him she was just a slip of a girl.

On the other side of the locked door, Dudley and Fitz-Herbert and their valets lumbered up and down the stairs, cursing with every step. Before Castleton, Prudence's eyes widened and her hands shook.

"The first thing you have to do is stop looking so bloody scared all the time," John said.

"Are you saying I asked for it?" Prudence asked angrily, eyes flashing.

"God, no," he swore vehemently. "I'm just saying you look at the world with these fearful doe eyes, awaiting the worst. Annie, the barmaid, on the other hand—she isn't taking nothing from nobody."

"Well, if I were as tall as she, and statuesque and—"

"Prudence," he said earnestly, gazing directly into her eyes, "you just can't be scared. Even if you're scared."

"That doesn't even make sense."

"If you don't think about it too hard, it makes perfect sense," he said.

Such were the words that gave him strength each day. There were a thousand and one things that might go wrong and a hundred opportunities for disaster to strike. People counted on him and this lucky streak of his, which was more likely to end with each passing second. It was a fact that he was constantly, painfully aware of. He could be paralyzed with fear and worry, or he could put one foot in front of the other and take his chances, roll the dice, play the game.

John eyed Prudence as she mulled this over. He wanted to explain everything. But the words wouldn't come. If his happiness were the only one at stake, aye, he'd tell her everything. But people were counting on him. So he kept his thoughts and stories to himself.

Besides, this moment was about giving Prudence strength, not unburdening his secrets. The sound of suitcases being lugged through the hall and down the stairs was a stark reminder of why.

"Men like him look to dominate someone else as a way to prove their own power," Castleton explained. He wasn't thinking only of Dudley but also of other "gentlemen" with a disregard for women. "It's not about lust or lack of control but dominance, pure and simple."

"But why *me*?" The anguish in her voice could break a man. Something in him just altered forever.

"I don't know, Prudence," he said softly, hating that he didn't have an answer. "We can't change what has happened, we can only do what we can to make sure it never happens again."

"What if I make him mad at me?"

"You will make him mad if you're doing it right," Castleton replied evenly. "But who cares about that? You just need to get away. I need you to be safe."

His voice might have betrayed an uncommon amount of emotion. This was all he could do. Give her strength, help her believe in herself.

"What do I do?" Prudence asked with an adorable and determined upturn of her chin.

"Are you scared?" John asked.

"Yes. Always."

"So?" He shrugged, arranged his features in an expression of boredom, and turned away.

"So? SO?" she echoed angrily, as he'd expected. He fought to keep his face inscrutable. *"So what if I'm scared*?" she cried. "That's everything!"

He turned to her.

"Now you're angry, Prue," he said encouragingly. "That's good. Anger will give you strength, where fear will make you weak."

"Ladies aren't supposed to be angry," she said, anguish in her voice.

"Ladies aren't supposed to do or be a lot of things, Prudence. Humanity is worse for it."

"Then what do I do?" Prudence asked, growing frustrated. "When do I hit you?"

"You hit when you have a good chance of landing a strong blow. But it's best if it doesn't come to that. You have to yell, Prudence."

John stalked toward her. His bruised and wounded appearance must have made it all the more frightful for her.

"Leave me alone!" It was a halfhearted shout. "Stop this!"

John hated doing this, but he took another menacing step toward her. Then another, then another, until they were standing close enough to kiss.

"Stand back!" This time there was force behind her words. This time, he almost did back off. But Dudley still hadn't departed the inn—they could hear him railing against the injustice of being beaten and forced into the rain.

John took a deep breath. He gazed down at Prudence and into her eyes. She was scared, certainly. But he also noted determination and a resurgence of that stubbornness that hadn't allowed her to get in his carriage when she had so badly wanted to.

"You have survived the worst thing that could happen to you," he said softly. "And you have carried on. Prudence, you are far stronger than you know."

That left her stunned and speechless.

"Now move," he said in a low voice, just before reaching for her wrist. She snatched it away.

"Move," he growled. "Like all those dancing steps you spent two-eighths of your life practicing."

John stepped toward her and she stepped back, and to the left. He advanced toward her and she darted to the right. Like some deranged waltz or quadrille, they moved around the room, dodging the furniture and each other.

All he wanted was to sweep her into his embrace and waltz with her properly. Like a gentleman with a lady he adores.

He didn't like *this*. But he hated the idea of her defenseless. He hated the knowledge that he wouldn't always be there for her. So all he could do was teach her now.

Prudence impatiently blew a wayward strand of hair out of her eyes. Her cheeks were becoming flushed.

"Can I hit you now?"

"If you can get close enough to," he murmured.

She advanced toward him. Those wide-with-fear doe eyes of hers were narrowed and shooting sparks. She was glorious, with her hair starting to work free from its arrangement, her flushed cheeks, and her determined strides. He wouldn't allow a smile. Not when she was so focused and determined. Not when she was, for once, more angry than scared.

"The next question is where," he said, once she was standing within striking distance. "You will never overpower a man with physical strength alone, so you have to hit him in his most vulnerable parts."

"His face?"

"No, his balls," John explained.

"Excuse me?" Her cheeks reddened, this time with embarrassment.

"No time to be ladylike now, Miss Merry-weather," he cautioned. Then, pointing to the pertinent place, he said, "You'll want to hit a man here."

Prudence swung her fist. With just a second to spare, he dodged her attempt to hit him.

"Hey! I'm trying to hit you!"

"It hurts too bloody much," he explained. "And I haven't given up on having children."

And just like that, she lost her anger and her focus.

"You want to have children?" she asked softly. "Do you plan to marry?"

That was another thing he feared—Prudence getting ideas in her head that he could never possibly live up to. It would wreck him to crush her hopes and expectations. His own hands clenched into fists—which made him swear from the pain Not wanting to get into it now, John just said, "We'll see what God has in store for me."

Both paused to acknowledge the sound of a whip cracking and a carriage starting off. Dudley and Fitz-Herbert were gone—for now. John didn't deceive himself; they would all be setting off on the same road toward London.

He prayed that Prudence never needed to know what he was teaching her.

"You can also try hitting a man in the eyes or the throat."

She tried, and missed. He dodged her attempts, while giving her guidance about what to do.

"Use the heel of your hand. And if you are going

to strike with your fist, make sure your thumb is on the outside," he said as he grasped her fist and, holding her hand in his, folded her fingers into a proper fist. "It will get crushed otherwise."

"The pain will make me angrier, which will help me fight," she said stubbornly.

"But if it doesn't heal properly, you'll never fit your hands into the kind of delicate gloves that ladies wear." Even though they were breaking all the rules here, she was still a Lady, and he'd do well to remember that.

"The horrors," Prudence said flatly. John couldn't help it; he cracked a grin. She half smiled and half sighed.

"Are you sure I cannot just run away?" Prudence asked wistfully with a longing glance out the window.

"In your long skirts?"

"It worked with the highwayman," she said. "I just slunk off, unnoticed."

"And I thank God for it. But you can't just run away from your problems," he said softly.

"It's been working rather well for me so far," she replied with a little shrug of her shoulders.

"Has it?" John asked softly.

Prudence sighed. She glanced at him, then looked away. He watched her gaze land on the locked door and skim over the bed before settling on the view from the window. He understood. Prudence wasn't too bothered by the rain, for she was content to remain here, away from London and the problems that had sent her running. As long as it rained, she didn't need to decide what to do.

"Are you really never going to return to London? What about your friends and family? I'm certain they miss you. Hell, they must be worried about you. "

"They would if they knew where I was. But they don't. And there's nothing really waiting for me in London."

"It's London! Everything is in London. There's nowhere to go except for London," he exclaimed. His hopes and dreams were pinned on the largest city in the country, and perhaps the greatest city in the world.

She smiled sweetly at him but revealed nothing about her life there and what did or did not await her. So many questions he wanted to ask, one of them being, why did he want to know so badly? At some point between their meeting on the road and this moment, she had gone from being just a girl to being the sun to his earth.

As if running away from the topic, Prudence changed the subject.

"What if none of this works? What if it happens again?"

"It won't happen again," he vowed.

"No one is ever there for me. Not even God. Only I am there for me."

"I'm so sorry." His voice cracked. He was sick with sorry.

"My friend Emma is always reading romantic novels. This, I believe, is the part when you promise to always be there for me," she said with a sad smile.

"I will be there for you," he said firmly. But he couldn't promise forever. He thought of Martha . . . and what he had left behind.

"And if you're not?"

"Then you had better learn to fight like the devil and run like the wind," he said.

"How do you know all of this?" Prudence asked. It wasn't an easy answer.

One year earlier
Blackhaven Manor

Young Lord Burbrooke had an affection for Martha. All the bucks did. She possessed a lovely figure, had the face of an angel, and a soothing voice. John had mastered the lethal stare early on. Often that was enough. And then it wasn't. His hands were constantly raw, fending off all her suitors. But that is what brothers did.

By suitors he meant . . . well, not exactly suitors. They weren't after her hand in marriage. Just a tussle. A roll in the hay. A romp in the hall. She had a way of driving men wild, forgetting sense and reason. And these "suitors" thought she was the kind of girl who didn't need a ring and promise of forever.

John kept them at bay. Until he hadn't been able to.

"What will I do when you're gone?" Martha asked. She sat on his bed while he packed a small case, pausing every so often to flex his hands, hissing with pain at the cuts and bruises. One of his fingers might have been broken.

He might have gone too far. Hitting Lord Burbrooke for flirting with his sister had definitely been going too far. Especially when by *flirting* he meant *accosting*.

She'd said no. Hell, she'd even said *please*.

Just thinking about it made him want to punch the wall. Worse: he could no longer stay at Blackhaven Manor now.

It was impossible for him to show his black-and-blue face in the breakfast room. It was impossible for him to pour brandy with hands too broken and swollen to fit into a pair of gloves. It was impossible for him to go about his business at the manor, with everyone terrified of him. He'd have to hastily depart and leave Martha able to fend for herself.

Thus, John taught her where exactly to hit a man so it would stun him with a breathtaking pain. He cautioned her to avoid being alone with one at all costs. Then he showed her how to escape from his grasp, how to dodge his advances, holler like a she-devil, and hit with all her strength.

"Why must you go?" Martha asked pleadingly.

"You know why," he said gruffly.

"It's my fault," she said glumly.

He snapped the valise shut and turned to look at her.

"It's not your fault," he said firmly.

"But—" Her voice was meek. So many questions in her eyes, and so many tears threatening to fall. It was killing him to leave. But it was impossible for him to stay.

Then, gently, he said, "I'll come back for you. And Mum."

"Where are you going, anyway? Where can you go?"

"I'm off to seek my fortune," John said, grinning faintly and cupping her face in his hands. "Then I'll come back for you and Mum and we'll live someplace nice."

"You've been reading too many novels," she said, with a roll of her eyes. He did spend every free moment with a book borrowed from the house's vast library. It wasn't like anyone else in the house read them.

"Maybe you haven't been reading enough."

"As if I had time . . ."

He picked up the valise. Hand on the doorknob, he paused. Looked back.

"One day, I promise you will have nothing to do but sit around and read novels in the most luxurious setting, with servants waiting on you hand and foot."

"You'd better go get that fortune, because I could

fancy that," Martha said. His memory wouldn't let him forget the tears he saw in her eyes.

He left shortly after that, taking one long look back at Blackhaven Manor. He knew he could never go back.

The Coach & Horses Inn

"How do you know all of this?" Prudence had asked. He couldn't bring himself to tell her. One answer would only lead to more questions that he couldn't answer without ruining everything.

"I just know," John said with a shrug before lowering himself into a chair. "My sister. When I had to leave, I made sure she was able to defend herself."

"Why did you have to leave?"

"There might have been a fight. Not unlike today," Castleton replied with a grimace.

"Did you duel?" she asked nervously. Lords were known to duel and then be forced to flee if their shots hit home. He could see her concocting a romantically tinged story with lords and ladies and duels for honor.

"It was less civilized than that," he said, his mouth settling into a grim line. Then he turned the tables on her. "What are you running from, Prudence?"

"What makes you think I'm running?"

"What else would you be doing here, when

you should be in London, drinking chocolate and reading gossip rags?" Castleton asked, his blue eyes settling on her and making her feel things. Warm, tingly, scary things.

Prudence looked out the window. It was too complicated to explain. She wasn't quite ready to tell him about Lady Penelope's Ball, and Cecil, and how her best friends had suddenly gotten married when she'd planned on them being a trio of spinsters. What it all came down to, really, was that thing The Beast had done to her and how her whole life had been reduced to making sure it never happened again. Unfortunately, she'd missed a lot of life that way.

And still it had almost happened *again*.

Because Castleton knew the awful thing that had happened to her and still smiled at her, she tried to explain, when she wouldn't have otherwise.

"There's what I want, you see. Then there's what I'm afraid of. Sometimes it's the same thing."

It was the closest she could get to saying, *Stay*.

She lifted her eyes to his; their gazes locked. He understood.

She heard the sharp intake of his breath.

"I want to hold you, Prudence," he said, voice rough. "I want to feel you in my arms, your breasts against my chest. I want to kiss you—gently and sweetly—and make sure it's everything a damn good kiss should be. I want to lose myself in you. But I want you to know pleasure first. I won't dare any of that unless you ask me to."

Just listening to him made her heart beat a little bit harder and a little bit faster. She could feel the blood rushing through her. Prudence also wanted those things. What would it be like to be held and not want to run? What was a damn good kiss like, anyway? What pleasure did he speak of?

For every desire was a wave of fear, threatening to drown her. Always she felt as if she was barely managing to keep her head above water.

"I'm not ready," she whispered.

He settled back in his chair, smiling.

"There's no rush," he said. "I have nowhere to be."

"You have to be in London for the exhibition," Prudence told him. She hadn't forgotten his excitement when he'd told her of his plans. She did not want to stand in his way.

Castleton leaned forward. There was a gleam in his eye. She was both curious and nervous to know what made him grin like that.

"Come with me," Castleton suggested.

"I beg your pardon?" He could not have actually suggested such a thing!

"I can't leave you alone, Prue," he said. "You should return to London anyway. It makes sense that we should travel together. I'll protect you."

"What if you are the one I'm afraid of?"

"Are you?"

"A little. I know what you just did to protect

me. But I've spent four years being afraid of men. It doesn't just end. Not when Dudley found me again. And not when—"

"When you've seen what force I'm capable of," Castleton finished with a deep exhalation. He glanced out the window—still raining!—and pushed his fingers through his hair, frustrated. Then he looked at her, really looked at her.

"I'm sorry," she said meekly.

"Do not be sorry," he said fiercely. "Something horrible happened to you, Prudence. You didn't deserve it. You don't deserve the repercussions, and you shouldn't be sorry because of them. It's not your fault. None of it." He paused to take a deep breath. She couldn't breathe. "It's fine if you're afraid of me. You should be—not because I'm going to hurt you but because of what you have experienced. But I'm just going to do everything I can to ease your fears and earn your trust."

This speech, of course, made Prudence weep. She turned away, hoping he wouldn't see.

No one had ever said those things to her—and how could they, when no one knew? For years she had kept her shameful secret locked deep inside. In quiet moments, her brain would go over it again and again, finding the mistakes she'd made and trying to uncover what qualities in her made her a target for a violent, controlling beast like Dudley.

Castleton's words weren't just words. They were ones she very badly needed to hear.

"Come to London with me. You can't stay here forever, wherever we are."

"Westbury," she mumbled.

"Right. You can't stay here forever, especially not when Dudley knows where you are."

Prudence stiffened. Dudley would be back in London eventually, too. But she'd rather face him there with her friends and Castleton by her side. Not here, alone.

"But what will people think? We cannot just travel together. It's not done." She might not have been a proper lady anymore, but she'd been trained to think like one.

"We'll tell everyone we're married," Castleton said, grinning. "How would you like to be Lady Castleton?"

For a fleeting second she forgot all of her fears and thought yes. "Prudence, Lady Castleton" had quite a ring to it. She imagined herself walking arm and arm with him through a ballroom, feeling secure and cherished.

Then she returned to the reality of her life. She should return to London, with protection. If Emma could pretend to be engaged for the duration of a house party, then perhaps it wasn't so crazy for Prudence to sensibly accept the pretense of a husband whilst on the road to London. No one in town would ever have to know.

"I could be Lady Castleton," she said. "It could be worse. I could be Lady Dudley."

Though she had uttered the words flippantly,

they were accompanied by a piercing truth: while she *hated* that no one had come to stop Dudley's first assault on her, it might have been a blessing. Society had such ridiculous rules: any couple caught in a remotely compromising position found themselves swiftly marching down the aisle. The circumstances didn't matter. A girl without her virginity and a husband was nobody at all. But no one had seen them, and thus no one could force them to marry.

She'd been spared being raped by him again and again—as would be his legal right.

Thank God she had been spared such a wretched fate.

"Let's have supper and then retire early," Castleton suggested. "We should leave at first light. We might be able to make it to London in a few days, taking a route other than the main road."

Prudence didn't sleep much that night. She lay in her bed, highly attuned to the sounds of the inn. The rain drummed on the roof; by now such a familiar sound she had to strain to notice it. There was a faint rumbling from the parlor—it was probably Buckley's snores. She did not hear heavy boots on the stairs or a knock on her door. There was only the sound of her breath and the beat of her heart.

Something had changed today.

Today, she had confronted her worst nightmares. And she had fought back. Someone had come to her rescue, for once.

Castleton had saved her, in more ways than one.

He'd stopped Dudley from hurting her again. He'd made it abundantly clear to Dudley—and herself—that she wasn't just a poor defenseless creature for him to prey upon.

She had confessed her deepest, darkest secret, and he'd *stayed*. She had always feared that if someone knew, they wouldn't want anything to do with one so shameful. On the other hand, she feared that men would think she would welcome their advances, as if she had lost the right to say no. Castleton had assuaged her fears on both accounts.

For the first time, she didn't feel so helpless. Castleton had taught her how to save herself, a gift almost as precious as telling her firmly that she wasn't at fault and she didn't deserve what happened to her. Knowing how to fight quieted the fear in her heart.

For the first time since the attack, she felt a spark of hope for herself. Prudence vowed to hold onto that spark and nurture it until it became a flame.

She could dwell on the terror—Dudley's cruel smile when he saw her, or his fierce grip on her arm, or worse. Or she could make a considerable effort to think of the good things. She had touched a man today for the first time.

She stilled at the thought. It was not accompanied by the usual shudder whenever she considered a man's touch. In fact, she felt a warmth in her belly and something she might have called yearning if she had more courage.

In the morning they would pretend to be man and wife as they traveled back to London. As expected, she felt a certain measure of trepidation at going off with a man whom she'd known only a few days—though she had a fine measure of his character. But there was also a little tremble of excitement. This might be the closest to marriage she would ever come.

The Faux Lady Castleton was about to make her entry upon the world.

Chapter 14

A HIGH PERCH PHAETON painted a glossy forest green with two white horses hitched to it was parked before the inn. Prudence eyed it from the porch, remembering how badly she'd wanted to ride in it—and how she'd walked for miles in the heat and rain rather than accept.

Even this morning, she hesitated when taking Castleton's hand as she climbed into the carriage. Lady Dare always chided Prudence for refusing a footman's offered hand and instead grabbing onto whatever was at hand to pull herself up.

But not Castleton.

"It's all right, Miss Merryweather," he said. She understood that he meant it was all right for her to climb aboard—she would be safe. And she also understood him to mean that her trepidation was perfectly acceptable. He understood.

For so long, Prudence had feared that someone would learn her shameful secret. It had never occurred to her that someone would learn it and that everything would be fine. She never considered that someone would understand *why* the littlest things were insurmountable obstacles to her.

"Well it feels good to be out of doors at least," Castleton remarked as he took a seat beside her.

"It's a bit wet," she remarked, and he laughed.

This morning the rain had lightened, which was lucky, since they had to go no matter the weather. Neither of them wished to wait around to see if Dudley would return. Much as she had tried to convince herself of the possibility of staying at the inn indefinitely, it was not truly an option. They would have to venture out on uncertain roads in a conveyance offering little shelter from the elements.

Besides, Castleton was right: she ought to return to her friends and family in London. And he had to make it in time for the Great Exhibition—rain or no rain. Because the carriage was open, with only a slight covering, it was necessary to sit so close to Castleton that she felt his leg pressing against hers.

It wasn't a bad feeling. It just triggered a bad memory.

For the first time, Prudence made a deliberate effort to separate the two.

"I confess this carriage isn't ideal for inclement weather. My apologies." Castleton gave her an apologetic smile. There was nothing wolfish or dangerous about it. It was just . . . nice. Nice was lovely.

"You couldn't have known it would rain for

forty days and nights, I suppose," Prudence remarked. She took one backward glance at the Coach & Horses Inn, taking in the sign hanging from the porch and the large parlor window from which they had stared out into the rain. The girl she'd been upon her arrival was not the same girl as she was now, upon her departure.

Funny that her life should change so dramatically in this little place.

Then Castleton cracked the whip and they set off. Prudence turned to face forward.

They took the road she had walked just a few days ago. It pained her slightly to see how fast they covered ground that she had taken hours to travel on foot.

"Where were you coming from, anyway?" Prudence asked. It only occurred to her now that she did not know.

"There was a horse race near Kingswood," he said. Then, with a lowered voice and a grim expression, he added, "I actually saw that Dudley fellow there."

"You did?"

"He was a bit sore that he bet against a certain filly," Castleton explained. "And I bet heavily on her."

"Was she victorious?" Prudence asked. She hoped the filly had won by a dozen lengths.

Castleton turned to face her, a half grin playing on his lips. "What do you think?"

"How did you know she would win?" Prue asked.

"Some people place their bets based on blood-lines, or because their friends own the horse, or because they think the ridiculous name sounds like a winner. But I look in their eyes." As he said that, Castleton turned to look into Prue's eyes. She gazed up at his and found them bright, and searching hers.

"What did you see?" Was she asking about the filly or herself?

"She was skittish," Castleton said. "There was something wild in her eyes. And I saw intelligence there, too. And the way she tossed her head—that girl had spark."

"I'm afraid I'm being compared to a horse. Or I hope I am," Prudence muttered.

"A lovely, champion filly. If you are, it's a compliment," Castleton said with another friendly smile. Once again, it made her feel warm inside. This time, she allowed herself to feel the heat unfurl from her belly and spread into her limbs. She didn't fight the smile that tugged at her lips either.

To say that Castleton was unlike any other man she'd met was an understatement. He was changing her—did he know? She didn't feel *whole*, but she felt less damaged. In fact, she rather felt as if springtime had arrived and she was thawing out after a long, cold winter. Castleton wasn't just making her feel nice things; he was quite possibly breathing life back into her.

There was no way she could ever repay him, but she could show her gratitude. Even if it meant admitting she'd been a liar.

"There's something I should tell you," Prudence confessed.

"I don't know if now is a good time," he said grimly. "I'm a bit busy at the moment."

"Doing what?" Prudence asked, a bit perplexed. He had his hands lightly on the reins while the white horses pulled the carriage along the very straight road.

"Busy driving," he said. And then, with a grin, he added, "And flirting."

Prudence laughed and playfully swatted his arm in mock frustration. It happened so fast that she hadn't realized she had touched him until it was done.

"Your flirting is comparing girls to horses!"

"Winning fillies with spark," he corrected with a wink. "Now, what were you going to tell me?"

Prudence took a deep breath.

"I can introduce you to the Duke of Ashbrooke. And Baron Radcliffe."

The horses bolted forward, and she was thrown back against the seat. Castleton must have tightened his grip on the reins. He winced—it could have been the pain from his hands, damaged in yesterday's fight.

Then he relaxed and exhaled and asked only one question: "How?"

"They are married to my best friends," Prudence said, further revealing herself. He now had the information to track down Miss Payton, when, as Miss Merryweather, she could have vanished in the London crowds.

"So I suppose you have more than a passing acquaintance with them."

"Well, we don't sit around drinking brandy and grumbling about how vexing women are, but yes, we are friendly."

Castleton threw back his head and burst out laughing. She thought her heart would combust from the sudden, intense pleasure of the sound and having made him laugh.

"I can't think of how else I might repay you," she said softly.

"Don't feel indebted to me, Prudence. I would have done it for anyone."

"I know," she said. And she did know that, completely. "That makes me admire you more. It's why I'm here."

He glanced down at her. Smiled. "I'm glad you're with me," he said softly.

"There is something else you should know," Prudence added.

"Look at you, with all the secrets," he remarked with a laugh.

"I could keep this one, I suppose. But when you meet the duke and the baron, the truth will come out." The Truth. That made it sound so dramatic.

"You're not really Miss Merryweather, are you?"

"It's my middle name. My real name is Prudence Merryweather Payton."

Beside her, he tensed. She felt it in his leg, touching hers, and she saw it in his jaw.

"Are you mad?" Prudence asked nervously.

"No," he said quickly. "I'd be mad if you gave your real name to a stranger you met alongside the road one afternoon."

"I never thought someone would understand me," Prudence sighed. Oh, Emma and Olivia knew her quite well, and they were knowledgeable about all her likes (chocolate, pastries, kittens) and dislikes (mean people, cold weather, tea without sugar). But they didn't understand her wounded soul the way Castleton seemed to.

Then again, how could they, when she'd never confided in them?

"When you've been let down, as you have, I suppose it's hard not to underestimate people," Castleton remarked, easily putting into words an entire knot of feelings she'd been walking around with for years.

"No one came," Prudence said softly. "I kept hoping someone would come and stop it. But I only just realized that if I had been caught with him, we'd have been forced to marry. Then he would . . ." She paused, searching for the word to describe what had happened to her. One that would not stick in her throat or pierce her heart to say aloud. ". . . he would hurt me again and again and again, and it would be his legal right to do so.

What a sick concept of honor." The unfair truth of that made her ache. "So I didn't cry out for help as loudly as I could have, and I never told anyone. I just wanted it to be over so I could get on with pretending it never happened."

Castleton looked ahead, stony-faced. The horses carried on. Just when she thought he might be unmoved by her confession—leaving her to feel utterly foolish for sharing it—she saw him wipe his eyes with the back of his hand.

"Do you know what they call me?" Prudence asked. This unburdening was terrifying—and then it felt good once those words were out. So when they kept bubbling up, she didn't try to stop them.

"The loveliest girl in London?"

She cracked a wry smile.

"Prude Prudence. Do you know what else they call me?"

"The most beautiful woman in the world?"

"London's Least Likely to Be Caught in a Compromising Position," she said dryly. "Doesn't that just slay you?"

"Yes," he said firmly. For a moment, a comfortable silence stretched between them. For years she had wanted to share the irony of the nicknames the ton had bestowed on her. It felt good to have finally done so.

And then softly, Castleton spoke up. "Prudence?"

"Yes?"

"I don't want to scare you," he said, "but I think I might be falling in love with you."

Prudence sat very still beside him, with her hands folded in her lap. She didn't know what to say to *that*. So she said, "Well, that is unexpected."

"For you, perhaps. I thought it was inevitable the moment I set eyes on you."

"You knew from half a mile away that the mess of a girl on the side of the road was lovable?" She glanced over at him, wondering if he was mad.

"I knew the minute you refused my offer for a ride and insisted on walking. You're one tough filly," he said. "You're a lovely, remarkable woman." This time it was her turn to look away and take in the scenery, although the tears slicking her eyes made it all a bit blurry.

"Prudence, thank you for offering the introduction. But you don't have to."

"I want to." She did want to, with her whole heart. "Besides, they love talking about the engine, and it bores me and my friends to tears."

"Emma and Olivia, right?" he asked, glancing at her to ascertain if he was correct.

"You remember," Prudence marveled.

"I was listening," he said with a shrug. And then his face broke into a wide grin. "Look ahead, Prudence."

"Is that sunshine?" she asked. Up ahead, rays of sunlight were streaming through gray clouds that were breaking up and drifting away.

Chapter 15

Dudley and Fitz-Herbert were lounging in a private parlor, enjoying a meal and killing time before the fight, though anyone who caught a glimpse of them would assume the fight had already happened.

Fitz-Herbert sported a black eye and a cut lip. Dudley's noble, patrician nose had been broken and hastily tended to by a harried Fitz-Herbert in the inn while the innkeeper had been hollering at them to get out, and they'd been hollering at their valets to hurry up already. So it wasn't set properly, and would probably sit at an awkward angle upon his face for the rest of his life. The black-and-blue eyes would fade, eventually. Already the bruises around his light blue eyes were fading to a sickening shade of yellowish green. There was no denying it: he looked ghastly.

Dudley took a swallow of wine and eyed the letter a footman had just delivered. He recognized his father's crest in the red wax sealing the vellum shut. It was with a distinct lack of enthusiasm that he opened it and scanned the words.

Letters from his father rarely conveyed good news. And if there was a bright spot, it was also tempered by an order. This missive was no exception.

"Bloody hell," Dudley muttered after he read it. Crumpling the paper in frustration wasn't satisfying, for the pain in his hands only reminded him of the beating he'd suffered.

"What now?" Fitz-Herbert asked. He was sprawled in a chair before the fire, lazily blowing misshapen smoke rings.

"My father has tracked me down."

"Is the old man here?"

"Of course he's not here," Dudley said in a tone that conveyed his low estimation of his friend's intelligence. "We all know the old man couldn't drag his fat arse away from Scarbrough Park even if he wanted to, which he doesn't. No, he sent a footman with a message."

"Impressive how they found you," Fitz-Herbert remarked, even though it wasn't.

"We told everyone we were coming here for the boxing match. It's not impressive at all, though it's incredibly annoying to be bothered with these tedious domestic matters when I am traveling."

"What does he want? I'm assuming he wants something from you. Otherwise, why would he write? Or has he suddenly developed a concern for your welfare and interest in your thoughts?"

Both gents burst into bitter laughter.

His father was not interested in his thoughts.

On the few occasions when he had ventured his opinion on the management of the estate, his father had called him an ignorant and inexperienced hack. Never mind that his inexperience was entirely owing to his father's refusal to share the duties of the estate or educate his son. Dudley had a piddly little estate that was his to manage, but it was so small and unprofitable that it was hardly worth the bother, especially when his father footed his bills.

And as for interest in his welfare? Dudley snorted. He was only important as the heir, which made him very important indeed. So important that his father impressed that fact upon hosts and hostesses around town, who would rather not invite Dudley but knew that they ought to—or else risk the disapproval of the ancient and respected estate of the Marquis of Scarbrough.

But as a person? As a son? The old marquis couldn't care less.

He was merely Lord Dudley, his courtesy title. He was the future Marquis of Scarbrough. That was all.

"Well? What's he say?" Fitz-Herbert asked impatiently.

"I am to escort my sister to a stupid ball," Dudley said, feeling emasculated just saying the words.

"So we'll arrive with her and then hit the card room." Fitz-Herbert shrugged. Then again, he didn't have any sisters to squire around town.

"A brilliant plan—if you were invited, which you are not. This ball is for her girl's school," Dudley said witheringly. "Lady Penelope's something or other."

"What do girls need to go to school for anyway?" Fitz-Herbert mused.

What followed was a list of carnal acts they thought ought to be taught at a ladies' school. This kept them amused for the duration of half an hour and half a bottle of wine.

But Dudley couldn't quite forget about the crumpled sheet of vellum there on the table amidst the dishes, cigar stubs, ashes, and wineglasses. It mocked him, that letter. It reminded him what a puppet he was. His father knew just how to make him dance to his tune, much as he was loath to do it.

"We'll have to leave soon in order to make it to London in time," Dudley said darkly.

"Soon? We only just arrived!" Fitz-Herbert exclaimed. He pulled a face, making plain that he was *not* pleased to be planning their departure already. "And I hope I don't need to remind you why we were delayed."

"Aye, because you wouldn't ford the river," Dudley said. If only they had taken that little risk. . . .

"We would have drowned."

"Instead we were beaten within an inch of our lives." Dudley fought the urge to press his fingers against the tender bruises on his face. Instead he looked down at his fists—red, gnarled, cut, swollen. These were not the hands of an aristocrat.

"And whose fault is that?"

Dudley just shrugged.

He remembered feeling so helpless—there had been the rain, and always orders from his father. He remembered because he always felt so frustrated that he couldn't *do* anything. And then Prude Prudence had bizarrely been there.

He had come up with that name for her. And it had stuck, for years now. He felt a bit of triumph at being a trendsetter amongst the ton, even if he didn't get credit for it.

She'd been there, and all he'd been able to think about was how powerful she had made him feel that one time, before. First she'd fought, and then she'd realized he'd been stronger and given in. How was he to have known that this time she'd had some hulk of a man ready at her defense? She was one of London's Least Likely, for Chrissakes. Those girls were destined from the start to be spinsters, everyone knew it. They existed to fill out the corner of the ballrooms, as if hostesses ordered them as part of their ballroom décor—potted palms, a punch bowl, wallflowers. In fact, he had often wondered—fleetingly, for he didn't *dwell* on such matters—if those wallflowers even existed outside the confines of a ballroom.

Which begged the question, what had Prude Prudence been doing at that country inn? That begged another question: what the hell did he care?

That letter was still on the table, intruding upon his line of vision.

"We'll have to miss the last day of boxing," Dudley said darkly. "If we go."

"Are you going to go?" Fitz-Herbert asked.

"Apparently, if I wish for him to pay my gambling debt to Lord Inverness, I will be there with bloody bells on."

"What do you owe him? I can't recall . . ." Fitz-Herbert wisely refrained from mentioning the numerous losses he'd racked up lately. It was just a losing streak; it would end soon.

"I owe him five thousand pounds because of an unfortunate hand I was dealt in a game of vingt-et-un."

"Ah, right. The game at Collins's house party. What a night that was. . . ."

It had been a splendid house party. There hadn't been any marriage-minded mothers with horse-faced daughters angling to trap a man into a leg shackling. This event had been strictly bachelors. Wealthy bachelors. They'd woken late in the afternoon and wagered through the night. The wine and the brandy had flowed freely.

And the women . . . Lord Collins had seen to it that there were women available. The sort that didn't say no or put up a fuss but just got a man off when he wanted and how he wanted.

The low point, of course, had been that game

with Inverness. Dudley remembered it clearly, even though he wished he didn't. Looking down at the cards in his hand. The dampness of his palms. Looking up at Inverness, who sat stone-faced with a winning hand. Looking at the blunt piled high in the middle of the table— paper, IOUs, and gold coins that had glowed in the candlelight. And then, on the other side of the room, at another table, playing another game: Castleton.

He'd been a stranger then. But Dudley just now matched the face to the name.

He'd been at that damned horse race in Kingswood, too. The man was just everywhere, wasn't he?

Dudley sat up suddenly. No. It couldn't be.

Or could it?

He'd read something in the newspaper about Castleton this morning. He'd had a raging headache at the time, so his recollection was a bit unreliable, but—

The newspaper! Dudley looked over at the fire burning in the grate. There were logs, twigs, and wadded-up sheets of newsprint.

He nearly knocked over his chair in his haste to grab the sheets from the flames. He burned his fingertips, he blew out the flames licking at the sheets, he scanned the tiny print until he saw the words "Fashionable Intelligence," and then he kept reading until that name caught his attention.

Dear readers, I have saved the best for last. For the first time in an age, tongues are wagging about Lord Castleton. After his extended tour on the Continent and lands unknown, the handsome viscount has sent word that he will shortly be returning to England aboard the ship Rahala.

"This says that Castleton has just returned to England. Or is about to."

"So?"

"We just encountered Castleton in a remote country inn," Dudley said. He'd never been great at sums, but this . . . there was something not right with the way the facts were adding up.

"Aye. And . . . ?" Fitz-Herbert was even worse with sums, facts, getting the point, and the like.

"He was at Collins's party. I remember him now. He kept quiet, except to rake in the winnings. And he was at that horse race."

"Do you have a point?"

"A man can't be in two places at once. This says Castleton just returned to England, but we know he's been here for at least a few weeks."

"Interesting," Fitz-Herbert remarked. Dudley felt a surge of pride, which was immediately tested when Fitz-Herbert asked, "What's the date on the newspaper?"

Smugly, Dudley looked down at the sheet. No. Bloody hell.

"I can't tell! It's bloody burned off."

"So it could be yesterday's paper. Or it could

be from six months ago," Fitz-Herbert rationalized. "One never knows when this far outside of London."

Dudley felt himself choking on garbled sounds of rage. His life was always like this moment—almost brilliant, almost clever, almost and always not quite. But this time, he had a nagging feeling about this Castleton—and a determination to pay him back for the damage he had inflicted upon his face.

"C'mon, let's go see the fight. It should be starting soon."

Aye, a fight. He was in the mood for that. Dudley crumpled the sheet of newspaper and left it on the table. Then he swigged the last of the wine, donned his jacket, and followed his friend out into the night.

John had rushed out into the night, sparing no thought for anything except for her. His jacket was open. His cravat had long since lost its complicated, starched arrangement. He no longer looked like a perfect gentleman. He no longer cared.

Had he been too late? When he finally arrived, there was evidence of a fight.

He crossed the room, shards of broken glass crunching under his boots.

John knew he was being watched. This scene unfolding was at once a long time coming, and only just beginning.

Chapter 16

THEIR ARRIVAL AT this inn was a long time coming, or so it seemed to John after days and days of being stranded elsewhere, his ever more intimate acquaintanceship with Prudence, and hours and hours on the road today.

And yet, as they were shown into a private parlor that a servant had just finished clearing of cigar ash, empty wineglasses, and a crumpled-up newssheet, he had the distinct feeling that things were only just beginning.

The girl before him was much more at ease and animated than the nearly defeated girl he had first met. Her every slight smile or shy glance had him hooked, craving more. He'd do anything for more.

Over a supper of simple fare and no wine, they conversed about . . . he hardly remembered the topics, just that he was falling, falling, falling for this girl who possessed a beauty, strength, and resilience that awed him. Knowing her as he did made those sweet smiles and shy glances affect him all the more. Blood rushing. Heart pumping. Breath catching. Did she feel it, too?

THIS WAS A new feeling. Prudence had never felt this before: light and lovely and finally understood. She had told Castleton her secret and he hadn't turned coldly away from her. She had entrusted herself in his care, and thus far, along miles and miles and miles of empty roads, he hadn't taken advantage of her. She was nervous about this evening.

What would happen next?

What did she want?

When it was time to retire, the innkeeper regretfully informed them only one room remained. He added that there was a boxing match nearby and all the inns around for miles were full up with spectators. Prudence did not understand the appeal of a boxing match; judging by the crowds, she was the only one who felt thusly.

Castleton said one room would be fine for him and his wife.

"You could have told everyone I was your sister," Prudence remarked as they climbed the stairs up to their room. Not that she wanted him to. Thus far she liked pretending to be Lady Castleton. But they could have done so.

"Have you seen the way I look at you?" Castleton murmured, leaning close to her. "I'd be arrested for indecency if I were caught looking at my sister like that."

Prudence blushed and tripped on a step. She hadn't considered herself desirable or an object of lust. But Castleton was attracted to her as a person, as a woman. It was plain in his gaze.

"That makes me feel nervous about sharing a room with you," Prudence said.

"Don't be nervous. Please. I couldn't bear it if I scared you."

He looked so earnest. She believed him. She had so much faith in him that she exhaled and was even able to breathe normally. But then she glanced up at him and noticed he was biting back words.

"What is it?" she asked.

They crossed over the threshold to their room—a spartan affair with whitewashed walls, rough-hewn wood floors, a bed, a chair, and little else. He set down the bags and turned to face her.

"I will wait for you, Prudence," he said solemnly. "As long as it takes."

"But . . ." The protest was a rush of breath over her lips. *It could be forever.* She might *never* be ready. She suddenly remembered the morning she'd spent kneading dough with Annie. She'd worked and worked and exhausted herself and nothing had changed. Until it had.

But she wasn't a ball of dough. She was a girl who had been hurt, who had the worst luck, and who might never be able to accept what Castleton was hinting at.

A wave of sadness enveloped her at the prospect. What a bleak life was ahead of her if she was forever tormented by the memory of Dudley's violent possession of her body.

What if she could take her body back? Her heart started to pound. What if she could reclaim it for her own? It was a question she could not answer. And she couldn't even think about it because what Castleton said next took her breath away and stunned her.

"But I want to touch you," Castleton said. "I want to touch you, gently, with love."

"Oh," she gasped. Gentle. Love. Castleton. Touch. Even though she was damaged. Even though she wasn't pure and innocent. Even though she wasn't any of those things, he was still falling in love with her and wanted to touch her.

Never, ever, ever had Prudence thought she'd find a man like him. If she had believed he was out there, she never would have run off with Cecil.

But she had. And he was here. Was she going to let him go? Was she going to be content with fear and shame forever? Castleton might be her chance to try again, be reborn.

"But I don't want to hurt you," he continued. "Or scare you."

His gentle demeanor soothed her. His relentless kindness made her feel safer than she'd felt in years. His blue eyes were smoldering. There was no denying it: he wanted her. He knew what had happened to her and *he still desired her.*

Would she ever find another man like him? No.

Would she ever have another chance to try to reclaim herself? Perhaps, if she didn't allow fear to hold her back. But why not start now? Why not seize this moment? Prudence thought of excuses but dismissed them. This was her chance.

So, mustering all of her courage, she asked, "How do you want to touch me?" She didn't know, and she wanted to.

"I would start by pushing aside that strand of hair that's been falling in your eyes all day," he said softly. "And I'd let my fingertips graze your cheek as I did."

That was gentle. That was safe.

"Like this?" Prudence asked as she enacted the movement he described. Her hair was soft. How many times had she pushed her hair away from her face? Countless. And how many times had she noticed that the skin of her cheek was soft and sensitive and responsive to a light and gentle touch? Once. Now. The slight caress of her fingertips against it sent a little shiver down her spine.

"Yes," he whispered. "Like that."

"What else?"

Castleton closed the door to their room. She was alone with a man behind a closed door. Prudence couldn't believe a few seconds had passed without her bolting. But her curiosity, desire, and determination were beginning to be stronger than her fear.

He took a seat in the upholstered chair on the far side of the room. Outside, the sun was setting, and the warm light filtering through the window made his skin seem warmer. His blue eyes were fixed on her.

Tentatively, Prudence sat on the bed.

Their gazes locked. His face was becoming familiar to her now: the blue eyes and dark lashes, the strong line of his jaw and the dramatic slant of his cheekbones, his firm mouth that often curved into a smile that made her feel warm inside. In this moment, she felt connected to him, even though they were on opposite sides of the room. Strange, that.

"Your neck is lovely," he began in a low voice. "I would want to kiss it, starting just below your earlobe." Since she couldn't kiss her own earlobe, Prudence pressed one fingertip there, lightly. She shivered, slightly.

"How would you kiss it?"

"Just a little press of my lips. I might taste you, too." Prudence sat very still, imagining the feeling of his lips pressing this sensitive spot. She felt a spark of *something* as she imagined his lips parting as he tasted her skin.

Then, feeling overwhelmed and faintly ridiculous, she dropped her hand into her lap. Who kissed people on the neck, anyway?

Apparently Castleton did. And judging by the darkening of his eyes and the heat in his gaze, he liked it. His voice was low as he continued with his seduction from the far side of the room: "Then I'd make my way down, with my mouth, to where your neck curves into your shoulder."

"I cannot kiss my own neck," she whispered.

"Use your fingers," he urged, wickedly. "Use your imagination."

Prudence was faltering. But she could do this if she just concentrated on his voice and her own touch.

"Fine," she agreed.

"Actually fine, or 'not fine but don't want to talk about it'?" Castleton asked with a lift of his brow.

The man knew women. She had to give him that. She also had to give him an honest answer. And after a moment of thinking about it, she said, "Actually fine."

His mouth turned up slightly. Her heart beat hard, but she *wanted* to do this. Whatever this was.

"Next I'd want to kiss you all along the curve of your shoulder."

She had never touched the curve of her shoulder before. Keeping the touch of her fingertips light, she dragged them back and forth. Then she freed the button of her spencer and shrugged it off. The short-sleeved gown underneath allowed her to touch her own bare skin.

Her skin, it had to be noted, was warm and soft. She had touched herself to bathe, with soap and with haste. She hadn't ever indulged in the pleasure of herself.

"What does it feel like on your inner arms, Prue?"

Within a moment, she knew.

"It tingles," she said, closing her eyes and really feeling it. "It's so sensitive. I had no idea."

"I'd touch you there," he said, voice rough. "Lightly. Just my fingertips."

With her eyes closed, she imagined he was the one slowly tracing his fingers up and down and around the delicate skin of her inner arms.

"I can feel it," she whispered. It was *nice.* It wasn't scary. It made her feel curious about touching more of herself.

"Tell me to stop." Prue opened her eyes and looked at him. Castleton was still in the chair, but his knuckles were white as he gripped the arms. That he was feeling this and was still planted in that chair on the far side of the room made her feel safe enough to do this. That he had given her a chance to stop made her feel comfortable continuing.

"It's fine," she said softly.

"Actually fine or 'not fine but don't want to talk about it'?"

"Actually fine." And it was actually fine. Prudence smiled. She heard his breath hitch.

"I would kiss you across your chest," he said, growing bolder now. "Just the skin exposed just above the bodice." Her fingertips took a leisurely trip to the previously unexplored territory of her skin, just above her bodice. This was the bit on display in ball gowns. The bit that occasionally men looked at until she turned away. This was the part of her the world had seen. Now she was going to take it back.

Fingertips along the bodice edge, right where

the muslin gave way to bare skin, she played with the edge of the fabric, weaving from one side to the other, ultimately seeking out the uncovered.

"Your skin looks so soft, Prue. Is it?" There was a slight anguish in his voice. She knew that it was because he wanted to feel with his own hands what she was feeling with hers. She was sorry, a little, if he suffered unduly. But this rediscovery of herself was magical, and for once she wanted to put herself first.

"It's soft," she told him.

"God, I want to feel you . . . ," he groaned. Her eyes flew open and she exhaled with relief to see that he was still in the chair. He pushed his fingers roughly through his hair.

"I won't," he said in a rush of breath. "Not until you ask me to."

"Why?" The word, the question came from somewhere beyond her brain.

"Because I'm falling in love with you," he said, his voice low, his words starting that heat inside again. "Because I respect you. Because you should be cherished. Because, because, because, because . . . Do you want to stop?"

Prudence paused to consider. No, she did not want to stop. The pleasure of each touch propelled her forward.

"What do I do next?" she asked.

"Keep your dress on," he said.

"I was planning on it," she remarked, the spell breaking slightly. Then what he said next swept her away, right back to this space lacking a sense of time or place. There was nothing but him, and her, and desire.

"If everything was just right," he said, "and if you wanted it, I would touch your breasts."

Prudence stilled. This was going far now. It was one thing to touch her shoulder in front of him. It was another to touch her breasts. Even Dudley hadn't touched her breasts. His hands had been full pinning hers against the wall and shoving up her skirts.

"How?" Prudence asked in a whisper. Honestly, she didn't know.

"Lightly," he said, his voice firm and slightly tortured. "Just your fingertips. Find the center." Even with her eyes closed, Prue knew that his were open and watching her intently. She felt nervous and . . . innocent.

She hadn't done this before. No one had ever touched her thusly. She was the first.

God, what a feeling of satisfaction that was.

"Yes," he hissed as her fingertips traced along the swell of her breast to find the pink peak in the center. Even with her bodice firmly covering herself, she knew it was right, because she felt a spark of electricity rocket through her. He gave her more instructions: "Circle slowly. Yes. Like that."

Her fingertips made slow circles of ever-increasing pressure around the center of her breasts until her nipples were stiff peaks and suddenly more sensitive. She inhaled sharply.

"Do you like that?" Castleton asked, still safely seated across the room.

"I wouldn't keep doing it if I didn't like it," Prue replied.

"That's my girl," he murmured. She smiled a lazy, happy smile. Her fingers did not stop.

"Tell me what you feel," he said. She didn't even know the words to describe what she was feeling, because it was nearly impossible to put into words things that young ladies like her didn't do.

"I feel the chains breaking free," she whispered. "I feel stiff buds in the center of my . . . breasts." She shyly stumbled over those words. Maybe she still retained some modesty after all. "I feel tingles all over from my breasts and . . . lower . . . and through all of my limbs." Her voice had taken on a breathy quality that was foreign to her ears. "It feels nice."

"Just nice?" His own voice didn't sound nice. It sounded ravaged by desire.

"It's been a long time since I have felt nice," Prudence told him with open eyes.

His own eyes were nearly black now, and completely fixed on her. She lowered her gaze slightly and saw that he was aroused. Oh, she'd heard it in his voice. But her eyes told her there was no denying that he was feeling this, too.

The door was closed. Everyone at the inn thought they were married and thus wouldn't step in to interfere if she screamed out. No one knew where she was or who she was with. If he wanted to take her now, he could. It would take force, but he could overpower her. The only thing keeping him in that chair and her fragile happiness intact was his self-restraint.

"Your stomach, Prue. I'd touch you there. All sorts of kisses."

She imagined his head, with its dark, unruly hair, bent over her belly as he pressed his mouth there. He'd be so close to her breasts (his mouth there, oh God!). He'd be close to that sensitive place between her legs. She was starting to feel things there. *Nice* things. A warmth. A yearning.

Funny how her body responded to her thoughts. But then again, it wasn't funny at all; it had been happening for years. Only now she was replacing thoughts of dirt and shame and disgust with thoughts of pleasure.

She commanded her fingers to touch her belly. It was rounder and softer than was fashionable. That didn't stop her from experiencing a lovely feeling as she explored this part of her body that she'd previously avoided.

"And then what?" she asked, her own voice sounding rough now.

"Your ankles have been awfully neglected," he remarked, an undercurrent of rough desire under his charming delivery. "Did you know they're very sensitive?"

"No," she said, reaching over to touch her ankles. "How do you know?"

"A man learns some things." She wondered

what else he knew. What wasn't he telling her, and whom had he learned it from? Was that . . . jealousy?

"They are sensitive. But not as sensitive," she said, thinking longing thoughts of touching her breasts again.

"Higher, Prue," he urged.

"Here?" She paused to touch her knee. That was not nearly as sensitive as her ankle, which was not nearly as sensitive as her breasts or the little spot below her earlobe. But wasn't it marvelous that she *knew* these things now?

"Higher still," he said.

Her fingers inched up along the silk of her stockings, swiftly approaching her garters and . . .

"I don't know if I can," she said, her voice and will faltering. Prue had opened her eyes. The sun was setting, but the room was still fairly light. Her skirts were already hitched up past her knees, giving him a peek at what no one else had ever seen.

"You don't have to if you don't want to," he said. And that was why she could. Because if she thought about it, she did, instinctively, want to follow this trail of desire he was blazing across her body. "But Prue, I want you to know pleasure. I want you to know that you are not that one time something bad happened."

Prudence knew she could ask him to leave the room and he would. He'd go downstairs and nurse a pint and leave her to finish this exploration on her own. Because of that, she felt comfortable staying as they were.

Besides, she might need direction, and there was this pressure building inside her. It was making itself aware in her belly and in that space that had once been violated. This was the first time she'd felt something good there. She desperately needed his instruction on how to relieve the pressure and how to keep feeling good.

She still had her dress on, he was still across the room, and she felt more beautiful and powerful than she'd ever felt in her entire life. Given how ugly and powerless she'd felt, that wasn't much. And yet, it was everything.

"Very well then," she sighed. "But close your eyes."

"Yes, ma'am."

"You can't 'yes, ma'am' me at a time like this," she squeaked, eyes opening to see him *still* in that chair and *still* aroused but grinning faintly.

"Yes, Miss Merryweather."

"That's more like it," she murmured, surprised at how she might have just murmured something coyly to an obviously aroused man.

"Where are your fingers, Prue?" His voice was lower now, rougher now. He sounded positively tortured. But she was in a state of bliss.

"I can't say," she said. But, having mustered more courage than she ever thought she possessed, Prue touched herself all around where she'd been violated. One spot, just above the opening, felt particularly pleasurable, so she stroked it and teased it, experimenting with different ways of touching. *All* of them made her feel hot and electric.

"Slow circles," he murmured. "Use a light touch. Feather light. So light you can hardly feel it."

"I've never done this before," she whispered. "Not even at night, not even in the bath, not even alone."

He groaned. "How does it feel? Please, tell me how it feels."

That was desire in his voice. She cracked her eyes open, glancing at him in a heavy-lidded haze of pleasure and self-discovery. Everything about him was dark and hard and tense. He *desired* her, and this—her own pleasure—was arousing to him.

Prue understood now the difference between domination and true pleasure. Right now, in this moment, with feelings of warmth and loveliness and *something*, she just couldn't be bothered with anything else.

"Tempting," she said. "And wet. I feel wet."

He groaned and said, "Keep going. Please." As if he had to ask! Before, she had felt stickiness between her legs, and it had been a bad thing. But this time, this wetness was accompanied by her desire, and it was her own. She didn't want to feel bad about something that was her own. And Castleton hadn't given her any indication that feeling was wrong or bad.

She kept going with the light circles around this magical place of insane feeling, not because he asked but because instinct compelled her to continue.

Then Castleton had a question for her that caught her off guard. His voice was gruff and pleading.

"Prue, can I touch myself? Please? I'll stay here. Away from you."

He was begging *her!* Never, ever, ever had she felt as powerful as she did in this moment.

"Yes," she murmured.

"You can look if you want," he said. "I don't mind."

It took her a moment to decide that she wanted to look. The room was darker now, as the sun sank down low. She saw that he had unbuttoned his breeches. Her breath caught in her throat. Part panic, part shock. He took himself in his hand. She saw, in the dim light, that it was big and firm. His hand closed around it and slowly moved up and down in the same leisurely movement with which she touched herself.

This touch had to be pleasing to him, because his head relaxed back and his eyes closed.

"How are you so shameless?" she asked.

"This is all good, Prudence. Our bodies were made to feel this way."

"What way?" she asked in a whisper.

"Hot. Do you feel that heat building inside?" She answered with a soft moan. "Do you feel a need for more of this feeling, even though it is driving you absolutely mad?" All of his words came out in quick gasps.

"I feel that," she said, breathless.

"Press harder," he murmured. She pressed harder, increasing the pressure with which she touched herself in wicked little circles around a sensitive place of pleasure she'd never before discovered.

She moaned. And there was no stopping it.

"One day, I'll press my mouth there," he said, and she gasped. "I will do with my tongue what you are doing with your fingers."

God, that sounded wicked. God, it sounded heavenly. God, that had never occurred to her, but now that it did, the thought of his head bowed between her legs, as if reverentially, wouldn't leave. And she couldn't help but imagine his firm, sensual mouth pressing kisses *there* and chasing away all the bad things.

Although her fingers were doing a damn fine job, too. She smiled. But then that faded as she lost herself in the sensations she was inspiring and the wicked imaginations of what he had to be feeling.

"Prue, what do you feel?"

"I feel like I can't breathe. I can't think. I can't stop."

"You're close. God, you're close. Press harder now, Prue, and *let go.*"

She pressed harder, groaning under the pressure of her touch and the pressure of something building inside her. It wasn't a bad pressure at all. It was lovely, like fireworks on a hot night, and because he said to let go and she trusted him, she let go, and then—

The force of it took her breath away. Vaguely, she heard him cry out, too. There was *nice* and then there was pleasure so intense and overwhelming that it took her breath away, cleared her thoughts, and ricocheted over every last inch of her body in the most exquisite way.

Her body, which she had started to reclaim.

Her body, which had known evil and now knew loveliness.

Her body, which possessed secrets she never would have known had it not been for Castleton's hoarsely whispered directions and his herculean self-restraint, which kept him on the far side of the room, giving her the freedom to explore, to discover, and to possibly start loving herself.

Chapter 17

The following day
The day before Lady Penelope's Ball

UNTIL THE PREVIOUS evening, stuff of the flesh had been bad, horrible, and a never-ending nightmare for Prudence. This morning, she wasn't fixed or healed or normal by any stretch. But she did know that there was at least one man in the world who didn't take gross advantage of a woman. And dear God, she had just discovered that her body could feel pleasure, too.

The world as she knew it had tilted sharply on its axis, jumbling everything.

There was much to reconsider, like how lucky she was that she hadn't married Cecil after all. She hoped he was all right. Surely he'd found his way back to his estate or town. But it was for the best that they'd never wed. They would never have made each other happy, and he would certainly never have taught her how to defend herself or pleasure herself.

Although now she didn't have a husband for Lady Penelope's Ball.

Perhaps she shouldn't even go. They might not arrive in time. She didn't have a dress. She still didn't have the gumption to go alone.

Prudence gave a sidelong glance at the tall, handsome man seated beside her in the carriage.

Or they might arrive in time, she could procure a dress, and . . .

John caught her glancing at him with a thoughtful expression on her face.

"I've been thinking," Prudence remarked.

"Oh no," he said with a nervous glance in her direction. She pursed her lips peevishly.

"I hate to ask you for anything," she began.

"This is ridiculous," he replied. "I want to give you everything. I hope last night demonstrated that."

"You're making me blush," Prudence replied.

Castleton glanced over at her. Her cheeks were indeed pink. It was adorable.

"Ask me anything, Prudence," he said. He meant it.

"Can we pretend to be married?" Prudence asked.

"We already are pretending to be married," he answered. "We've been telling innkeepers all over the countryside that very 'fact.'"

"Can we keep pretending when we get to London?" Prudence pressed on.

She had already promised him an introduction to Ashbrooke and Radcliffe, and he was confident that she wouldn't go back on her word. He had nothing to gain from this but Prudence's happiness, which was reason enough for him to say yes. Still, he hesitated.

"Is there an occasion, or is this an indefinite arrangement?"

"There is a party," Prudence began to explain. "An anniversary party. It's a stupid thing, and I'd already given up on attending, let alone attending with a husband, but then last night . . ."

Something had changed last night. He had felt it, too. He'd been with women before—he was a man, and one with a pulse at that. There had been flirtatious and obliging housemaids, and barmaids, and, recently, the occasional widow who'd taken advantage of the freedom of her station and whom he'd been happy to oblige.

But he had never felt such a soul-deep connection with another person—never mind that the woman in question had been across the room and in a haze of her own.

He couldn't even imagine what must have occurred for Prudence.

She didn't finish explaining what had happened last night. But he sensed what her question would be.

"Do you want me to attend as your husband at this party?"

"Yes," she said, exhaling.

"I'd be honored," he said, glancing down at her. It was a huge risk to take. Pretending to be married whilst staying at country inns they would never return to was one thing. But pretending to be married for high society? It was begging for trouble.

But he could still imagine her cries of pleasure. He still hadn't tired of gazing into her lovely brown eyes. He still hadn't held or kissed her.

He couldn't say no to her. She caught his eye and smiled shyly. He returned her smile. But he felt something intense inside. Desire. Heartache. Regret. All of it, in one sharp pang.

He was falling for her. Nothing could come of it.

She was opening up to him, but all his secrets were still locked away. He couldn't confess to them—surely he would then watch her retreat to the place of fear and mistrust from which she was only just starting to emerge. He couldn't take that from her. She might never recover.

He also couldn't confide in her because then Prudence certainly wouldn't want anything to do with him, and he couldn't, as a gentleman, leave her alone with Dudley roaming the countryside. Aye, John would keep his secrets until she was safely returned to her family in London.

He shouldn't have gotten close to her. But he had, and now he dreaded losing her.

Castleton shook his head, chasing the thoughts away. The sun was shining in a cloudless blue sky. They were on their way to London. She would provide him with the introduction that would change the lives of himself, his sister, and his mother. He could provide so much happiness if just given the chance.

"Tell me all about this party," he said. "And spare no detail—we have hours yet to travel."

"It's to commemorate the hundredth anniversary of Lady Penelope's Finishing School for Young Ladies of Fine Families. Emma, Olivia, and I attended. And every year at this anniversary party they recognize all the girls that have wed. And no one, in the history of one hundred years of the school, has remained unwed this far into their fourth season."

"Not one?" he asked, suspecting he knew where this was going.

"Well, me," she said with a heartbreaking sigh.

"You won't go alone," he promised. "We'll waltz every waltz together, drink champagne whilst looking at the stars, and I'll call you my Lovely Lady Castleton very loudly at every opportunity so there is no mistake."

"Suddenly I find that I am no longer filled with dread at the prospect of this ball," Prudence murmured. "Funny, that."

"I'm happy to oblige."

"It's just a stupid ball, I know," she sighed.

"It's more than that," he replied knowingly.

"It's an imaginary target I had to hit," Prudence explained. "Or it's a measure of my worth. You know it's very awful that a woman's worth is only determined by whether she's married or not," Prudence lamented. "It's ridiculous that a woman's entire life should be reduced to her marital state and the delivery of heirs."

"Indeed," he agreed, knowing a little something about how the world could demand less of people than they were able to give.

"But I believed it, too. So much so that I tried to elope," she confessed, and his heart stopped in shock for a second. "But then the mail coach was robbed and . . . I managed to slip away into the forest. And then I met you."

It was a moment before his heartbeat and breathing returned to normal. That information stopped him sharply. So *that's* how she'd come to be roaming the countryside unaccompanied. It was an explanation that only raised more questions. At his command, the horses slowed, and he turned to face her.

"Wait a minute, Prue. You have a fiancé running around the countryside, presumably looking for you?"

She hesitated. "Oh, I doubt he's looking for me. Cecil didn't really want to marry me. I suppose I didn't really want to marry him either."

"Then why agree to marry him?"

"He wouldn't hurt me. And I just didn't want to be alone at this party. I didn't want to be the one failure—the one blemish—in the history of the school."

But marriage . . . she would have traded a lifetime for just one night. John had half a mind to track down this "fiancé" and thrash him within an inch of his life for leaving a woman to face a highway robbery alone. Then again, thank God he'd done so, so that John could find her. But bloody hell, the lengths she went to in order to face this party.

And for what? There was one crucial point she was forgetting.

"You still will be unmarried, even if we pretend," he said, regretfully pointing out the truth.

"Yes, but no one else will know," Prudence said softly. "It's important that no one know."

"What about Emma and Olivia?"

"They'll understand," Prudence said confidently. "And they won't tell."

"What about after?"

"I can't think about after. The event looms so large in my mind that I cannot see past it," Prudence confessed.

"Or we could just get married in truth." The words were out of his mouth before he could bite them back. It was just a flippant suggestion. A crazy idea, a mad remark, a borderline lie.

But the deep sense of righteous that settled within him suggested it wasn't crazy or mad or flippant but right. It felt like . . . the idea of home. A safe haven, a refuge, a place he'd always yearn to return to. Yet any good feeling was swiftly replaced with a cold, hard knot of regret: he could not marry her.

"You can't possibly mean that," she said with a little laugh of disbelief. "Not . . . me."

"Why, because of Dudley?" He glanced over at her; Prue's cheeks had pinked and her gaze was fixed on her hands, clasped in her lap. "I hate what he did to you, Prudence. But I don't think less of you because of it."

"You're mad," she said softly. He didn't miss the slick sheen of tears in her eyes.

"Tell me, Prue, is my winning streak continuing?" John asked with a grin.

"We'll see," she said primly. Her lips were pursed, as if fighting a smile.

"We'll see," he echoed. "Oh, God. The lady wounds me."

"We can't actually get married," Prudence said, matter-of-factly.

"Why not?" He was treading upon dangerous territory but couldn't—wouldn't?—find the path back to safety.

"Oh, I don't know. A dozen reasons, at least."

"Name one," he said. John could think of a few himself—namely that once she really knew him, she couldn't marry him even if she wanted to. But there was this stubborn little spark of hope that kept insisting maybe, maybe, maybe.

Maybe they could find a way to ride off into the sunset, happily married as man and wife and madly in love. No, what he felt for her was clouding his judgment and occupying all his thoughts.

"We haven't even kissed," Prudence said. "Not really. The kiss in the stables was nice, but . . ."

John smiled. That kiss had been all too sudden, and all too brief. It hadn't the soul-deep, lose-one-self kiss he—and Prue—needed. His hands eased up on the reins and the horses slowed.

"A real first kiss is something that is very easily remedied," he said easily. "If you want."

There was a long moment in which the horses walked on, John's heart thudded hard in his chest, and Prudence remained quiet and still beside him. He'd give anything to know the details of the battle likely being waged in her head and heart.

Then, in a low voice, she said, "Pull over."

"The most romantic words I've ever heard," he murmured as he guided the carriage over to the side. The road stretched ahead and behind as far as the eye could see. There was not a single other carriage. On either side were vast fields and meadows, alive with birds and the buzz of bees, but not another human in sight.

She glanced up at him, her brown eyes full of feeling. He could discern that she was fearful, but resolute. She was nervous, but desirous. She was refusing to be scared, even though she was scared. Tugged at his heart, that.

"Just one kiss. If you don't stop . . ." Her breath hitched, and she was aware of how alone they were. John was keenly aware of how much his self-restraint in this moment could either save her or devastate her completely. It didn't help that he wanted to lay down his jacket on the soft, mossy, grassy ground under that tree, lay Prudence down, too, and make love to her with the sun on his naked back.

By *wanted*, he meant hard with desire, his body urging him instinctively to lay with her. He couldn't breathe, he wanted her so badly. There were all those inches of skin that he wanted to taste and touch.

But the only thing as strong as his desire was his self-restraint.

Nevertheless, he told her, "If I don't stop, you'll hit me like I taught you."

She nodded solemnly. He spoke again. "To really enjoy a kiss, you've got to be able to surrender to it. I want you to enjoy this kiss. Which is why I'm giving you this."

John pulled out the knife he kept in his boot and pressed the handle into her palm. He wanted her so badly. The only other thing as strong as his desire was his determination that Miss Prudence Merryweather Payton have the exquisite first kiss she had been denied. If he had to risk an injury for it, so be it.

"If I don't stop when you tell me to, then feel free to use this. But, Prue, you have to tell me to stop if it all becomes too much."

Prudence nodded yes because she wasn't sure she could speak at the moment. She wanted *this* kiss with a fierceness that surprised her. The setting was beautiful, if a bit remote. And the man . . . she was falling for this man.

Because of him, she felt stronger, which made her feel safer, which made her feel able to enjoy the little things, like a handsome man's smile or the sensation of his leg brushing against her skirts, or being able to ride in his carriage rather than stumbling along desolate country roads, alone.

Castleton pressed the handle of the knife into her palm and her fingers closed around it, feeling the heft of it. She held it aloft between them, the sharp point of the blade inches from his chest. His heart.

"I want this kiss," she whispered. He seemed to be waiting to hear it.

His lips quirked into a faint smile. She noticed that his eyes crinkled slightly at the corners. Today his eyes perfectly matched the color of the sky. Castleton was handsome, there was no doubt about it. He made her think of happily ever after.

He started by pushing a strand of hair away from her face. His knuckles gently grazed her cheeks, just as he had described. It was just like her own touch: soft and hesitant. The gesture was sweet.

Pleasant as it was, her heart was pounding in her chest, equal parts fear and anticipation. The knife in her hand wavered. Just when she started to panic, her gaze locked with his. Those blue eyes gazing at her kept her steady.

"Close your eyes," he said softly.

By some miracle she did, shutting out the scenery and, fortunately, the nervous thoughts dashing through her head. Instead, she focused on more sensual matters, like his scent and how she could feel him leaning in close to her. She was aware of his heat and the soft rush of their breaths.

She opened her eyes for a second to see that his chest was just touching the tip of the knife.

Any second now would be her first real kiss. This was a moment she feared had been lost to her forever. She savored it now.

Castleton's lips swept softly, lightly, gently across hers. Had she not been so attuned to him, she might have thought it just a slight summer breeze. But then he was there with more warmth and more pressure, making it impossible for her to think of anything other than him.

With his fingertips, he lightly caressed the slender column of her neck and up and down her arms. The delicacy of the touch made her aware of the tension she carried. He kept kissing her. She sighed, allowing herself to soften under his touch. She hadn't felt soft in quite some time.

Then the kiss deepened, like little sparks starting to smolder.

This was a delicate give and take, in which she tasted him as much as he did her. She worried, fleetingly, about knowing what to do, then she just followed his lead, finding the rhythm, sucking his bottom lip after he nibbled on hers, and sighing every once in a while because this was happening and it was beyond what she'd ever dreamt of.

After all, how was she to know that a kiss could be so gentle, yet seem to stoke the fire in her belly? How was she to know that a good kiss could make her feel alive again?

Prudence, now either losing her wits or growing bold from the pleasure coursing through her, dared to touch him. It seemed absolutely imperative that she feel the firmness of his chest or thread her fingers through his hair.

Without realizing it, she opened her palm and dropped the knife. It fell with a thud on the carriage floor. She opened her eyes to see John watching her—what was she going to do?

Would she pick up the weapon and put the sharp blade between them? No. She was going to do what she really wanted. Prudence threaded her fingers through the soft strands of his hair, pulling him close to continue. He turned slightly, to press a kiss on her inner wrist, and murmured her name, his voice heavy with desire. "Prudence."

His mouth collided passionately against hers.

Prue allowed herself to get lost in the surrounding birdsong, her occasional sigh, and the sound of their breaths. She felt the warmth of the sun, the softness of his hair, and the firm line of his jaw under her palm. She felt him, tasted him, fell a little bit in love with him and this pleasure. God, she could do this for hours. God, how long had they been on this road, kissing like wild young lovers? Time seemed to have stood still.

Castleton seemed to have the same thought; he pulled away, then pressed one last kiss on her lips and whispered, "We should keep going . . . and continue this later."

Prudence nodded. Her heart started drumming in anticipation of what would happen later, once they reached the next inn. Something would have to happen, because that kiss made her want more.

Chapter 18

FOR THE FIRST time, Prudence wanted more. She had first felt the sparks when their lips had touched. Next, the slow burn as the fire had started to catch. She'd felt positively smoldering all day. Simmering. Waiting. Wanting. More.

Things had been tense and awkward over supper in a private parlor. Did he also feel things had only just started? Prue had only just begun to have these feelings; she still lacked the vocabulary or courage to speak of them. Thus they'd made idle conversation about how much longer until London (one day, two at most), what they would each do upon arrival (how they delicately avoided conveying expectations of the other!).

Then they ascended the stairs to their separate bedchambers. This would be the inn that had two rooms available, one for each. Gone were her hopes of somehow having *more* without having to explicitly invite him into her bedchamber. If something happened, she was curious and desirous enough to explore, but she didn't possess the courage to invite him into her bed. Yet.

Later that night, she lay in her bed alone and unable to sleep. She strained to identify all the sounds of the inn: the low rumble of voices in the parlor, the footsteps in the hallway, the occasional burst of a woman's laughter. Occasionally she feared she heard Dudley's voice—he was out there somewhere, wounded and angry, and she couldn't quite forget it completely. She was glad to have Castleton's protection for the return journey to London. Now that she thought about it, what would she have done if they hadn't happened upon each other?

It was a fate too awful to contemplate: Dudley, finding her alone, no one to save her.

What would happen in London? She would return to a life with Lady Dare and her two friends, who were revoltingly happy in love. Would she still see Castleton?

Or would she return to the wallflower corner, anxiously avoiding Dudley and dreaming of this wild week in the countryside when no one knew where she was or even *who* she was.

Except for Castleton, who already knew her better than anyone else did.

Castleton, who had almost but not quite proposed to her this morning.

Castleton, whose kiss brought her back to life.

In the dark, Prudence touched her fingers to her lips, savoring the memory. Over and over she played in her mind the first sensation of his lips upon hers. Over and over she recalled his warmth, his taste, his gentle touch. Over and over she remembered the way a kiss, lips against lips, could be felt all over.

That kiss had started something.

Something that hadn't been finished.

Something she wanted to finish. Or start. Prue wasn't sure if another kiss would be the beginning or the end, or the beginning of the end.

It was just a kiss.

But it wasn't, or it wouldn't be, if she had the gumption to slide out of this bed and knock on the adjoining door to his room.

To her surprise she did just that.

Her bare feet hit the cold, hard floorboards. The night air was cool against her skin, and the flimsy chemise she wore offered little coverage.

What was she doing? This was madness. She ought to get back into her bed and be thankful for a room of her own with locks on the doors.

Instead she knocked on the door adjoining their chambers. This desire was thrumming through her veins now, fire where there had once been ice. The sparks that had started earlier had given way to a slow burn, smoldering all afternoon and evening. Now conditions were just right for the bright embers to explode into roaring flames.

A MAN COULD dream. A man could dream of a woman in his bed, lips plump from his kiss, her hair unbound and splayed across his pillow. A man could dream of his hand on her hip, easing into her, losing himself completely as he discovered her.

A man could dream that Prue knocked on his door.

John stirred from his half-waking, half-sleep state, roused by the sound of her little knuckles rapping lightly on the wood. He lay in bed for a moment, telling himself he had to be dreaming. Prue could not possibly have been knocking on his door; even he was not this lucky.

But he was.

John leapt out of bed, pulled on a shirt, and strolled over, opening the door to see her standing there in just her chemise. His mouth went dry. God, she was tempting him. He fought, and lost, the battle to avoid stealing a glance—his gaze traveled from the flimsy straps to her breasts, lower still to the fabric clinging to her hips.

"Are you all right?" John asked, his voice rough.

"Yes," she said. Then, "No."

"What is it?" His pulse had chosen this moment to start pounding.

"I want to kiss you." With those softly spoken words, his heart stopped. His breath caught. Aye, a man could dream. And sometimes a man's dream could come true.

John reached for her and placed one hand on the span of her waist. He took a step closer to her. She stood on her toes, rested her palms on his chest, leaned in, and tilted her face up to his.

Just this kiss, just this kiss, just this kiss. With his

pulse beating wildly and his body demanding more, John kept repeating those words to remind him. *Just this kiss, just this kiss.*

He claimed her mouth with his.

WITH THEIR LIPS locked, Prudence felt, strangely, as if their souls were connected. It was impossible to feel lonely when her soul was connected to someone else's. It was so intimate the way his tongue tangled with hers. Every move, every breath, every stroke of his tongue or hers only made her want more. And the taste of him . . . she could not believe she knew the taste of him.

Strange how she could feel a kiss everywhere, all over, inside and out, even though they weren't really touching anywhere else.

Minutes passed, perhaps hours, in which her world began and ended with kissing this man in the dark.

There was more after the kiss; she knew that. For the first time she yearned to experience it. From his every kindness to this long, leisurely kiss, she just knew that with John, it would be different. It would be good.

Still, she was nervous, unsteady on her feet and not quite certain of how to get from here to complete bliss.

"Tell me to stop," he whispered, and it was possibly the most romantic thing he could have said.

"Don't stop."

"Tell me what you want." His voice had deepened.

Tonight, Prudence knew what she wanted.

"I want to feel everything like it's the first time," she whispered. "A good first time."

HIS BREATH HITCHED in his throat. He couldn't breathe. For a moment, John couldn't move. God, he wanted that more than he wanted anything. *Anything*. He wanted to be the man that kissed her sweetly, held her hand, showed her such passion and pleasure that everything bad before was gone, forgotten, washed away.

It was an honor, this. More than he deserved. The trust she had placed in his hands was humbling. He was terrified of breaking such a lovely, fragile thing.

"I want to feel what I felt the other night," she whispered. In the dim light, he could see a little blush stealing across her cheeks. "I want you to touch me."

Once he touched her, there would be no returning to *before*. Whatever they had already become to each other, they would be more. It would be impossible to leave Prudence once he made love to her, but that would mean giving up his other dreams.

He paused at that thought.

"I don't want to hurt you," he said.

"I know. You won't." She smiled so sweetly. He was helpless to resist. Besides, a gentleman honored a lady's wishes. . . .

John pushed a wayward strand of hair away

from her skin, his knuckles grazing her cheek. Soft, so soft. She turned her cheek into his hand, pressing her lips to his wrist. He cradled her face and kissed her deeply, drinking her in, like he would never get enough.

Prudence stood still, experiencing the fireworks again, and this time she enjoyed the hot, shimmering, sparkling explosions that left her breathless and entranced.

John pressed a kiss on the soft spot where her neck curved into her shoulder. She sighed, a dreamy smile on her lips, asking for more with a tilt of her head that gave him more access. He pressed kisses along her shoulder—she felt a series of hot little sparks.

Taking her by the hand, he led them to her bed. He sat on the mattress, she stood facing him.

She gazed into his darkened eyes. He was asking her for permission, asking her to be certain.

"Kiss me. I want you to kiss me how you described."

His hands were clasped on her shoulders, and his fingers slid under the straps of her chemise, easing them off.

John kissed her . . . a dozen little kisses . . . all along the edge of the chemise at just the spot were the fabric gave way to her skin. Aye, she felt a dozen sparkly explosions. His lips, soft and warm against her skin.

Prue threaded her fingers through his hair, as

she had been wanting to do. It was no small thing, wanting to touch someone and being able to.

"Prue?" he asked, her name a question. As was the way he started to slowly tug down her chemise.

"Yes," she whispered.

THE WHISPER OF her *yes* was more fuel to the fire of his wanting. He had fantasized about this moment, wanting to see her unclothed, wanting to touch her with nothing between them. He gazed at her, hair unbound, breasts uncovered and her skin glowing in the candlelight.

"You're beautiful, Prue."

She sighed, smiling faintly, another pink blush blossoming across her skin.

He had wanted her and fantasized about this. Wanted her and restrained himself. Wanted her and told himself it was impossible, then he'd kept on wanting. This moment, this vision of her, was an image that had kept him up late, was what he'd thought about in that liminal state between waking and sleeping.

Now the moment was real and here, and he wasn't sure if he was dreaming.

He ducked his head to her breasts, tentatively pressing his mouth.

Prue gasped. Her fingers, threaded through his hair, tightened.

This was real. A faint smile tugged at his lips. He dragged his gaze up to her face.

"Don't stop," she said impatiently. "I want you to do that again."

And again and again and again.

EVER SINCE JOHN had wickedly suggested this, Prue's mind had drifted to it, imaging him and her and his mouth there. Now it was real and it was beyond, just beyond what she had imagined.

She stood before him weak in the knees, with his hands clasped around her waist as he kissed her breasts, his warm mouth teasing the dusky centers until they were stiff peaks. The sighs and the moans she heard . . . oh, that was her . . . this feeling . . . more of those shimmering, sparkling explosions, lighting up the sky.

Eventually she was truly weak in the knees and light-headed from all those little shallow breaths. The bed was just there. . . .

Did she dare?

Prue reached out and placed her palm over his heart. She felt it beating wildly. It soothed her nerves knowing he was as nervous and desirous as she. Then she clasped a handful of fabric and tugged. It wasn't fair that he should remain so clothed when she wasn't.

He grinned. Oh, she felt that, too. Then he removed his shirt and oh . . . she wanted to feel him. Run her fingertips along the planes and ridges of his muscles, the slight dusting of hair on his chest, feel his hot skin under her palms and perhaps tease him with her mouth the way he had just done to her.

Prue leaned over, pressing one little kiss on his chest, then gazing up at him. His eyes were closed, lips parted.

"Don't stop," he whispered. She didn't. One thing led to another, and she was so overcome with desire that she forgot to be afraid. It seemed so right, so inevitable that they should come to lie on the bed together, side by side, kissing as if they had all night and the rest of their lives, too.

"I want to feel what I felt last night," she whispered.

"Which part?"

"The best part."

His hand caressed the length of her side, moving slowly down to touch her where she was most sensitive. His touch was feather light, so light she wondered if she was truly feeling it. Oh, but there was no denying it: the pressure within her was building and the heat she felt was intensifying. Her hips started to move in an instinctive rhythm against his hand.

And then he stopped.

"Don't stop."

John shifted their positions so that she lay on her back as he slowly pressed kisses across her belly and down to where his fingers had just been bringing her to heightened sensations of pleasure.

She remembered something John had whispered that night: *One day, I'll press my mouth there. I will do with my tongue what you are doing with your fingers.*

And then, oh God, he did. He expertly moved his tongue in slow, lazy circles around the bud of her sex.

At first Prue could not quite believe this was happening, that she was allowing it and then that she was so desperate for it to continue that she thought she might die if he stopped. The relentless, teasing touch was stoking that fire that had been smoldering inside. Flames, flickering. Her breath, catching, shallow. The pressure building inside. And the more he satisfied her desire to be touched, the more she wanted.

To her surprise, Prue found herself wanting, aching to have him inside her. It was a deep and primal want for this moment, with this man. But how to find the words to tell him?

"I want . . . ," she gasped. "I want you . . ."

She wanted to say more. But then came the fireworks: the scorching, sparkling, shimmering explosion of pleasure that had her crying out and nearly lifting off the mattress with the force of it.

God, what satisfaction that was, to hear her cry out with pleasure, calling his name and God's. He didn't think his heart would ever return to a normal beat.

Especially with what she said next.

"I want . . ."

"Tell me what you want," John said, his voice a rough whisper.

"I want to feel you inside of me," she said softly.

His heart began to pound. But he didn't feel that as much as other parts of his anatomy demanding attention.

"Prue . . ." She didn't have to do this. He needed her to know that. Because if she didn't want to do more, he had to know. Now.

"I want new memories. I want to feel you. I want—"

"I want you, Prue." It was all he allowed himself to say. John didn't want to scare her with how badly he desired her. He was harder than he'd ever been, her every little sigh and moan making his cock throb.

Everything in him—nerves, instincts, whatever—wanted to claim her. Sink into her warmth and move until he lost his mind and spent himself inside. He bit back a growl from the back of his throat. He wanted Prue in such a primal way.

She kissed him sweetly. Then she whispered yes. And he whispered yes.

Her heart was beating wildly as she straddled him. In this position, she could be in control. Prudence was a little nervous, as if this was her first time. What if it wasn't better than before? What if it was too much? Her body craved this, but her memories . . .

"Tell me to stop," he said.

"Don't stop."

She felt his hot, hard length at the vee between her thighs. Prue tensed, remembering . . . then he stopped. His hands still grasped her hips, but he didn't enter her. She hadn't said stop. But he was so attuned to her that he just knew. And he listened.

Prue knew she could trust him, allow herself to take pleasure in this, finally, feeling whole and feeling in love.

It was a slow torture for them both as he slowly, so slowly, pushed inside, giving her every chance to say no. . . . She said yes.

God, she said yes.

Slowly, so slowly, their bodies joined together and he began to move inside her, finding a steady rhythm. Her hips rocked against his. He felt her hands caressing his hot skin.

There was only this moment. The past was gone, over, couldn't hold a candle to this moment when they were in love and they were one. She wasn't the only one to feel that pressure building intensely, more and more with each controlled thrust. Prue wasn't the only one to finally feel whole, and right, and in the midst of one perfect moment.

He wanted it to last forever.

There was nothing else, just her, how she felt around him, the scent of her skin, the soft tendrils of hair brushing against his chest, her luscious body in his embrace. Nothing else mattered. He claimed her mouth for one more deep, passionate kiss before he cried out her name and pulled away.

Later that night, Prue drifted off to sleep, a smile

on her lips and John by her side. Tonight, she had set aside her fear to let love and desire take over. She didn't know what the morning would bring, but tonight, in this moment, everything felt perfect.

John lay awake beside her, listening to her soft breath as she slept. He knew that everything could change in an instant. But this feeling . . . with this woman . . . it was worth everything he would have to give up.

Chapter 19

The following day
The day of Lady Penelope's Ball
The day before the Great Exhibition

THERE IT WAS: London. After miles and miles of empty country roads and small village inns, they had finally reached the city. After days and nights risking everything, John had finally arrived in the greatest city in the world and the scene of his last great gamble. Was this arrival the beginning of the end . . . or just the beginning?

John reached for Prue's hand, interlacing their fingers.

He exhaled slowly, forcing the tension to dissipate from his limbs.

Tonight, they would masquerade as man and wife. It was madness, that. If his wits hadn't been so addled with love, he would never have agreed to it. But how could he say no to the woman he loved? How could he ever explain why this was so damned dangerous?

Tomorrow he would meet with the duke and the baron about the engine. He only needed enough time to make that deal. If he could just secure his fortune, then he could have a chance to secure his future.

He hoped, with every damned heartbeat, that his future included Prudence. But he didn't see how it could.

THERE IT WAS: London. The city where she had been born and raised. Now she felt like she saw it as if for the first time. The city seemed alive—pulsing with activity in the streets, glowing under the morning sunlight, a dull roar of noise from the thousands of people and beasts within, going about their business.

She and Castleton rode in silence. She had questions, but she didn't want to ask them for fear of the answers. But it was there, on the tip of her tongue, waiting for her to screw up the courage. *What happens now?*

Prudence was glad when Castleton transferred the reins to one hand and clasped her hand in his. With a squeeze of his hand she felt more confident. He loved her. She loved him. What could stand in their way?

Prudence straightened her spine, sitting tall in the carriage beside this handsome man as they rode into London. For the first time in her life, she hoped people saw her in this moment of triumph.

After successfully navigating the bustling city streets, the carriage rolled to a stop before the town house she shared with Lady Dare at Number 12, Berkeley Square.

"Until tonight," Castleton murmured, pressing

his lips to her inner wrist. His smoldering gaze promised so much.

"Tonight," she whispered.

They confirmed their plans—he would come for her at eight o'clock that evening, and together they would journey to Lady Penelope's Ball.

Tonight she would show them all—and herself—that she was not a failure. Not at all. She, Miss Prudence Merryweather Payton, had survived the worst thing that could happen, and she'd found true love anyway.

After an extended tour of the Continent and other foreign lands, Viscount Castleton has returned to London at last! He brings with him a lovely American bride, who is eager to take the ton by storm.

—"Fashionable Intelligence By A Lady of Distinction"
The London Weekly

Dudley had been right. God, it felt good to be right! He'd had a hunch that "Lord Castleton" was not, in fact, who he claimed to be. It was that scrap in the newspaper. It was the simple truth that one man could not be in two places at once, especially if the two places were Wiltshire and a ship crossing the Atlantic.

It was a simple matter of suffering through a tedious conversation with his sister on the gossip: "Oh yes, Lord and Lady Castleton have returned just days ago," Megan said, chattering on as she was wont to do. "Aunt Marleton and I went to visit, and whilst there we learned that Lady Bessborough will be having a ball to officially welcome them. Did you know, Dudley, that Lady Castleton is American?"

"Fascinating," he said. Indeed, it was.

"Whilst we called upon Lady Castleton, I saw the Duchess of Ashbrooke and Lady Radcliffe. We all chatted about Lady Penelope's Ball—it's tonight. Remember, you promised Father that you would accompany me. I can't believe those wallflowers have landed such husbands and I am stuck with you. But I hope to be married soon and . . ."

Dudley stopped listening. It was a fair bet that Prude Prudence would be in attendance. He also thought it was a fair bet that "Lord Castleton" would accompany her.

Did Dudley mention that he was right about "Lord Castleton"? The man had broken his nose, made a hideous mess of his face, cast him out into a torrential storm, and failed to respect his betters. And now revenge was Dudley's with just one visit, peer to peer.

"Lord Castleton is not at home to visitors," the butler intoned when Dudley came calling. The old man had taken one look at his face—his cut, broken, and bruised face—and made the declaration without even looking at his card.

"I am Lord Dudley, heir to the Marquis of Scarbrough, and I have information that Lord Castleton wishes to know."

A moment later he was shown into the *real* Castleton's library. Castleton took a seat by the fire, and Dudley sat opposite.

He could see immediately how the fake Lord Castleton had done it. The two men bore a striking resemblance to each other.

"Welcome back, Lord Castleton. Or should I say, it is good to see you again?"

"I don't take your meaning, Lord Dudley." Castleton clearly wished to be engaged with something else.

"Fortunately, I am here to enlighten you," Dudley said with a grin. But Castleton grimaced, reminding Dudley how gruesome he looked, and why. It only renewed his determination.

"If you don't mind getting on with it, I would be much obliged, what with having just returned from spending years abroad. My wife is eager for me to introduce her into society, my secretary has a mountain of correspondence requiring my attention, and my estate manager is keen to review years of account books with me."

"I hate to be the bearer of bad news, Lord Castleton, but I must inform you that in your absence, a man has assumed your identity." Dudley paused for dramatic affect. Castleton's brow lifted. Then he settled into his seat. Suddenly, he had time for this interview. Dudley continued, "He has been roaming the countryside, claiming to be you as he fleeces gentlemen at card games at bachelor house parties, wagers on horse races, stays at various inns. He has also resorted to violence. Against peers of the realm."

"I suppose I can look to you for evidence."

"And Lord Fitz-Herbert as well," Dudley said gravely, nodding. He fought hard to keep a malevolent grin from spreading across his face as he continued digging the fake Lord Castleton's grave. "Fitz and I had come across him availing himself of a woman—against her will. She was a gently born woman, so we intervened on her behalf. There was an . . . altercation."

Lord Castleton paled.

"And the woman?" He was concerned for her. How touching.

"I wouldn't wish to compromise her further by revealing her identity," Dudley said. "I hope you do not mind that I have come to relate this to you. As a fellow peer, it pains me to see the Castleton name dragged through the mud by this desperate pretender."

"Yes . . . Yes . . ." Castleton was lost in thought. The viscount stood, walked over to the sideboard, and poured them each a glass of brandy.

"I had thought you might wish to be aware of this," Dudley said, accepting the drink.

"Indeed. I am greatly indebted to you for bringing this matter to my attention. Something must done before this man inflicts more damage upon my family name. And before this affects Lady Castleton's entrance into society."

"I know where to find him," Dudley said with more certainty than the truth merited.

"Do you?" Castleton looked up. God, the hope in the man's eyes!

"I do," Dudley said solemnly.

Castleton was forever indebted to him now, and the fake Castleton would see the inside of Newgate by nightfall. Again Dudley struggled to keep his countenance grave, as befitting the situation.

Revenge . . . being *right* . . . made him downright gleeful.

Castleton's voice was steely when he said, "Find him. And bring him to me."

Mother,

By the time you read this missive I will be married. Miss Prudence Payton has consented to be the future Lady Nanson. We will marry by special license at Mowbry Hall and will journey to London shortly thereafter. . . .

—A letter written and sent prematurely by Cecil, Lord Nanson, the contents of which quickly became widely discussed amongst the ton.

Near Berkeley Square

Fuck. Not tonight. Not now. He knew it: the second a man starts to believe that his good fortune will go on forever is the second the winning streak comes to an end. This, then, was his moment when everything crashed and burned.

The minute John let his guard down was the minute the men on horseback surrounded his phaeton. A few other men climbed up onto the seat next to him—where she had been, just hours before, holding his hand.

They requested he hand over the reins. The request was punctuated with the cold barrel of a pistol pressing against his temple.

His winning streak was, officially, over. So very over.

But what if he had something greater on his side than fortune or mere luck? What if love really did conquer all?

John kept these thoughts to himself as his carriage was hijacked and he was driven to a posh house in Mayfair that he ought to have recognized.

As he was shoved out of the carriage, the devil himself was there, sneering down at John from atop a horse. He gripped the reins and a whip.

"Thank you, fellows," Dudley said. "The real Lord Castleton will handle matters from here. If you'll excuse me, I have a ball to attend. Lady P something or other."

My dear Lady Penelope,

Have you heard the news? Miss Payton has, at the very last possible moment, obtained a husband for herself. I do know you were so very worried about the reputation of your school—every graduate in one hundred years, married by her fourth season is quite the achievement. We had prayed for this, and the Lord has answered.

I do hate to trouble you whilst you are in the midst of last-minute preparations for the big anniversary ball tonight, but there is news I believe you must be made aware of. I'm so vexed to relay this additional gossip regarding your student, but I must.

Miss Payton—though I suppose she is Lady Nanson now—was spotted today, alighting from a carriage before her home in Berkeley Square. She was unchaperoned, accompanied by a gentleman who was certainly not the foppish Lord Nanson and who quite brazenly kissed her hand most intimately.

Yours,

Lady M

Number 4, Mount Street
Scarbrough House

Dudley leaned against the mantel in the drawing room, sipping a brandy and smirking at his reflection in the mirror. To be sure, he was not looking his best. He looked like a beast, thanks to that bastard "Castleton." The bruises would fade. "Castleton" would be locked up. Then Dudley would be the one laughing last.

Pulling out his timepiece, he noted that Megan was taking far too long in her preparations for this evening. Not that he was in a rush to escort his sister to her little school party, but there would certainly be more entertainments there than looking at one's ghastly face in the mirror. He'd rather be playing cards at his club. Or paying a visit to Madame X's—for play of another sort. He was in the mood.

But perhaps there would be diversions at this silly soiree.

Miss Payton would be there. And he had ensured that she would be there alone.

Dudley turned when he heard his sister sashaying into the room wearing a frothy explosion of ruffles and lace. She was accompanied by their father, who was a large man with a perpetually serious expression and prematurely gray hair. Megan shrieked when she saw him, clasping her gloved hands over her mouth.

"What the devil happened to your face?"

"Good to see you, too, sister," Dudley remarked. "Is that the thanks I get for leaving my boxing match to rush back to London for your silly little party?"

"Did you rush into a wooden beam repeatedly on your way?" Megan retorted. She huffed and turned to their father, who was regarding Dudley with his usual dismayed expression. "Papa, he cannot go with me with his face in such a state. I'll be too embarrassed."

"I would hate to embarrass her," Dudley concurred.

"After you've come all this way?" the marquis queried, his voice laced with sarcasm.

"Indeed, I would have preferred to remain in the country," Dudley replied.

"But you are here and your sister cannot go alone. It's just not done," his father said firmly. "One never knows the devils lurking out there."

"Aye." Dudley just sipped his brandy. One never knew.

Megan pouted. "Papa, can you attend with me?"

"Sorry, Daughter, but I have estate matters to tend to."

"I could help you with those," Dudley offered. The hopefulness in his voice caused him some embarrassment, which he washed away with a strong sip of brandy and a scowl.

"You can help me by taking your sister to the

ball," the marquis said, dismissively as always. "And if you can find a lady who'll have you, I beg of you to consider it. You have to marry eventually. Might as well get it done."

"How romantic," Dudley replied, sarcasm dripping from his voice.

"Just don't scare off my beaux," Megan sighed.

"I'll be in the card room the whole time anyway," he muttered. Although he did want to be present when Miss Payton arrived. Alone. Without "Castleton."

Emma, Olivia,

Have returned to London. So excited to see you this evening at Lady P's. Dear friends—I have news! And someone I'd like for you both to meet.

Yours,

Prue

Chapter 20

LADY EMMA, FORMALLY known as the Duchess of Ashbrooke and previously known as London's Least Likely to Misbehave, turned to her friend, Lady Olivia, with a furrowed brow and a frown and asked, "Where is Prudence? Have you found her yet?"

Olivia, now Lady Radcliffe and previously known as London's Least Likely to Cause a Scandal, had just returned from a turn about the ballroom. She was gasping for breath.

"Young ladies do not pant like dogs," Emma admonished. Olivia managed a scowl even though young ladies did not scowl either.

"Oh, pfft. Emma. I. Have. News," Olivia said breathlessly.

"What is it?"

"I know what Prue's news is—*and* who she wishes us to meet!"

"Is she married?" Emma asked, eyes wide. "She must be married. And who is the lucky man?"

"Lord Nanson," Olivia said triumphantly. Prue had sent them each a rather cryptic missive this afternoon. Olivia and Emma had been wracking their brains trying to guess at what Prue had to tell them.

"Lord Nanson!" Emma exclaimed. And then, in a lower voice, she asked, "Who is Lord Nanson? Do we know him?"

"We are not acquainted. I understand that he prefers Bath. But they are, of course, in town now."

"How do you know this?"

"Whilst in the ladies' retiring room, I overheard Lady Montague telling Lady Falmouth that a letter arrived at his mother's saying, and I quote, *'By the time you read this missive I will be married. Miss Prudence Payton has consented to be the future Lady Nanson. We will marry by special license at Mowbry Hall and will journey to London shortly thereafter. . . .'*"

"It sounds so whirlwind! Doesn't it? They must have fallen madly in love," Emma said with a big smile and sigh of contentedness. "I knew it. I knew we would all be happy and married by tonight."

"I cannot wait to see her. I cannot believe she has not yet arrived."

"Perhaps she and Lord Nanson were distracted," Emma said with a giggle.

Olivia adopted her loftiest expression and said, "Young ladies do not speculate on the marital activities of others."

"Thank you, Prissy Missy," Emma retorted. And then, impatiently she asked, "Where is Prudence?"

Number 12, Berkeley Square

Prudence anxiously awaited Castleton's arrival and wondered if there was any other way to wait other than anxiously. Perhaps impatiently, or eagerly. Tonight, as the minutes ticked by and Castleton had not yet arrived, she thought *anxious* wasn't quite a strong enough word.

Castleton had promised. He would be here.

She had no doubt. Right? She pushed aside thoughts of the other instances when men had failed to come through for her.

Not wanting to wrinkle her new gown, Prudence stood and took a turn about the drawing room. By some miracle, her favorite modiste had had a gown that another customer had returned. With a few quick alterations, it fit her to perfection.

Just wait until Castleton saw her!

Prudence couldn't resist another glance at herself in the reflection of the tall windows overlooking the square. The dress consisted of frothy layers of deep violet silk and chiffon, adorned with glittery amethyst stones. Underneath she wore a newly purchased pale pink silk corset and other delicate underthings. For the very first time, she felt radiantly beautiful.

It wasn't just the silk or the sparkling gemstones or the pretty new dress. It was the pink flush on her cheeks of a woman in love, the coy smile of a woman with a secret, the lips of a woman who had been kissed, a sparkle in her eye because she was loved and she knew it.

This wallflower had blossomed.

But her smile faded when the butler, Farnesworth, interrupted her waiting.

"Would you like some refreshment whilst you wait, Miss Payton?"

Prudence glanced at the clock on the mantel—a quarter past eight. It was fashionable for one to be fifteen minutes late. He would be here momentarily.

"I would love a glass of sherry," Prudence told the butler, thinking it would soothe her nerves while she waited these last few, anxious, impatient, eager moments before he arrived and they kissed before setting off for the ball, where she would show them all that she wasn't the one failure in one hundred years.

Thirty minutes later, she had taken numerous turns around the drawing room while imagining all the possible reasons why Castleton should be nearly an hour late. Perhaps the horse had thrown a shoe, or the carriage wheel had broken, or he had gotten lost, or stuck behind an outrageously slow-moving vehicle. There might have been a carriage accident, or a fire, or . . .

She hoped he wasn't hurt.

Or did she? Because if he wasn't hurt and he wasn't here, then she would have to face the fact that another man had disappointed her yet again. And this time, she was in love. . . .

Farnesworth returned. It was a particularly awkward moment when the butler looked at her with pity.

"Would you care for something to eat, Miss Payton? Another glass of sherry, perhaps?"

Prudence had visions of how the evening would unfold if she said yes. She would eat alone in the drawing room, wondering what had become of Castleton and imagining all her classmates celebrating at the ball. Another glass of sherry might dull the ache of feeling forgotten, but it was more likely to muddle her wits and reduce her to a weeping mess. Then, after a lonely meal and tipsy from drink, she'd probably just give up, remove the dress that had made her feel so beautiful, and crawl into bed, alone.

In the morning, she would wake up feeling like a coward. She had already wasted too many days living in fear and making every effort to avoid anything remotely uncomfortable or scary. She'd had good reason, but enough was enough.

She thought of the words Castleton had whispered fiercely to her: *You have survived the worst thing that could happen to you. And you have carried on. You are stronger than you know.*

If Prudence was strong and courageous, she would go to the ball. And she was—Prue had survived a highway robbery, walked for miles on her own, and survived a violent assault only to overcome the hate in her heart to fall in love.

Aye, she would not wait for Castleton, who

might or might not come. (*He had promised! Where was he?*) She would go to the ball and see her friends—lud, how she missed them! And she would catch up with her schoolmates. Perhaps she wouldn't spend the entire evening languishing like a wallflower—surely Ashbrooke and Radcliffe would dance with her.

It wouldn't be the night she had dreamt of, but it would still be a triumph for her.

"No, thank you, Farnesworth," she said. "But I would like the carriage brought around, please."

Lady Penelope's Ball

This was the moment she had been dreading ever since that invitation had arrived earlier this summer. *Lady Penelope requests the pleasure of your attendance . . .* Pleasure? Ha! Prudence stood in the grand foyer waiting for the butler to announce her. Her stomach had worked itself into a gnarled mess of a knot. Even though she had arrived late, there was still a long receiving line, giving her plenty of time to fret.

Where was Castleton?

Why had he not come?

What if something had gone wrong? What if something hadn't?

Was he breaking his promise?

Was she a fool to have trusted him?

How many times did she have to learn that men

never arrive just in time, at the very last moment, to dramatically rescue a girl from whatever disaster she faced? First Dudley, then Cecil. Now Castleton?

No, she couldn't quite believe it. But the evidence was swiftly mounting.

She may have mustered her courage in the comforting surroundings of her drawing room, but now she felt her determination slipping away. Her knees felt weak and her stomach ached from nervousness, but she was proud of herself for attending. She was still terrified and awkward and unsure of a thousand things, but those emotions were no longer ruling her life.

Under the silk and chiffon folds of her gown, her feet tapped anxiously on the parquet floor.

Perhaps he'll arrive soon, she hoped, even though she knew better.

Dear God, please let him arrive soon, she prayed, even though she knew better.

"Lord and Lady Crawford," the butler declared.

Prudence inched closer. Her palms were damp under her satin gloves.

Where was he? Castleton had promised. She had believed him. Even now she couldn't quite fathom that he would leave her to face this night alone. This night, in which she was confirmed as the one unwed graduate of Lady Penelope's class of 1820 and the only girl to fail at her one goal in life.

"Lord and Lady Mulberry" the butler declared.

Lord and Lady Mulberry strolled into the ballroom, arm in arm.

Oh God, it was her turn now. The butler looked at her expectantly. Should she tell him Miss Payton or Lady Castleton? The matter was no longer merely a name but some epic dilemma about her identity, her faith in Castleton, God and Men, and her confidence in herself.

Did she believe in Castleton?

Did she still have faith in love and happily ever after and heroes that arrived in the pivotal moment? Or had Dudley so thoroughly broken her that she was going to lose all hope?

The butler cleared his throat. He was waiting, unaware of her massive dilemma. People were growing anxious behind her—they wanted to drink champagne, and dance, and gossip with their friends.

She had to give a name *now*. She had to decide *this very minute* if she still believed in happily ever after.

"Lady Castleton," she whispered to the butler in a fleeting moment of hope and faith.

"Lady Castleton," the butler announced. Loudly. A few people nearby turned to look. Upon seeing *her*, their laughter began and moved through the crowd in a slow ripple.

Prudence had made an art of not being noticed in the hopes that she would avoid exactly this moment. Everyone was staring—except for the people poking their friends and urging them to look at her. Then they all laughed. Why?

What was so funny? Prudence held her head high and refused to cry.

She could see them talking about her, whispering behind their fans. What were they saying?

Her palms were damp beneath her gloves, and there was a foreboding ache in her belly. Mechanically, she stepped forward into the ballroom and began to weave through the crowd, searching for her friends.

The curious stares and the hissing whispers followed her. She overheard snatches of conversations:

"Lady Nanson . . ."

"Castleton returned days ago . . ."

". . . thought she was American."

"Prudence! You're here!" Emma cried. Olivia was with her. Radcliffe and Ashbrooke were deep in conversation nearby but looked up and seemed pleased to see her.

At the sight of her friends, Prudence let out a deep breath she hadn't been aware of holding in. Leaving London—and even lying to her friends—had been the right thing to do. But she had missed them, and she was scared, and they were here. They were *home.*

"We were afraid you wouldn't come!" Olivia admonished. Prue gave a little smile, not daring to tell her she almost hadn't. In fact, she almost wished she'd been back in her room at the Coach & Horses rather than being the subject of whispers here.

"Where is he?" Olivia asked immediately. Prudence's smile faltered. She had written to her friends promising to introduce them to someone. Right. Well done, Prudence. *Where was he?* And was it wrong to hope that he was lying comatose in a ditch?

"We cannot wait to meet your husband, Lady Nanson," Emma said with a wink.

"Cecil?" What the devil were they talking about—and how did they know about Cecil? Prue looked from Emma to Olivia and back again. They were both beaming, idiotically so. Their happiness at her *finally, finally* having married was at once wonderful and tragic.

"We heard you married at his estate by special license," Olivia said, eyes shining.

"It sounds like such a whirlwind romance. Was it? Tell us everything," Emma gushed.

Prudence looked around for a chair. She needed to sit down. If news had reached the ton that she was Lady Nanson and she'd just announced herself as Lady Castleton . . .

Prudence now looked around for a place to discreetly cast up her accounts. There was nowhere, so she closed her eyes, hoping to shut out the unmitigated disaster unfolding. She was jolted back to reality by Olivia.

"News just reached his parents this afternoon, and I just heard about it in the ladies' retiring room," Olivia said.

"Didn't I tell you we would all be married and in love by tonight?" Emma said with a happy sigh. "I do love being right. I think it suits me."

Prudence didn't have the heart to tell her the truth.

"Where is he? Do you see him?" Olivia asked, having noticed Prudence glancing around, wondering if she would see Cecil. Or Castleton. Oh, any one of her two fake husbands.

Unfortunately, Prudence spied Dudley instead.

Her instinct was to turn and flee, like a frightened little lamb with a wolf approaching, openmouthed, sharp teeth glistening. That would just encourage him to chase, wouldn't it? She had run around ballrooms for years avoiding him, and then he had somehow found her in a small village miles from London. There was just no running away from him, which meant she would have to stand her ground and fight.

Stop looking so bloody scared all the time.

She drew strength from Castleton's words, as if he'd been right behind her, whispering in her ear, instead of echoing in her memory. *Why wasn't he here?*

Even as Dudley stalked through the ballroom toward her, Prudence forced herself to stand tall and proud, as if she wasn't utterly terrified.

His face was a revolting mess of cuts and bruises, made all the more menacing by the look in his eyes: he was thinking of *before*, and doing it again, she could tell.

Her confidence wavered as Dudley came to stand before her. He had the power to destroy her, and they both knew it. This was the moment of confrontation she had feared, and she was on her own for it.

Had Castleton anticipated this moment when she would have to face the devil on her own? Is that why he had prepared her for this moment? Had he known all along that he wouldn't be with her?

"Miss Payton, we meet again," Dudley said with a smile that did nothing to enhance his gruesome face or ease the cold knot of fear in her belly. "Or should I say Lady Nanson? Or Lady Castleton?"

It so happened that there was something worse than being unwed for Lady Penelope's Ball: being unwed with rumors that she was married to two different men.

"I thought Lord Castleton only just returned from America," Emma said, looking quite puzzled. "With his wife. How would you have met him, Prue?"

"Did your friends not hear you announced as Lady Castleton?" Dudley asked.

Prudence ignored him, her attention fixed upon what Emma had said. Castleton hadn't mentioned anything about just returning from America. That was odd. It seemed the sort of thing one would bring up.

Also the sort of thing someone might bring up: *a wife.*

How did her friends know all of this? How did she not? It was taking everything in her—every ounce of strength, every last nerve—to remain upright.

"I thought you married Lord Nanson," Olivia said, furrowing her brow. "Prudence, what on earth is going on?"

"Where is Lord Nanson?" Emma asked. "Or Lord Castleton?"

"Castleton is not here this evening," Dudley said smugly. He obviously knew something and was taking a perverse pleasure in lording it over her. "In fact, I'm quite certain he has been indisposed and won't be attending."

What had happened to him? Where was he? What had Dudley done to him?

There were too many questions, too many little things that were not adding up. She was aware, vaguely, of her world beginning to fall apart. There would be vicious rumors about her . . . Castleton was gone . . . had he lied to her from the start?

"Since he is not here," Dudley continued, "you must be in want of a partner, and I hear a waltz starting. Would you care to dance with me?"

When, as a young girl, Prudence would make a mistake with her lessons or get into a spot of trouble, her governess, Miss Georgette, would always say kindly, "Dear Prue, it's not a mistake if you learn from it."

Needless to say, Dudley was a mistake she wished she hadn't made, and God help her, she wasn't going to throw away her safety and happiness because of a stupid rule of etiquette. Again.

Dudley held out his hand with a sick grin on his face, his malicious intentions too clear to her. Prudence remembered Castleton instructing her not to give him an opportunity to grab her. So she kept her hands behind her back and said, loud and clear, "No."

Not *No, thank you* or *I'm afraid I mustn't* or any of the other delicate words and phrases that might soften the impact of the refusal. She simply said NO, bluntly rejecting his invitation.

"I beg your pardon?" Dudley reddened.

Gentlemen's dance invitations were never refused, especially by a wallflower on her fourth season who might or might not have two husbands but who was certainly a person of scandal and ridicule.

But Prudence knew there was something worse than being unwed on her fourth season, and it was having her innocence taken against her will, living each day with fear in her heart, and not knowing love.

"I said no," Prudence said, her voice stronger now. Castleton wasn't here, but she could imagine him encouraging her. Emma and Olivia stepped in closer to her, forming a wall of wallflowers. Ashbrooke and Radcliffe stepped close, towering behind her, ready to fight this battle for her.

"You're a very rude young woman," Dudley said sharply.

Prudence lifted her chin and said, "And you cannot truthfully call yourself a gentleman."

Someone nearby gasped, but Prudence couldn't look to see who—she was far too distracted by the blood rushing to Dudley's head, the pure hatred emanating from his eyes, and the barely contained fury in his body. She had angered him.

Don't be scared even when you're scared. Don't be scared even when you're scared. Don't be scared even when you're scared.

Even though Prudence wanted to run, she stood her ground. In some way, Castleton was here after all. And she wasn't alone: her friends stood behind her. A crowd of guests, including Lady Penelope herself, began to gather, watching this scene unfold.

"What is happening, Prue?" Emma asked, keeping a warning gaze on Dudley.

"You didn't tell them, did you?" Dudley sneered. Then, leaning in close, he whispered the most vile, viscious things in her ear. She felt his hot breath on her neck. The scent of wine and cigars on his breath took her back to that night. "They don't know what happened between us years ago. For if they knew—if anyone knew—it'd be wedding bells for you and me. And I could have you as much as I wanted. Whenever I wanted. However I wanted. Wherever I wanted."

Prudence didn't think; she acted. She rammed her knee into Dudley's groin, just as Castleton had taught her. Not expecting such a show of force, Dudley went down, swearing, gasping, clasping where she'd struck him.

Just for good measure, she struck upwards with the heel of her hand, hitting Dudley solidly in the nose as he went down. There was the most wretched cracking sound, a garbled scream of pain and blood. Prudence paled at the sight of his blood on her new gloves.

"Where did you learn to do that, Prue?" Olivia asked in an awestruck whisper.

"Certainly not at Lady Penelope's school," Lady Penelope reprimanded.

Prudence looked up from the oddly pleasing and arresting sight of her tormenter writhing in agonies at her feet.

"You gave us an excellent education, Lady Penelope, but in some aspects it was insufficient," Prudence replied.

The ballroom had fallen silent—even the orchestra had ceased.

Prudence lifted her gaze to all the shocked and curious faces staring at her.

That was when the screaming began. The sound of shattering glass rent through the room, and all hell broke loose.

Chapter 21

Number 24, Bruton Street

THE REAL LORD Castleton's residence was a four-story home built of limestone, with large glass windows and a pitched slate roof. It quietly and impressively radiated wealth, power, and confidence, as did the viscount's country estate, Castlemore Court. Both grand homes were the sort John never had a prayer of owning himself.

He was escorted into the real Lord Castleton's study. It was a well-appointed and dignified room covered in dark wood paneling, with built-in bookshelves with hundreds of leather-bound volumes protected by beveled glass doors. The Aubusson carpets were thick and plush under his feet. The furniture was exquisitely crafted—a large wooden desk, a smattering of small side tables with green marble tops, chairs upholstered in green silk and velvet.

John had spent plenty of time in the finest rooms of the finest houses. Tonight, he was all too aware that he might never set foot in a room like this again.

Lord Castleton stood upon his arrival. John was invited to sit in a chair. A massive desk stood between them, reinforcing the real Castleton's inborn superiority.

"So you are Castleton," the real Castleton began. He leaned back in his chair and steepled his fingers. "I find that interesting, because *I* am Castleton."

John felt the old urge to be deferential, to begin and end every sentence with *"my lord."* It was how he'd been brought up. How he'd been trained, like a dog. But something had changed in this past year, when he'd acted as if he'd been the viscount. John couldn't shake the proud and assured posture or the confidence he'd gained from every instance when he'd been welcomed, and every round of cards that he'd won.

John elected to say nothing. Instead, he kept his expression inscrutable—though he couldn't resist a glance at the clock. A quarter past the hour. Prudence would be waiting, and he had promised.

Then the real Castleton spoke, and John shifted his attention back to him.

"You can just imagine my surprise when I return from abroad, only to have learned that someone has been traveling round the countryside, impersonating me."

Dudley. His name, a curse.

"I also learned that I, or you, rather, have been fleecing my fellow peers of their fortunes."

At that, John scoffed.

"I did not cheat," John said in such a manner to suggest that it was beneath him as a gentleman, a man of honor, and a man of intellect. "I was invited to play, I did so with skill, and I fairly won. I'd almost go so far as to congratulate you on your newfound reputation for cards."

"So you admit to impersonating me, the rightful Castleton?"

"I said I would almost," John remarked. He held Lord Castleton's gaze as if he'd been his equal. Nothing could have been further from the truth.

"I've also heard that you've been assaulting women and brawling, leaving one man bruised, bloodied, and with a broken nose." John's eyes narrowed and chest tightened. He wanted to deny the charge of assaulting a woman, but he could not admit aloud to impersonating his lordship. "I've been told that he was then ruthlessly shoved out of the inn on a cold, rainy night. What a lack of Christian charity," the viscount continued.

Definitely Dudley. Dim-witted Dudley must have seen that notice in the paper and figured it out. Then he must have called upon Castleton the minute he'd set foot on English soil. John had to hand it to the scoundrel as far as revenge went.

"Most nights in England are cold and rainy. It's hardly remarkable. I trust you haven't forgotten that whilst you were away."

"Do you deny these charges?"

John simply looked at the viscount, conveying with his glance alone that it was beneath him to be questioned like this. The real Lord Castleton smiled.

"Your impression is excellent. Your manner of speaking, the way you carry yourself, the way you look. I'm not surprised you were able to pull off the fraud."

The word *fraud* hung in the air like a hangman's noose swaying in the breeze. John could be brought up on charges of fraud. Castleton seemed to be interested in questioning him first, like a cat toying with a mouse. John wouldn't be surprised if he was in Newgate before midnight.

He wouldn't give a damn if it hadn't been for Prudence.

John glanced at the clock again, the minutes ticking by. Would she be waiting anxiously in the drawing room? Would she retire for the evening, sad and disappointed?

Or would she go to the ball alone? His breath caught. Dudley would be there. She would be there. He might not be there. And if she went unaccompanied, would she be announced as Miss Payton—or Lady Castleton? The exposure and subsequent embarrassment would be devastating to her.

He had to stop her.

He had to explain.

He could not explain.

Castleton leaned back in his chair, comfortable and content to let this interview carry on for as long as required to obtain the answers he sought. John's throat tightened "I've heard you also have a Lady Castleton of your own," the viscount said.

This made John impatient, angry. He couldn't say anything without compromising Prudence. God, what if she had gone to the ball and introduced herself as Lady Castleton? She'd be a laughing-stock. A sweat broke out on his brow. He had to get to her.

"Ah, speaking of Lady Castleton . . ." John's head jerked in the direction of the woman who had entered, for he had become accustomed to thinking of Prudence thusly and half expected it to be her.

But it was a dark-haired woman with alabaster skin, and she looked curiously from one man to the other.

"I'll just be a moment, dear," Castleton said. As if sensing the tension in the room, she murmured her apologies and stepped out, leaving the door slightly ajar.

Then the viscount turned his attentions back to John, who wrenched his attentions away from the clock.

"You do look familiar," Castleton remarked.

"I could say the same," John replied, slightly testy.

Indeed, the resemblance was uncanny. Both possessed the same dark hair, the same bone structure, the same build. Their eyes were different, but otherwise they could pass as brothers. Hanging over the mantel, the portrait of the late viscount did nothing to dispel the possibility that the three were related.

"Brandy?" Castleton offered as he poured himself a glass from the crystal decanter on his desk.

"Is it poisoned?" John questioned.

The viscount cracked a smile and said, "No."

"Then yes, thank you." John didn't want the drink, but something happened when two men drank together—it bonded them. At this point, John's reign as Castleton was well and truly over. His only hope lay in ensuring the man didn't press charges. He thought of the engine, the money in the bank he'd saved, his mother and sister, and he thought of Prudence. There was a rich future awaiting him, though he could lose it all in an instant.

Could it be taken from him? John hadn't made much study of the law when running from it.

Castleton took a sip of his brandy and said, "Care to tell me why you did it?"

"Well, you weren't using it," John quipped.

"Waste not, want not, right?"

"My thoughts exactly," John murmured. Castleton paused, regarding John thoughtfully.

"Why do we look so bloody alike that you got away with this for months? Everyone knows everyone. I went to school with half of the fellows that you gambled with. Our families have known each other for generations."

"My mother spent some time at Castlemore," John said gravely, allowing Castleton to put two and two together. It was a gamble, telling him this. Whilst it might play on a familiar connection, it also exposed his father as the sort of lord who cheated on his lady wife for a romp with the housemaids. And above all, John had no proof. His mother hadn't told him who his father was. He just knew that looking at Lord Castleton was like looking in a mirror. Especially tonight, when John was dressed in a gentleman's evening clothes.

Castleton narrowed his eyes and said, "I think I remember you." John didn't have time for a jaunt down memory lane, especially when no good could come of it. He had to get out of here. Prudence and that ball awaited. "Are we brothers?"

"I don't know," John said honestly. "It's possible."

"And you've spent the years since masquerading as me."

John wasn't about to tell him how desperate he'd been the first night this charade had begun. The world didn't give him a bloody chance, so he'd taken one. He didn't think this born-and-bred aristocrat would understand or sympathize. Instead, he said flippantly, "It passed the time."

"What are you going to do now?"

"I suppose that depends on you," John said evenly. Tightly. Impatiently. He glanced at the clock again. Prudence would think he'd abandoned her. She would think that heroes never came through. That fragile happiness she'd fought so hard for would be lost.

He was nobody's hero. He was a fraud.

The only thing that mattered was his word, his promise, to Prudence.

"I'll be honest, I have no wish to deal with this," Castleton said, sighing mightily. "I've just traveled halfway around the world and made all sorts of promises about England to my lady wife. And now her entry into society will be compromised because of these rumors. She was nervous enough already."

"My sincere apologies to your wife," John said. He meant it; Prudence had let him know how tricky and dangerous society could be. Given the way Castleton nodded, he knew the man understood.

"You keep looking at the clock," Castleton remarked. "Is there somewhere you must be? Or are you calculating how much time you have before the authorities arrive?"

"There is a woman," John said, and his voice betrayed too much emotion. "A lovely, vulnerable woman who is depending on me."

"Ah, romance," Castleton remarked dryly. If he was about to display a soft heart or a capacity for cruelty, John knew not. When he heard the arrival of Bow Street Runners, John didn't wait any longer. Taking advantage of Lord Castleton's momentary distraction, John made a run for it.

He'd been on the run for a while now. . . .

Chapter 22

THE FIRST TIME John styled himself as Lord Castleton, it was born of the desperation that can only come of a black, wet, and cold February night.

The freezing rain was relentless; it soaked straight through his clothes, leaving his skin damp and chilling him to his bones. Nevertheless he stood outside that village inn, letting the weather do its worst, as he looked through the windows at everyone gathered around a roaring fire.

Nearly every room at the inn—from the parlor to the dormer windows on the top floor—was lit with the warm glow of candles. He imagined steaming hot baths, dry beds with warm blankets, and wealthy lords and ladies blissfully unaware that anyone would be out of doors in weather such as this.

John would give anything for a hot bath that might thaw him out and bring him back to life. He'd give anything for a warm, hearty meal. Maybe even a pint, if God really wanted to show him some favor. For the past few days he had subsisted on old bread, tepid water, and whatever he'd hunted or foraged along the way from Blackhaven Manor to this village. He'd gotten by on odd jobs for the past few months, but lately the work had dried up.

He'd give anything for a bed, too, where he might stretch out his weary legs and allow his body to relax. Hell, he'd even take the floor, as long as there was a roof over it. After all, he was used to that.

John patted his pockets, not knowing why he even bothered. They were as empty as they were yesterday, and the day before that, and all the days previous.

His wanting for warmth and food was so great that, despite logic, reason, and past experience, he felt along the lining of his coat, lest a stray coin or two had slipped through a hole in his pocket. No such luck.

Runaway footmen didn't tend to travel with much blunt.

Penniless runaway footmen with the law on their tail couldn't avail themselves of the comforts of a village inn either. If he could just get to London, or Manchester, or even America, his humble beginnings wouldn't matter and he'd have a chance to make something of himself.

But first he had to endure this night, and this cold, driving rain, and the dim awareness of being frozen from the inside out. Even his bones felt cold, and he'd swear he could feel ice in his veins.

John stood there, hands shoved in his pockets, muttering a string of words so foul they'd make a sailor blush. He bloody well swore at God for his damned bad luck.

God damn that bastard Burbrooke for assaulting his innocent sister. That pompous prick didn't deserve to breathe the same air, let alone touch her. Claim her, as if he owned her. John choked on a gulp of icy air.

But he did own her, didn't he? All the servants were reliant upon him and his father for wages and letters of reference should they attempt to leave and find work elsewhere. Lord Burbrooke was a stingy bastard, with both wages and favorable letters of reference.

It was a certain kind of purgatory in that house, a far cry from Castlemore Court, where life had been fine, FINE, until John had started to look a little too similar to the young lord and master. It was an uncomfortable thing for the family to look at the face of the viscount's bastard son over the breakfast table, where he served them. Lady Castleton had taken issue. So had the young lord. John—and his mother and sister—were asked to leave.

They found stations at Blackhaven Manor with Lord Burbrooke and his family. It was not a happy household, to say the least. From the lord and master, to the butler, to the scullery maid, everyone was miserable and mean.

When Lord Burbrooke learned what had

happened—and that his heir had been beaten to within an inch of his life—he called in the magistrate, leaving John no choice but to depart immediately, without references, or wages, or a place to go. John should have been glad he was out, but knowing his mother and sister remained without him to defend them tempered any exhilaration he might feel at his freedom.

His mum and sister would have to stay on at Blackhaven Manor as housemaids, marked for trouble because of what John had done. Unless there was a way he could get them out. He had to get them out. Somehow, someway, he'd figure out how to earn enough money that they could be safe and live together as a family again.

Or were they too lowborn to deserve even that?

But it burned, God, it burned to know they were there without protection. The world had few opportunities to offer a footman too smart for his own good, and too easy with his fists.

The burning, at least, kept him warm. Made his hands bunch into fists, which kept his fingers from freezing completely. But he was still cold, and still angry.

Bloody way of the world where some men were born lucky and some weren't and that was that. John was smarter than most of the idiotic peers he'd had to serve, thanks to books carefully pilfered from the library, read by stolen candlelight, and returned. He took knowledge however he could get it—eavesdropping on conversations about influential people, current events, or foreign countries, because all the lords and ladies thought that his livery made him deaf and dumb. He read old newspapers before they were used to line trunks or start fires.

But who had all the money? Who had the power?

Who was the one standing in the rain, penniless and dreaming of a fucking meat pie as the greatest luxury in all of God's creation?

Just because his lowborn mother worked and was unwed when she gave birth to him. He probably had the blood of the viscount in his veins—but it hardly counted.

So life wasn't fair. Grossly, massively unfair.

The question was: what was he going to do about it?

Skulk about in the rain until morning? Fueling his anger until it consumed him alive? The sensible thing to do would be to find a stable where he could bunk for the night in a vermin-ridden pile of straw and make his escape at first light.

The prospect did not enthrall.

Because what would he do tomorrow night, or the night after? This was England. There were many cold, wet nights in his future. It wasn't that he needed a feather mattress. He was an intelligent man, not an animal, and a life of illicitly nesting in straw bales wasn't something he was about to settle for.

The world might have little to offer him, but that

didn't mean he would be content with the scraps. It didn't mean he wouldn't try to seize more.

His eyes narrowed as he kept watching the window. A quartet of wealthy peers sat down at a table before the fire. Even from where he stood, John could see their faces, red and round from a life of excess. The innkeeper hovered, serving them brandy. The gents smoked, drank, and played cards without a care in the world.

As a footman, John had seen and served many peers; dukes, marquises, earls, were all frequent guests of both Lord Burbrooke and Lord Castleton. Upstairs, the fancy folks dined on the finest food, drank the finest wines and spirits, and had the most inane conversations. Downstairs, John had the rest of the staff in peals of laughter as he mimicked their manner of speech and the ridiculous things they said, all in the clipped, commanding tones of an upper-class British accent.

John was willing to bet there was no room at the inn for the likes of him, but there was always space for the aristocracy.

No one knew him. He was a nobody. Nothing.

But what if he wasn't?

Really—*what if he wasn't a nobody?*

The anger turned to something else. A spark of possibility. What if he were a lord and peer of the realm? Or more importantly: what if everyone believed him to be?

In the cold, and the dark, and the wet, John Roark laughed.

Threw back his head and laughed. His hands out of his pockets, by his sides. This was the moment his luck was going to change—or he would land in jail. Either way, he'd have a roof over his head.

When he was done laughing, John squared his shoulders and walked across the road with determined strides. With every step he shed the trappings of his old self: the righteous fury of someone held down, the deferential attitude drilled into him since he was literally born into service, the knowledge that he didn't have a farthing to his name and that it was a name that carried no weight and mattered to nobody.

To hell with his old self.

His boots thudded heavily on the wooden steps because he walked with a purpose, with determination, with the resolution that his every step was more important than anyone else's.

The door crashed open, thudding into the wall, because a display of force often went a long way. John stepped across the threshold.

Warmth. Light. The mouthwatering aromas of food, the convivial atmosphere of warm people with full bellies, pints of ale, an assured place to sleep.

Instead of feeling *wanting*, John felt *expectation*.

He would have these things. He would have them tonight.

Everyone in the main room turned to look at the unfortunate sot who had been out on a night like this. Everyone included the innkeeper, a barmaid, an assortment of tradesmen and merchants, and a pack of dissolute peers seated at a table before the fire, card game in progress.

The innkeeper, a reedy little man bustled over, shutting the door behind John. He took a look at John's wet and worn attire, which labeled him as a poor nobody even when it was freshly pressed.

John drew himself up to his full height of six feet two.

"Good evening, but I'm afraid—" the little man stammered, John's appearance suggesting *peasant*. But if he was doing it right, John's expression was all haughty lord.

"I am Castleton."

The declaration was made in the cultured manner of a British aristocrat, an accent John had spent years practicing. *Castleton* wasn't just a name—it was an essential truth, a history, a statement of his wealth, a declaration of his honor and worth. It was more than a name, more than a man, and the way John uttered *Castleton* made all that crystal clear.

It was also a complete lie.

Castleton was the title of the man who might be his father and was now possessed by a man who might be his brother and who had left the country years ago. Castlemore Court was where John had grown up, and he knew it like the back of his hand. John knew all the family stories. Hell, he even had the same name as his possible half brother.

He just didn't have the title. Until now.

The lords a lounging looked up from their game in surprise. "Castleton!" Another exclaimed, "You're back!" And yet another said, "It's been an age!"

Castleton nodded in acknowledgment. It helped that he and the viscount were of roughly the same age and, though it was never commented upon, remarkably similar in appearances. It also helped that the real Lord Castleton had left England to travel some time ago.

"I'd like a room and a hot bath," Castleton informed the innkeeper.

"Right this way."

"Come down and join us once you've cleaned up a bit," one of the blocks called out.

"Of course," he answered.

That was all it took: *"I am Castleton."*

A declaration one moment, and the next, he was soaking in a hot bath and the chill in his body started to ease. He had a tray sent up and almost died with pleasure and gratitude when it contained a large bowl full of thick, hearty stew accompanied by fresh bread, salted butter, and a big tankard of ale.

Life for Lord Castleton was good. It was much better than life for John Roark, runaway servant. Why not continue to be Castleton? Finally warm and full, John could think of no good reason not to.

An hour or two later, his clothes had dried

enough for him to return downstairs, where he joined the gents playing cards before the roaring fire.

"Pull up a chair, Castleton, and tell us what the devil happened to you."

He spun an exciting story of his travel on the high seas, full of threatening storms, mad ship captains, and a pirate attack or two. Never having experienced these things himself, he drew upon the books he'd read and the stories he'd heard told over the dinner table. He spoke of his Grand Tour and all the European capitals where he'd drunk the finest wines, dined with aristocrats and influential thinkers, and made love to breathtakingly beautiful women.

Meanwhile, he divested his fellow players of fifty pounds, thanks to the books on mathematics he'd nicked from the library, and Benny, one of the stable hands, who'd learned to count cards. While he had stood about, waiting to pour wine or brandy or port, John had performed calculations in his head to keep himself from going mad at the tedium of it all.

It helped that his companions this evening were deep in their cups and he was not (though he certainly partook of a glass when offered). It helped that they played recklessly, for the thrill of it, rather than to earn enough money to pay for their room at the inn.

By the end of the night, John won enough to pay for the inn and perhaps get a new suit of clothes, which would be essential for his next great gamble: he had secured an invitation to continue on and join them at Lord Collins's house party—gents and women of loose morals only.

And so it began.

As Lord Castleton, he went from card game to card game, house party to house party, living the life of a debauched lord with no claims on his time. His winnings accumulated and were put away to earn interest. After a few smart investments, his wealth increased.

Within a month, he was able to move his mother and sister out of Blackhaven Manor and into a small cottage in a different village, but that still wasn't the life he imagined for them. However, frugality and discretion were the order of the day. He was saving, and investing those savings, for something big. The only way to win a fortune was on a massive venture.

Like the Difference Engine.

So he saved and saved, earning just enough to possibly acquire a factory, or shares in the business of the engine—anything that would ensure he was so filthy, unfathomably rich that he would never be cold, hopeless, soaking wet, and starving again.

Chapter 23

On his way to the ball

JOHN NO LONGER gave a damn about being cold, or wet, or starving again. To hell with his plans, his hopes and dreams. The Difference Engine didn't matter now. He hated to leave his mother and sister, but they would have access to the money he'd already won, earned, accumulated. He might see the inside of Newgate by morning—and God only knew what would happen after that. It didn't matter. None of it mattered.

Only Prudence mattered.

He had to keep this promise to her. It was all he had left to give.

John was under no illusions: it was only a matter of minutes or hours before she knew the truth about him. She would know that he had been too cowardly to confide in her, when she had bared everything to him.

He deserved to lose her.

But she did not deserve to be left alone on this night, of all nights.

John took advantage of Castleton's momentary distraction to escape through an open window. He sprinted across the garden to the stables

behind the house, where he took the first animal
he saw—a massive and restless black stallion.
They took off at a gallop.

The black stallion surged beneath him, taking
long, powerful strides. Hooves hit dirt, sending
rocks kicking back, before launching once more
into the air. Digging in his heels against its gut,
Castleton urged the horse to go faster still. His
own muscles burned from the pressure of gripping the horse between his thighs. His bruised
and damaged hands were tangled tightly in the
horse's mane.

There had been no time to saddle up. Opportunities were meant to be seized. He'd grabbed onto
this one with both hands.

His heart pounded hard, fast. Echoed in his
head loudly, so loudly. But not loud enough to
drown out the sound of Prudence's screams of
fear, or her cries of pleasure, or the soft, lilting
sound of her laugh. Some things a man never
forgot.

The stallion heaved loud, heavy breaths that
John could feel underneath him. This was a great
distance at a tremendous speed, even for a fine
animal like this one.

He would be late. The minutes had ticked by
too fast. But he would be there.

Pedestrians flung themselves out of the way
when they saw the massive beast bearing down
on them. Carriages stopped abruptly or turned
swiftly, wisely getting the hell out of his way. This

stallion leapt over fences and expertly dodged other carriages. The horse galloped at full speed through dark, narrow alleyways and wide, expansive avenues.

The wind whipped through his hair and stung his clean-shaven face.

Faster, faster, faster, faster.

Yet he felt as if moving through water—slow, thick, lethargic movements. But the wind was at his back and he was on his way to her.

Finally, the house—castle, practically—came into view. The stallion galloped down the drive, gravel flying under his hooves. Ahead, John saw the grand entrance to the house, thick with carriages, loitering drivers, and butlers that would refuse entry to anyone not explicitly invited.

He did not have an invitation.

And on the left, the ballroom stretched out, a long, rectangular room with massive glass windows stretching from floor to ceiling. Thousands of candles were lit, illuminating the guests in all their finery, having a merry time. They had no idea that Prudence was there, dying a little inside, and that he had to save her.

Digging in his heels, he urged the horse to the left. Moving as one, they charged up the vast expanse of green lawn toward the ballroom.

Up ahead the ballroom loomed. On the terrace, guests mingled. John watched more details come into sharp relief as he got closer. He saw dapper gentlemen with blunt cigars in their fingers, then the bright red tips, then plumes of smoke curling up in the evening sky. Women stood by, delicately clasping flutes of champagne; he got closer and could see their jewels sparkle, and he could hear their posh, never-worried-a-day-in-their-lives laughter.

John and the beast breathed hard, hurling toward them at a furious and punishing pace.

He saw as they all became aware of him— gasps! And then it dawned on them that he was not going to stop. The screaming began as they all fled from his path.

Tall windows, stretching from floor to ceiling, were open.

At the last moment, John urged the stallion to jump up the stairs to the terrace. He sailed up and across, not touching down until they landed in the ballroom.

The horse's hooves clattered on the parquet floor. More than a few women screamed, and some genuinely swooned. A footman with a tray of champagne glasses was knocked off his feet into a table of lemonade. At the sound of the screams and the shattering glass, the ballroom hushed.

Everyone stood frozen.

Everyone included Prudence.

Dudley was writhing on the floor at her feet and clutching his balls. A grin tugged at John's lips as he understood what had happened. He hated that she'd had to face him alone, but he was glad to have taught her to defend herself.

Just in case he wasn't there. . . .

But he was here now.

John dismounted, patting the horse with gratitude. The stallion breathed heavily and pawed the floor as John walked determinedly across the ballroom to his woman. Anyone in his path stepped aside immediately.

Prudence, lovely Prudence, was his. Whoever he was. She belonged to him the way two people who loved each other belonged together. Had she felt it, too?

He stopped before her. She whispered his name. "Castleton."

"He's not Castleton," Dudley said through gritted teeth as he clambered back to his feet.

Prudence furrowed her brow, perplexed.

"I thought I told you to stay away from her," John said, his voice low and threatening.

"I don't take orders from pretenders," Dudley said with a smirk.

There was only one response to that: John swung, his fist connecting so solidly with Dudley's already bruised jaw that the force of the impact lifted Dudley off his feet before he fell backward onto the floor.

Prudence turned to face John. He was in no condition to see her now. His clothes were a mess from the mad ride to get to her. He was breathing hard from the exertions. And bloody hell, his fist was throbbing like the devil.

"You're here," she whispered. As if she had

doubted him. It slayed him that she'd had reason to.

"I promised, didn't I?" He lifted her outstretched hand for a kiss. Her lips parted slightly. Like her, he was thinking of how he really wished to kiss—the completely-lost-in-you-never-need-to-breathe kind of kiss.

"Why does he say that you are not Castleton?" Prudence asked, looking up at him with those scared and wounded doe eyes of hers. His heart ached, literally ached. He could feel it thudding slower and slower in his chest, giving up in the face of a battle that could not be won.

"Waltz with me," John said softly, reaching out for her.

"Answer me," she demanded, chin trembling.

"Please. I will explain." He could hear the raw desperation in his voice. Could she? He tried to smile. "Let's not waste two-eighths of your life."

"There's no music," Prudence said. The orchestra wasn't playing. No one in the ballroom was speaking. Everyone was watching this scene unfold, in which a man they didn't know crashed into their party and begged for a waltz from the girl no one had ever given much notice to.

John held out his hand.

He waited with his hand outstretched and his invitation plain for anyone to see.

Prudence looked around the ballroom, bewildered. Then she lifted her gaze to his. His breath hitched. Could she believe that he'd never meant to deceive her? Could she see that he loved her?

If she would just take his hand, there was hope that this wasn't the end.

Prudence placed her hand in his. He swept her into his arms. Gazes locked. He nodded, and they began to waltz. One could hear the slight shuffling of their steps: *one two three, one two three*. The crowds backed away, allowing them room. The orchestra started to play.

Waltzing was something John had learned whilst standing along the perimeter of the ballroom near doors that might need to be opened or closed. Later, he would attempt the steps with a spirited housemaid. He remembered one night when Sally, a lady's maid, had laughed as she'd said, "When will I ever need to be able to waltz?" He had replied, "You never know. And when the moment comes, you'll be glad you learned."

The moment had come. He embraced Prudence, one hand low on her back, another firmly clasping her palm. The last time they had danced had been at the Coach & Horses Inn, in some village, and he remembered her not wanting to be held too close or too tightly.

Tonight was different, because they were lovers now.

Also, he couldn't risk that she would run away before he could tell her.

Also, this might be the last time he ever held his beautiful girl. It was essential that he be close enough to breathe her in, feel the warmth of her skin and the silk of her skirts catching around his ankles, see all the freckles across her cheeks.

"You are especially beautiful tonight," he murmured.

"I've never been so happy to see you," she whispered. "But why did he say that you are not Castleton? And why did you not deny it? Why did they laugh at me when I announced myself as Lady Castleton?"

John ignored the sickening feeling in his gut and how this lie of his had spiraled so far out of control. He wanted to tell her about that night when he had been so desperate. He wanted to tell her about all the moments he'd considered confessing everything to her.

Instead he paused and memorized how she gazed up at him. Her velvety brown eyes. The light dusting of freckles. The plump mouth with kisses that undid him. This moment might be the last he ever saw of her.

John took a deep breath. It was time to tell her the truth.

"I am not who I said I was, Prudence," he said gravely. Her lips parted and her eyes widened. He felt her tense in his arms. There was no time to be a coward now—he would tell her the truth. "The real Lord Castleton has just returned from travels abroad. I can't say he's pleased to learn that I've been assuming his identity for the past few months."

Her lips parted, but it was a moment before words emerged.

"If you are not Castleton, then who are you?"

This was the moment he lost her. John hesitated, taking a moment to remember her eyes at this moment: warm and brown and full of emotion. Her lips were full and the color of a plum, and he wanted to kiss her forever and ever.

"John Roark," he said, his voice rough. "Former footman."

"A footman?" Prudence gasped, with a nervous little laugh.

Slayed him, that.

He smiled sadly and sighed. She had been raised with a bevy of servants. Footmen were mute men in uniforms who made doors open, transported luggage from carriage to bedchamber and back, and served food and poured wine. They never spoke, and, in their livery, all looked the same.

"Please let me explain," he pleaded. Begged.

But the full force of his deception was hitting her now. He could see it: all the little explosions of truth, laying to waste all the beautiful moments they had constructed together.

"You lied to me," Prudence whispered. "This whole time, *everything we have done*, you lied to me?"

He could see her remembering all their intimate moments, from her confession to her cries of pleasure. Every kiss, every secret revealed, every little happiness—and he had been lying to her at every moment.

"Only the title I appropriated was a lie," he said firmly. "Everything else—every word, *every touch*—was truth itself."

"I laid my body and soul bare to you," she said, her voice stronger now and her eyes flashing. "And you lied *the whole time*. You lied about something as fundamental as who you *are*."

"But I didn't. With you, Prue, I was the truest version of myself—the version the world never cared to see. With you, Prue, I am the man I could be if given the chance. The name was a lie, one started long before I met you, and one I dared not reveal when you had no other protector."

He had left her speechless. Breathless. There was more for him to say.

"I love you, Prudence," he declared with a crack in his voice. "I, John Roark, upstart footman, love you. I want to marry you."

"Ha!"

The sound of shocked amusement burst from her lips. Knife in the heart, that "*Ha.*"

Of course the lovely, well-bred Miss Payton would say "*ha!*" at the prospect of marriage to a servant.

"I know you, Prudence, in a way no one else does. I know who I am, too. Don't you think I haven't been completely tortured knowing that I can never marry the woman I love? Don't you think it didn't kill me keeping this secret from you? I am painfully, achingly aware of my deception and how society and prejudice stand between us and some sort of happiness. I know it," he said bitterly. "I just hope that love is stronger than everything holding us apart."

"I feel . . ." She glanced away, and sighed, and whispered, "I feel used again."

He wanted to be sick. Nevertheless, he persisted. "The truth is—"

"The truth? Really? Now?"

"The truth is, I love you," he said, gazing into her eyes, unflinching. "All of you. I know you, Prudence. And I am only telling you this now because I want you to know that you are loved fully and completely for who you are—the good, the bad, the ugly, the beautiful. I am so sorry that this lie came between us, but without it, we would have never known each other, so I cannot bring myself to regret it completely. It will haunt me until my dying day that I am not enough for you. I came tonight, Prudence, to keep my promise. And to make sure that you know that you are loved."

Her eyes were now bright with tears. But the stubborn Miss Merryweather wouldn't let them fall.

"Tonight I announced myself as Lady Castleton. Because I believed you, I am now a laughingstock." He winced. She saw. "And the thing was . . ." She stopped and bit her lip. Her cheeks flushed. Dying, he was dying. "I knew better," she said in a low and bitter voice. "I knew better. God doesn't answer. Heroes never come. I am always on my own."

Prudence broke free of his embrace. With one last glance at him, she turned and walked away. Her friends followed immediately behind her. Everyone else in the ballroom swept aside to let her go.

John wanted to run after her. But that *"Ha!"* held him back.

Chapter 24

THE THREE FORMER wallflowers gathered in Lady Emma's bedchamber. The duke was dispatched to another chamber whilst the three girls climbed into Emma's massive four-poster bed, wrapped in blankets and dressing robes.

A fire roared in the grate, providing warmth and soft light.

Glasses of sherry were poured into three cut-crystal glasses.

"Tell us everything, Prudence," Emma said.

"Everything," Olivia added for emphasis.

"Starting from when you left for Bath last month," Emma said.

Prue sipped her sherry, as if a little more time and a little more of the sweet wine would somehow make it easier to finally tell her friends the truth. It was a night for truth telling, it seemed.

The dull ache in her belly from earlier this evening had only intensified.

She had fallen in love with a man she didn't know.

While she had been revealing every truth, he

had been concealing a fundamental fact about his existence. Prue didn't even know what to call him in her thoughts—not Castleton, obviously. John? That seemed too intimate. Yet they had been so intimate.

Prudence didn't know what to think. She ought to be mad, for she had been deceived. And she was mad at him for lying to her. But a portion of anger was directed toward herself. She knew better than to trust a man, to love a man. . . .

But she couldn't forget the freedom she'd felt at revealing her secrets. Hiding the truth was exhausting. She was so tired of being tired.

She also couldn't forget how she'd told John what had happened to her and he hadn't shunned her as damaged or spoilt. Perhaps, then, it was time to confide in her best friends. She was still scared: What if they could no longer be friends with her after they knew? What if they always looked at her in a certain way, or treated her gently, as if she were damaged? With her friends, who didn't know, she could just be Prudence. If they knew, she might be poor, pitiful, pathetic Prudence.

Prudence gazed up at the anxious faces of Emma and Olivia. They were *dying* to know what had happened in Bath, and with Lord Nanson and "Castleton."

Don't be scared. Even when you are scared.

"I know you want to hear about . . ." Prue paused, stumbling over the name. ". . . that man who made the dramatic entrance tonight."

"'Dramatic entrance' being a vast understatement of epic proportions," Emma remarked.

Prue smiled wryly and nodded. "But I have to tell you both what happened during my first season."

As if sensing the weight and sadness of what she was about to tell, the mood in the room shifted, and Emma and Olivia's expressions became somber, on edge, waiting.

"Dudley raped me," Prudence whispered, putting into words that thing that had happened to her and saying it aloud for the first time.

She looked from Emma to Olivia, fearing judgment. She saw expressions of sadness, and shock and pain—and compassion. Wordlessly, as of one mind, they shifted to sit on either side of her and wrapped their arms around her in a warm and loving embrace that made some truths clear. Her friends would not leave her. Her friends still loved her. She had the strength now to tell the rest.

"Not ravished, not seduced, not even took advantage," Prudence said in a low, bitter voice. "He took my innocence against my will."

"Oh, Prue," Emma moaned, resting her head on her shoulder.

"I'm so sorry," Olivia whispered, holding her close.

"Why didn't you tell us?" Emma asked.

"I was afraid no one would believe me," she whispered. "Or worse: I was afraid people would believe me and I would be forced to marry him.

If no one knew, then I could pretend it never happened. I just wanted to forget."

"We wouldn't have let that happen to you," Emma said strongly. Prue doubted they could have done anything during their first seasons—the lot of them had been nobodies without influence, voice, or power. (*Like John?* That thought, unbidden, interrupted her.) But they would have tried, certainly.

"How can people be so cruel as to force a girl to marry her rapist?" Prudence asked, a little sob catching in her throat. "As if some hasty arrangement to patch up her reputation were the answer to such a barbaric act."

"What a strange, cruel world we live in," Olivia murmured.

"I didn't want to have the attentions of another man after that," Prudence continued. "Being a wallflower was my refuge. I let my figure grow round, and I never looked any man in the eye. In the wallflower corner, I was surrounded by other girls, and no man ever dared to approach. Everything was fine until—"

"All the pressure to marry for Lady P's ball," Olivia said softly, regretfully.

They fell silent, remembering an evening earlier this season when they drank sherry and pledged their determination to marry this season *or else!!!*

"I was ruined. Spoiled. I could not marry," Prue said. "I cannot marry."

"Oh, Prudence, how wretched that must have

made you feel," Emma added, clutching her close. "I am so sorry."

"We are both so sorry," Olivia added mournfully.

What was left unsaid but understood: it was one thing to face spinsterhood with her best friends by her side. It was quite another when they had married for love and she was alone. The last wallflower.

"I know neither of you ever meant to hurt me," she said. "I didn't want to be the only one unwed. I didn't want to be a failure, yet I couldn't bear the thought of being touched or having to submit to a man. Again."

"But where did you meet that handsome stranger?" Olivia asked.

"That handsome stranger who looks at you as if he is deeply and irrevocably in love with you," Emma added.

"First, I tried to elope with a man I met in Bath. Cecil was . . ." She didn't know quite how to explain him. "A marriage of convenience would suit us both. I didn't think he would ever claim his marital rights."

"Lord Nanson?" Emma asked, and Prudence nodded yes.

"But then our carriage was robbed. I managed to escape." Prue didn't wish to get into Cecil's betrayal or her night in the forest.

"That explains why his letter arrived in town, but neither he nor his bride came with it," Olivia said.

Prue smiled ruefully. "It seemed like a good idea at the time to provide notice of our intentions."

"Let me guess: that handsome stranger drove by and saved you," Emma said. "It sounds like a novel."

Emma read lots of novels.

"Not quite," Prue answered. "He did drive past and offer to drive me to the nearest town, but I had to refuse. Then I made my way to the nearest inn. He was there."

"Why didn't you let him drive you there?" Olivia asked, perplexed.

Prudence sighed, about to give her friends a glimpse of the turmoil she'd lived with for years now. "Because, since Dudley, I could not be alone with a man. I just couldn't."

"Even if it meant walking miles in the scorching sun?" Olivia asked.

"Miles of scorching sun immediately followed by a mile in a downpour," Prue added.

"Oh, Prudence . . ." Emma and Olivia sighed so sadly at the same time, as they started to understand what it was like living with that fear and its icy grip on her heart.

"Because the rain made the roads impassable, we were stranded together at an inn for a few days. In that time, I think I fell in love with him," Prudence said, a little hitch in her voice. Aye, this was a night for truth telling. She just didn't know what to do with that love. . . . Was it still real if he wasn't the man she believed him to be?

The faintest of smiles graced her lips as she recollected the little moments—the waltz at night, wondering if Buckley ever woke up, sobered up, and left, how Annie was faring now. There was the moment she confessed her darkest secret and John didn't judge her for it. She remembered how he'd taught her to defend herself—and she thanked God that he had. Had John known even then that he wouldn't always be there for her?

She'd never forget the pleasure he'd shown her. How was she ever supposed to live without it now?

But all those memories led up to his heart-stopping revelation tonight. *I am not who I say I am.* Her smile faltered and her heart felt rather like it was breaking. "Rather, I fell in love with the man I thought he was. I'm sorry, I'm not ready to talk about him yet."

"Have more sherry," Emma said, topping off their glasses.

"What are you going to do about Dudley?" Olivia inquired.

"What do you mean?" Prudence asked.

"He is still plaguing you, Prudence. We saw him tonight," Olivia said.

"John helped me discover the strength to stand up to him," Prudence said softly. "And he taught me how to defend myself."

"That's very good, but everyone saw what you did to him. He will be angry. What if he retaliates?" Olivia asked softly.

Once again, fear started to spread in Prue's heart. Dudley would be livid—and John was no longer around to protect her.

Emma's brow furrowed as she considered something else. Then she spoke up: "But what if there are other girls?"

Prue glanced at her friend in shock. What if there were other girls walking around, trying to piece together a life after Dudley's damage? And what of all the girls—like John's sister—who suffered similarly at the hands of demons like Dudley? It meant she wasn't one lone weakling, and it meant he was a monster.

It also meant something had to be done.

"Oh, my God," Prudence gasped. "What if there are other girls?"

What if there were other girls who would never meet a man like John, who, in spite of being a monumental liar, had made it possible for her to love herself again? He had shown her patience and compassion. What if these other girls never met a man like John who knew her dark secret and *loved her anyway*?

For the first time, Prudence's heart began to ache not for herself and what she had lost but for the other girls who had suffered the same and might never know love.

"You have to do something, Prudence," Olivia urged. "He's just out there, walking around, angry, possibly terrorizing other young girls . . ."

"Should we kill him?" Emma asked. Prue and

Olivia turned to face her. She was completely, utterly serious.

"Emma, I don't think that's a good idea," Olivia remarked. "It will make a dreadful mess, for one thing."

Prudence thought of his blood on her new satin gloves, and rage flared. "I could do it," Prudence said.

"We can't let you do it either," Olivia countered. "Newgate is disgusting, and you are too young and lovely to swing from the hangman's noose."

"Besides, death is too good for him," Emma said. "Now that I think about it. We need something more devious, with more lasting devastation. He has to suffer."

The girls fell silent, sipping their sherry and considering all the ways in which three young women could take justice into their own, ladylike hands and make a peer of the realm suffer unfathomable tortures and humiliations, as he so rightfully deserved.

Finally Olivia broke the silence. "This is a bit unoriginal, but why don't we do what has always worked before?"

"Send a letter to *The London Weekly*?" Emma queried.

"We know they publish *anything*," Olivia pointed out. "And we know everyone reads it."

They knew this because they had previously sent in the most outrageous items of "news" to the paper—some on purpose, others by accident—

only to read them in print a few days later, over breakfast, along with the rest of London.

"I don't want anyone to know what happened to me," Prudence said. "Tonight was mortification enough—I honestly don't know how I can show my face in society again after foolishly announcing myself as Lady Castleton, being rumored to have married Lord Nanson, and having inflicted bodily, bloody harm on a peer of the realm. I probably ought to leave town. Indefinitely. Forever."

"Hang society! You have us," Olivia said. "And something must be done about Dudley. *The London Weekly* is the perfect way to get the word out about his true character. We shall leave it up to the decent people of the ton to shame and shun him."

"Send the letter anonymously," Emma suggested. *"Dear London, beware of Lord Dudley."*

"I'll even rewrite it in my perfect handwriting," Olivia offered. "That way it cannot be traced back to you."

That was a kind offer, but the minute the letter appeared, speculation as to the author would begin. After the events of this evening, all fingers would point to her. Prue had been out for four seasons now, and she knew how these things worked.

"If word got out, Dudley would be shunned, surely," Emma said. "I know Ashbrooke would ensure that no one received him. But only if he knew."

"Radcliffe, too," Olivia added. "Just imagine—a world without Dudley."

A world without Dudley. Well, if that didn't sound like Heaven, Prudence didn't know what did. Already the world seemed like a better place because her friends knew her awful secret and stood by her, taking her problems as their own, determined they should solve them together.

"Once we take care of Dudley," Emma said, and her matter-of-fact use of *we* was the sweetest thing Prudence had ever heard, "we'll figure out what to do about that handsome stranger whom you are obviously in love with."

"I don't think there's much to be done," Prudence said. Her voice wavered. John had deceived her. After everything she'd been through, it had taken so much for her to trust him, and he'd been lying throughout.

John had taught her to defend herself—but not against the likes of him. A charmer, a pretender, a rogue footman in gentleman's clothing.

He had touched her. He had taught her how to touch herself. She thought she'd been discovering her own pleasure. A stranger had been watching her, urging her on. She had given herself to him, body, heart, and soul. And she didn't know who he was.

She could not marry him. She could not entrust herself to him again.

Prue's friends were a comforting presence, but even they could not stop the ache in her heart. She had triumphed over the devil tonight. But the victory was bittersweet, for she could think only of the man she had loved.

And lost.

And who might never have been the man she'd believed him to be.

Chapter 25

The day of the Great Exhibition

AFTER A QUICK escape from the ball, John had spent the hours after midnight wandering around the city until the sun started to rise. So many nights he had lain awake dreaming of London and how triumphant he would feel to finally arrive. He kicked a small rock in the street and it ricocheted off the cobblestones, flung aimlessly to and fro before stopping in the gutter.

John might have made it to London, but he was anything but triumphant. He was lower than ever, lower than he'd been on the dark, cold, wet February night he'd stood outside that inn and refused to be constrained by his station. But for a slip of paper that was a marriage license or a law that left nothing to by-blows, John might have been something. He probably had the blood of a viscount in his veins, but it counted for nothing.

Like Prudence and her quest for a marriage license bearing her name. That little slip of paper was the difference between a respectable life deemed successful and a lonely existence as a pitiful spinster. It was just paper. It didn't change who he was, or who she was.

Couldn't she see that?

John kicked another little pebble, and it went skidding so far ahead that he didn't see where it landed. John had risked everything, gambling big, and he'd sustained the kind of losses a man never recovers from.

So he'd never enact his plan to manufacture the Difference Engine. Now that he would be known as the man who'd assumed the identity of a peer of the realm, it was doubtful he'd even find work as a servant now—which was probably irrelevant, as either prison or deportation to Australia was probably in his near future.

It was the loss of Prudence he grieved the most. She was the reason his chest felt tight and his throat was constricted. He felt like he was choking and his eyes were hot. She wouldn't let the tears fall—well, neither would he.

It was her lips he dreamt of, sweet, plump, perfect for kissing. And those rare and magical smiles of hers. He'd never felt more powerful than when he'd made her smile, or laugh, or cry out in pleasure. It was a very real possibility that he would never touch her again, breathe in her scent, or hear her voice. Thus it was a very real possibility that life no longer held any purpose or meaning for him.

John knew he should have told her the truth sooner. But he also knew that his reason for hiding his past was sound. Prudence would have run off (as she had done last night). She would have found herself alone in the country, where highwaymen and Dudley roamed. She would have refused his assistance or protection (as she had done from the start).

Keeping his secret had kept her safe.

Revealing it had cost him his future.

That memory of her breathless "*Ha!*" smothered any hope he might have still nurtured.

Having walked all over London, John suddenly found himself at the docks. The place was just stirring to life. Sailors and unsavory characters went about their business. Ships rocked gently on the river.

The sun was starting to rise. Was this the light of a new day dawning—one where he was liberated from the secrets he had kept and the past he'd been running from? Or was this the beginning of another like all the ones before?

It was the matter of minutes and a few inquiries whereby John learned of a ship departing for America that afternoon.

He bought a ticket.

Galloway's Coffee Shop

With a few hours to kill before leaving England and Prudence forever, John found a coffee shop and settled in with a mug of black coffee and an assortment of newspapers so freshly printed they left ink smeared on his hands.

The light was dim—it was just after dawn on an overcast day, and there were hardly any candles about the shop. John squinted at the issue of *The London Weekly* in his hands, just barely making out the small moveable type. The headline was easy enough to read, though: *The Great Exhibition Opens in London Today.*

The article detailed all of the inventions and notable personages expected to be in attendance, and the author went on at length about the achievements on display, how England was the greatest nation on earth, how all these innovations would lead to a bright future. This was a celebration of unprecedented advances in technology, a showcase of man's brilliance and his greatest achievements.

John couldn't lie: it burned to read those words. He felt, once more, as if he were back at the Coach & Horses, pacing in front of the window, looking out at the incessant rain and watching it wash away his hopes and dreams.

That was just one of the obstacles he had overcome. For an upstart footman, running like the wind with the law chasing after him, he'd made it pretty damn far.

So it burned to be so close and to miss it. His stomach ached with wanting to be there.

John patted his pocket, feeling the ticket to America.

He ought to write a letter to his mother and sister. Tell them about the change in plans. He would send for them once he was settled.

He took another sip of hot black coffee, and that burned, too. Then he turned the page, finding the gossip columns there. He kept reading. There was a sea of names he didn't recognize, names of people he would never meet, soirees he would never attend, a life he would never live.

John glanced up, around the dark coffee shop. It was full of plainly dressed men with mugs of coffee and thick stubs of cigars in their rough hands. They all had newspapers, and they were all reading about a government they couldn't participate in, plays and operas they were unlikely to see, information about ships coming and going without them.

The ticket was still there, in his pocket.

He had a choice.

He had a way out.

One name in bold print in the gossip did catch John's eye. Then another and another and another:

What were they to call Miss Prudence Merryweather Payton?

"Prue," he whispered, answering the question posed by the newspaper. Then he continued to read.

Do we call her Prude Prudence?

He swallowed hard, remembering the moment in the carriage when she'd told him of this cruel name. She'd been so matter-of-fact about how awful it was, and he'd hardly been able to breathe from a painful mixture of anger and empathy, knowing what had happened to her and knowing the cruel names they taunted her with.

London's Least Likely to Be Caught in a Compromising Position?

John nearly crumpled the newspaper in his fists when he saw that in print.

Doesn't that just slay you? she had asked. Yes, by God, it did just slay him. That girl of his—in his heart of hearts, Prudence would always be his—had survived the worst thing that could happen. She'd carried on with a strength and stubbornness that were simply humbling and awe-inspiring.

John felt that ticket in his pocket, but this time he felt ashamed for running.

He was always running, wasn't he? From one gamble to another, waiting for the big reward that never came. But could he afford to stop running now?

Do we call her Lady Nanson?

So that was the name of that pipsqueak fiancé of hers who'd left her roaming the countryside on her own. Whoever this Nanson was, he didn't deserve a woman like Prue. The question was: did John?

Everyone knows not to call her Lady Castleton.

The burn of the smoke and cigars . . . the burn of the black coffee in his throat . . . it was nothing compared to the fiery flames of regret charring him from the inside out. He had set her up for humiliation on the night she'd most wanted to impress. He wanted to spend a lifetime making it up to her. But did he deserve such an opportunity?

What do we call this wallflower?

With that, John did crumple the damned paper into a tight ball that left black ink all over his hands. He tossed it into the fireplace and watched it erupted into flames.

John watched it burn, and under his breath he muttered, *"You call her Mrs. Prudence Roark."*

Chapter 26

OF ALL THE things on display, none commanded more attention than the Difference Engine. It was difficult to look away from the gleaming brass machine that stood eight feet high, seven feet long, and three feet deep. It was surrounded by a throng of curious people, eager to watch the machine perform calculations.

The Duke of Ashbrooke, the machine's brilliant inventor and a renowned charmer, held a crowd of men and women captive with his explanation of how the machine worked and how it would change the world for the better.

Nearby, Baron Radcliffe, a quiet genius, was immersed in a serious conversation with members from the Royal Society about all the parts he had designed, constructed, and assembled to make a working machine that performed all manner of calculations correctly, every time.

Emma, Olivia, and Prudence stood off to the side, taking it all in.

"Don't they look so happy?" Emma gushed.

"They look ridiculously happy," Prudence concurred. "Perhaps even triumphant."

She felt a twinge of *something*, thinking of John and how badly he had wanted to be at this exhibition, to see this machine and to shake the hands of the inventors. She remembered her envy at his ambitious and audacious plans for his future, when hers had been a long, bleak expanse of loneliness. But what was his future, now that he was exposed as a lying and lawbreaking footman?

Amongst the other memories weighing on her mind was her promise to introduce John to Ashbrooke and Radcliffe as a debt of gratitude for rescuing her from Dudley. He had refused her offer.

Prudence, thank you for offering the introduction. But you don't have to.

I want to. She did want to, with her whole heart.

Prue wondered now if she had made it impossible to confide in her by extending this coveted invitation to Lord Castleton, a noble peer of the realm. By revealing his true identity to her, he might have risked loosing the opportunity to gain an introduction to Ashbrooke and Radcliffe.

Or was she simply making excuses for him, twisting the facts around and taking the blame upon herself? He ought to have told her the truth the night Dudley had attacked her the second time.

Where is he now? she wondered. Had he been arrested? Had he fled the country before they could capture him? That would be the sensible thing to do, and she wouldn't blame him for it. Why, then, did a small, rebellious bit of her heart still wish that he would stroll in here, to the Great Exhibition, and magically make everything better?

"They're so very handsome, too," Olivia sighed. She and Emma were lost in a world of adoration for their husbands. Their handsome, charming, brilliant, not-lying-about-their-identities actual in-the-eyes-of-God husbands.

Prudence smiled tightly and turned away. She was happy for her friends. Truly. Deeply. Happy. But at the same time, she was sad for herself. Why did it always have to be so *hard*? For every step forward, Prue seemed to take two steps back.

Her every hope for happiness had been taken from her. Again.

This time she was well and truly ruined. This morning Emma and Olivia had tried to hide the gossip columns from her, but Prue had caught a glimpse and seen enough.

One of London's Least Likely was rumored to have wed two different men, one of whom was already wed to another. She had attacked the heir to the Marquis of Scarbrough in public. Men fought duels for less.

The reporters didn't know what to call her: Prude Prudence, London's Least Likely to Be Caught in a Compromising Position, Lady Nanson, Lady Castleton.

Prudence heaved a heartfelt, tragic sigh. She longed to go back to being Miss Merryweather in those moments when she had started falling for John, before everything had started to go wrong.

"What is bothering you, Prudence?" Olivia asked. "You seem awfully glum."

"And who do you keep looking around for?" Emma asked, looking around herself.

"That's a ridiculous question," Olivia replied. "She's obviously hoping that handsome stranger of hers will arrive."

"Well then, he's probably the reason she's glum, Olivia," Emma retorted.

Correct on both counts.

"I do hope he turns up," Emma said.

"I as well," Olivia agreed. "I'd like to meet the man who our Prudence has fallen in love with."

If only they knew that the man she had fallen in love with was a footman! Who had lied to her about who he was! Would they still wish to meet him then? Emma was a duchess—she couldn't consort with lawbreaking servants. Olivia's own reputation was only just recovering after her outrageous attempts to ruin it earlier this season. It was one thing to ask for their support for a horrid secret from years previous. Asking them to publicly support a man in John's situation was quite another.

But honestly, when had Prue become such a snob?

"I'd like to plan a wedding," Emma said, sweetly oblivious to the impossibility of Prue's marriage to anyone. At all. Ever.

"Your wedding wasn't enough?" Olivia asked.

"My wedding was a spontaneous, thrown-together affair," Emma answered.

"There won't be a wedding," Prudence said flatly. She thought of all her attempts and all her talks with God. Every time she had come close to marriage and a possible happy ending, the rug was yanked out from under her feet. She could just imagine God laughing and thundering, *I jest, Miss Payton, I jest!*

Prudence was in no mood for humor.

"Why won't there be a wedding?" Emma demanded.

"Yes, why not?" Olivia echoed.

"Because he lied to me," Prudence said, confessing. "He told me that he was Lord Castleton."

"Which we now know he is not," Olivia said.

"A man with a secret identity! How delicious," Emma said.

To which Prudence replied, "You read too many novels."

"Or perhaps you don't read enough," Emma retorted.

"Ahem," Olivia interrupted. "Who is this man, if he is not Lord Castleton?"

Prudence glanced from one friend to the other. They were waiting impatiently for her to reveal the full truth, because they were the best of friends and thus they oughtn't keep secrets from each other.

Fine. FINE.

"Not only is he *not* Lord Castleton," Prudence said. "He is a footman."

Emma and Olivia remained very quiet for a moment. A long moment. Their expressions were inscrutable as they processed this information. Prudence sighed. *This* is what she'd feared. Their judgment. Like all gently bred young ladies, they had been raised to marry and marry well.

A baron qualified as marrying well. To land a duke was the height of marital success. To marry a servant was to lower oneself tremendously. It might not be right, but it was the way of things. Alas, Prudence thought with a sigh. Alas.

Finally, Emma spoke. "He's a very handsome footman."

"He certainly knows how to make an entrance," Olivia added.

"And the way he looks at you, Prue . . ." Emma sighed. "I'd say his gaze sparkles."

"No, it smolders," Olivia countered.

"It was very plain that he loves you," Emma said. Olivia agreed.

Prudence's heart started to pound. They obviously did not care one whit about his station—or lack thereof. All they were concerned about was whether his gaze sparkled or smoldered when he looked at her.

Prudence knew that he couldn't have faked the love in his eyes when he'd looked at her. That much was true. But was that enough?

"Oh, look, he's coming this way!" Olivia exclaimed, pointing at him, even though young ladies didn't point.

"And he's looking very determined," Emma murmured.

The trio turned to watch his approach. The crowds were thick, especially around the engine, but they melted out of his way. Prudence watched him cut through the hordes of people, wearing the fine clothes of a gentleman. If she hadn't known better, she would have assumed he was a peer of the realm—a duke, even! There was something in the way he carried himself—with such assurance and authority that they were all lucky to breathe the same air as he. She tried to imagine him in livery.

But then one look in those blue, blue eyes of his and there was no denying that this was a man who mattered.

And then he was standing before her and she found it hard to breathe, in a lovely, aching way. Her mind knew of his treachery, but her body remembered only the pleasure of his touch.

"Hello, Prudence," he murmured.

"Hello," she replied softly.

John had finally, *finally* made it to the Great Exhibition. The Difference Engine was *right there,* yet he only had eyes for Prue.

She was so obviously a proper lady—from the complicated arrangement of her hair to her very fine green dress and delicate gloves—that he almost lost his nerve. Her natural polish made him painfully aware of how he had faked his upper-class accent (though it came naturally now) and adopted the other outward trappings of a gentleman.

Prudence looked beautiful, though he preferred her with her hair unbound and her skin bare in the candlelight, anticipating his touch.

That memory, so vivid he could almost see it and feel it anew, reminded him why he was here. They belonged together. They had connected in all the ways that mattered.

John was here not because of some long-standing ambition, or a great hulking machine, or that introduction she had promised before she'd known who he really was. John was here because he loved her. One didn't get on a boat and sail halfway across the world, never to return, without saying goodbye to the person one loved.

Of course one had to *say* the word "goodbye," whilst he was just standing there and gazing at her like an idiot.

It had to be noted that she gazed back at him.

That is, until another young lady with fair hair elbowed her in the ribs. The action was meant to be discreet. It was not. A woman with darker hair stepped next to Prudence. The two of them looked at Prue, then at him, and back again.

"May I present . . ." Prue faltered with the introductions.

"I am Emma," the dark-haired one said, "and this is Olivia."

It was a notable lack of formality, and he suspected that the women were Prue's friends, the

Duchess of Ashbrooke and Lady Radcliffe, and that Prue must have told them about him.

"And this is . . ." Again Prue faltered. He knew why; how was she to introduce him, if not as Castleton?

"John Roark," he said.

"We are *so happy* to meet you," Olivia gushed.

"Indeed, it is a *great* pleasure to make your acquaintance," Emma added.

Prudence blushed furiously.

"Come, I shall introduce you to Ashbrooke and Radcliffe," Prudence said. She started to walk away, but he stepped quickly after her, reaching out for her hand.

"Prue, wait."

She didn't pull her hand away. She turned instead to face him.

He glanced over at Emma and Olivia. They had obviously noticed his intimate use of her nickname. After A Look from Prue, they shuffled back, allowing John a modicum of privacy. Not that the Great Exhibition was a place for a private conversation, but this was his only opportunity.

"Prue, I'm not here for an introduction," he said urgently.

"It's all right," she replied kindly. Or was that pityingly? "I gave you my word. It's a matter of honor."

"I don't want to meet them," John insisted.

"Then why are you here?" Prudence asked, obviously surprised that he would turn down the opportunity and confused as to why.

"I came to say goodbye," he said softly. That disastrous scene last night couldn't be the last time he ever saw her.

"Goodbye?" Prue echoed, sounding surprised.

He swallowed hard. He didn't want this to be goodbye. He'd give anything for this to be the start of something. But in the event she never wanted to see him again, he would go. John would not skulk around like Dudley, reminding her of the time she had been so vulnerable and taken advantage of.

So John reached into his pocket and pulled out the ticket to show her.

"I'm leaving for America," he explained.

"When?"

"This afternoon."

"That's so soon."

"Unless . . ." His chest was tight. His heart was pounding hard. He, who seized every opportunity, was giving up and putting his fate in the hands of this woman. His future was her choice.

John held his breath, praying she would say, *Stay* or *Farewell* and he would know which way to run this time—into her arms or down to the docks. What she said next surprised him.

"You should meet the duke and the baron before you go. I know how much it means to you."

PRUDENCE'S HEART WAS pounding in her chest. She thought it might burst right through. She understood the unspoken words following his *"unless. . ."*

He lied he lied he lied he lied he lied. She couldn't forget that.

But she loved him. He had breathed life back into her when she'd thought she might just give up and die. Ladies didn't marry servants, but when had ladylike behavior ever made her happy?

What was she to do? And however was she to decide their fate before this afternoon?

She would introduce him to the duke and baron. Perhaps she could think while they conversed. It was certainly impossible to think when John's blue eyes were looking at her like she was the sun, moon, stars, and everything else that was beautiful and true in the world.

She linked her arm with his and led them over to the Engine.

"Ashbrooke, Radcliffe. I hope I may present Mr. John Roark to you," Prudence said. "I am forever indebted to this man for the kindness he has shown me and the protection he has given me. He has grand ideas for your engine that I think you will wish to entertain."

"Roark? I am not familiar," Ashbrooke said. Nevertheless, he greeted the man openly.

"Mr. John Roark, former footman, former impersonator of Lord Castleton, and tremendous admirer of your work on the engine."

Prue wasn't the only one to smile.

She was quite certain her heart was the only one pounding at such a furious pace, though.

"How did you hear of it?" Ashbrooke asked.

"I've had extensive conversations with members of the Royal Society. I've read numerous publications about it as well," John explained. "I knew you were onto something when the machine was decried as useless and impossible."

That seemed like just the right thing to say to prove to Ashbrooke and Radcliffe that he was serious and understood them and the potential for the machine. A passionate, animated conversation ensued, in which Prudence overheard things about physics that flew right over her head. He might have been a footman, but he had somehow obtained a gentleman's education—perhaps even more. She wondered how he had managed it. She wondered what kind of man managed to bring himself up from being a servant to speaking intelligently about the sciences with a duke.

The conversation concluded with a coveted invitation for the former footman: "Call on us tomorrow at Ashbrooke House. Three o'clock."

She didn't mention the ticket in his pocket for a ship destined for America. Neither did he.

She and John then stepped back away from the crowds surrounding the Difference Engine.

John clasped her hand in his, lifting it to his lips for a kiss. She felt sparks. It was bittersweet.

"Prudence, I cannot thank you enough." The gratitude was plain in his eyes, and she was truly glad to have helped him with the small manner of an introduction, even though nothing might ever come of it if he boarded that boat.

"You're a footman," she said, as if the truth was still sinking in. "One who knows of physics, and engines, and other advanced scientific things."

"I was. I suppose I am."

"And your mum and your sister?"

"Housemaids." He glanced away for a second before returning his gaze to her. "We worked at Castlemore Court before leaving for Blackhaven Manor. I looked too much like the real Lord Castleton," he said wryly.

Prudence let it all sink in. He was probably the illegitimate son of the real Viscount Castleton. She began to understand how he'd been able to pull off such a monumental charade; according to the newspapers this morning, he'd been pretending to be Castleton for at least six months, deceiving scores of the nobility. Prudence only had more questions for him now.

"If I could do it all again," he began, "I would have let you in on the secret from the beginning. But then what chance would we have had to be together?"

"It's hard, isn't it," she mused, "when the world doesn't allow much room for a person to live the life they want."

She thought of all the strict rules imposed on a woman, defining her innocence, her marriage-ability—or ruination. She thought of the strict social barriers separating the aristocrats from everyone else, and she thought of servants who were just supposed to fade into the background.

She wanted to be more than her qualifications as a wife, more than the status of her virginity.

He wanted more, too. *Was that so wrong?*

"I love you, Prudence," he said, clasping her hands. "You deserve better than me. You deserve a man of your rank who will adore you and care for you and not cause embarrassing and destructive scenes at balls. You deserve children who will attend finishing school and won't have to live with the shame of their father's humble origins."

She *did* deserve all those things. But that wasn't all that mattered.

"No one else will ever love me like you do," she said softly. She could now see the possibility that perhaps, in time, she might find another man with an open mind and an open heart who would take her as his wife. But it wouldn't be the same. She wanted this man, who'd taken her as a fragile, wounded creature and with patience, kindness, and love had made her strong enough to live without him.

"Because you are lovable, Prue. I want you to know that."

She knew that now. She also knew that she loved him. No other woman would love him the way she did. Before Prudence could tell him these things, shouts erupted, and the crowd swelled and surged dangerously.

"There he is!" Someone shouted, pointing directly at John.

Then an officer hollered the fateful order: "Arrest him!"

Chapter 27

PRUDENCE OUGHT TO have been exhausted after the events of the past twenty-four hours, or the past week, or the past few years of her life. Instead, she found herself electrified, for now her life had purpose.

For so long it had felt like she'd dragged herself through each day, always fighting her fear, with many little victories, numerous defeats, and never winning the war. It all had felt so hopeless. But then, suddenly, there was a transformation. A phase change. Suddenly Prudence knew how to make everything right, and she felt absolutely determined to do it.

She could not stand idly by while John, a good—though flawed—man was imprisoned. She could not stand idly by while scum of the earth like Dudley strolled around, free to wreak havoc on the lives of innocent young women.

It was time for her to take matters into her own hands.

The offices of The London Weekly
57 Fleet Street, London

Three young ladies arrived at the offices of *The London Weekly*. A terrifying man standing guard at the door questioned their purpose and, satisfied with their answer, granted them entry.

Emma, Prudence, and Olivia then waited for an interview with Mr. Derek Knightly, owner and publisher of the most popular newspaper in London. It had been doing well enough, until he'd hired a quartet of women to scandalously write for the publication, producing exposés, reports of weddings, the most salacious gossip, and an advice column. Then the paper's popularity skyrocketed. Very few members of the ton had made the acquaintance of this lowborn upstart—yet they all lived and breathed by his printed word.

"Are you certain of this, Prudence?" Olivia asked anxiously.

"Yes," she said confidently. "And besides, it was your idea that I write a letter. Why are you having second thoughts now?"

"Because we were under the effects of sherry then," Olivia replied.

"I think it's noble. And brave," Emma said firmly.

"Thank you." Prue flipped open the folded sheet she held in her gloved hands and scanned the lines once more.

She had written about what Dudley had done to her. She had written about why she had kept this secret for so long: what if no one believed her? Worse: what if someone had? It was a cruel thing that her only options should be to marry her defiler or suffer in silence, alone.

She condemned his despicable act and the unspoken rules that declared her ruined, spoilt, and useless because of this. She was more than this one bad thing that had happened to her.

She'd even written about John. To her surprise, his lies hadn't been the topic she'd focused on. He knew the truth about her. Anyone else would have judged her, cast her aside, or taken this admission as permission to take further advantage of her. John had loved her.

One man had diminished her; another had nurtured her.

One man had perpetrated violence against her; another had taught her how to defend herself.

One had planted fear in her heart; another had shown her love.

One had a title, a country estate, and a fortune; one had nothing of value, but everything that really mattered.

By the time Prudence had signed the letter, only one question remained: was she really going to cut love out of her heart because of the circumstances of a man's birth?

Yes, he had lied about who he was. But hadn't she also done so all these years?

John had also told her the truth. And with this letter, so did she.

DESPITE THE FACT that they were not acquainted, Prudence found herself standing before Mr. Derek Knightly's desk in his Fleet Street office. Little was known about him, but she reckoned he had a soft heart for women and an open mind about their involvement in newspaper publishing.

Mr. Knightly stared at her with brilliant blue eyes. He put her in mind of ~~Castleton~~ John, with his bright, inquisitive gaze and unruly dark hair. Apparently, being lowborn was another point these two men had in common. There were very quiet rumors that Knightly was the bastard son of an earl.

But to look at Knightly now, one would never know. Everything about his office—a spacious room decorated in the finest furniture—declared him to be the wealthy, powerful man that he was. She wondered whether John would have an office like this, and a power like Knightly's, if he did manage to buy his factory and produce those engines.

Prudence remembered the passion and determination with which John spoke of the Difference Engine. John could be like Knightly if given the opportunity. Ashbrooke and Radcliffe were currently working on securing his release from prison by appealing to Lord Castleton. She was about to make a tremendous public declaration—

after all, she was already quite ruined, had little left to lose and everything to gain.

"Well, Miss Payton?"

Not Lady Nanson, not Lady Castleton. Miss Payton.

"I would like you to publish this letter," Prudence said, finding her voice. She handed the folded sheet to Mr. Knightly. Her hand shook only slightly.

He flipped it open and quickly scanned the words she had composed in a frenzy this afternoon. Then those bright blue eyes settled on her.

"This will ruin him," Knightly said gravely. Interesting choice of word: *ruin*. She would have been ruined if word had gotten out. She had felt *ruined*.

"It will be what he deserves," she said with a lift of her chin.

"You will cause an uproar amongst the ton," Mr. Knightly pressed on. Did he really think she was unaware of that? Oh, she knew.

"People should know what he has done," she said. "I think it will be worse if this letter doesn't cause a ruckus."

"And what if they say that boys will be boys, reformed rakes make the best husbands, and then you see him around at all the parties?" Mr. Knightly asked, and this time he seemed genuinely concerned for her well-being.

"That is a risk I shall have to take. I am tired of standing by on the side of the ballroom, silent and fearful, while everyone else waltzes past me. I am tired of being afraid. I thought I didn't deserve love, Mr. Knightly. But now I know that I do. I came to *The London Weekly* not because it's the most popular but because of the Writing Girls you had hired. I thought you would understand a woman's voice needing to be heard."

Mr. Knightly stared at her for a moment. Lud, those eyes had a way of getting to a girl. Had she said the right thing? The wrong thing? His lips quirked up into a slight grin, which reminded her of John. After last night's humiliation and heartache, and this afternoon's dramatic turn of events, she had no more patience for more charming, upstart rogues and their mysterious half smiles and sparkling blue eyes.

"Are you going to print my letter or not?" Prudence demanded.

Knightly grinned. Then he leaned forward and said, "Let's run this bounder out of town, Miss Payton."

Chapter 28

A<small>LL OVER</small> L<small>ONDON</small>, from dining rooms to coffee shops, there was a symphony of sounds. First, gasps of shock. Next, the sound of the newspaper being snapped straight so one could be sure they were reading the words correctly. This was followed by teacups set firmly in their saucers and cutlery rested on the edge of the plate, for the contents of this morning's issue of *The London Weekly* demanded one's complete attention.

The letter began with *"Dear London"* and proceeded to provide a shock.

> *There is something you must know. Lord Dudley, heir to the Marquis of Scarbrough, violently took my innocence against my will. As I am a gently bred lady, he has also robbed me of my prospects of marriage. As a girl, he left me feeling damaged and unworthy.*
>
> *I am writing this letter out of fear that I am not the only victim of Lord Dudley's violent attempts to control and dominate innocent young women.*

Had I not found the love of a kind, generous, and good man who has helped me love myself, I wouldn't have had the determination and courage required to give voice to a secret I've kept for so long.

At a breakfast table on Brooke Street, Miss Marchwood, spinster, sat very still, newspaper in hand, trying very hard not to cry into her teacup. Her father was immersed in the business section, and her mother was reading a letter from Aunt Bess. To their dismay, Miss Marchwood had never married, even rejecting a number of suitable men. She had never explained why.

For the first time, she understood that she was not the only one.

I beseech you to send a message to Dudley and others who treat women so cruelly. Refuse them. Refuse them entry to your homes, your clubs, your ballrooms. Refuse to condone and enable violent behavior against the innocent, perpetrated by "gentlemen" who act with callous disregard for others.

Just as a woman's worth ought not be judged by her innocence and marriageability—a man's worth isn't to be found in his station or wealth but in his honorable actions.

Signed,

Your daughter, your sister, your friend

In Berkeley Square, Lady Dare set down the newspaper and peered over her spectacles at her niece, who had come in to welcome her after her return from Bath late the previous evening. As was their habit, Prue lounged on a settee, and Lady Dare remained abed. They shared the newspaper whilst sipping chocolate and nibbling on breakfast pastries.

Lady Dare hadn't always been the most attentive guardian, and she'd never been the maternal type. Prue's governess, Miss Georgette, had provided all the warmth and care. But Lady Dare had seen to it that Prue had received the finest education, wore lovely gowns, and had been properly brought out in society.

But now Lady Dare wondered: was something like this the reason Prudence had gone from being a lovely, spirited girl in her first season to one who had become very quiet and rather adept at not drawing attention to herself? Lady Dare had noticed, she had wondered. But she just hadn't known how to broach the subject in such a culture of silence.

Besides, Prudence had been *fine*.

But a young lady oughtn't just be fine. She ought to be splendid, gloriously happy, and madly in love.

This article gave Lady Dare a chance to bring up an emotionally fraught and delicate matter in a very roundabout way. It would allow her to say things she didn't know how to say otherwise.

"This girl is very brave," Lady Dare said resolutely, jabbing at the newspaper with her finger.

"Which one?" Prue asked cautiously.

"The one who stood up to Dudley." Lady Dare watched her niece closely. What she saw broke her heart. There was a slight tremble in Prudence's chin, as if she was about to cry.

"Oh. I'm so glad you think so," Prudence replied in a small voice.

"I do. And anyone who thinks otherwise is an ignoramus," Lady Dare added, just in case there were ignoramuses who thought otherwise. Knowing the half-wits in the ton, there would be.

Prue cracked a smile.

"I wouldn't turn away a girl like this. I would tell her that he's despicable and she is lovely anyway. I would also tell her that she deserves every and any happiness. She must give everyone a chance to love her."

"You're very kind," Prue said softly.

"Nonsense. I am merely human and concerned for my fellow humans."

With that, they returned to drinking chocolate and reading the paper. However, Lady Dare stole glances at her niece, who seemed to be a little bit brighter.

Ten o'clock in the morning
Lady Dare's drawing room

While there were numerous dim-witted people amongst the haute ton, there were also some shrewd minds who were able to put two and two together. Was it a coincidence that Miss Prudence Merryweather Payton had done a grievous injury to Lord Dudley at a ball and then, just days after, such an accusatory letter appeared in the newspaper?

Many did not think it was a coincidence.

Many thought Prudence was grossly impertinent, had forgotten her place, and ought to be reminded of it. Others wished to seek the intimate details. A few more wished to offer their support to a brave young woman who had stood up to a known bully.

It was not fashionable to pay calls before noon at the earliest. But it was never fashionable to be the last one to hear the latest news or converse with the most recent person of scandal. Thus, society called upon Prudence en masse at a dreadfully early hour.

Impertinent or not, one of London's Least Likely had become London's Most Talked About.

They crowded into Lady Dare's drawing room, gossiping shamelessly whilst waiting to see if Miss Payton was "at home" to their call. She dared not descend into the viper pit that her drawing room had become, though she did stand at the top of the stairs, listening to the base accusations and declarations of support that drifted up to her through the open doors.

"Miss Payton, there is another caller."

Farnesworth extended the silver tray bearing

one thick vellum card engraved with a lady's name in a fancy script.

If it was someone else calling about that article she had published this morning . . . then no, she was not at home to callers.

But if it was one of her friends calling with news about John, then yes, she most certainly was available to see them. Upon John's dramatic arrest at the exhibition yesterday, she had told her friends' husbands just enough information about her relationship with him that they'd felt immediately impelled to use their rank and power on her and John's behalf. The more she thought about him, the more her heart and mind returned to the same conclusion: she loved him. He was the only man she would even think about marrying.

To hell with society if they disapproved. Especially if society was the collection of vipers and dragons in her drawing room.

Prudence picked up the card Farnesworth presented.

Lady Castleton.

That was interesting. Possibly terrifying. Potentially terrible.

Now if only she was truly as brave as Lady Dare believed her to be.

"I shall see her in my private sitting room," Prudence said. "And please send up tea."

THE REAL LADY Castleton was a slender, petite woman with dark glossy curls, an alabaster complexion, and large green eyes. Prudence guessed that they were approximately the same age. She was also an American, judging by her accent and her forthright manner.

"I understand you were also going by the name of Lady Castleton," she began without preamble, which Prudence found both surprising and also refreshing.

"The short answer to that is yes, I was," Prudence replied. "Would you care for tea?"

Lady Castleton nodded yes and said, "My husband is livid about it, as we have just arrived in London and all of our callers are inquiring about his time spent gallivanting around the countryside, gambling outrageously, starting fights with fellow peers, and consorting with a woman who is not actually his wife. There is a tremendous amount of confusion. We are quite horrified by the manner in which the Castleton name has been used."

"That must be difficult for you and your entry into society," Prudence said. She knew as well as anyone that name and reputation were everything to the haute ton. They mattered even more than money.

"I'm so glad you understand," Lady Castleton said.

"Unfortunately, I know how harsh they can be," Prue replied.

"I hope you can understand that I am eager to resolve this mess and clear our name. We intend to reside in England, and it shall be a long and lonely life if I am not received."

This was the moment that Prudence had most feared. It could determine John's freedom—possibly even his life. What easier way to have this matter put behind them than to have the man responsible locked away in prison indefinitely, shipped off to Australia, or swinging from the end of a rope?

But I love him. Prudence drew her strength from this one, basic truth. He had saved her from Dudley and had even saved her from herself. It was time to return the favor.

"There is another matter I'd like to discuss with you, Miss Payton. Lord Castleton and . . ." She, too, wasn't quite sure how to address John, as evidenced by her hesitation over his name.

"Mr. Roark," Prudence supplied.

"I could not help but notice that he and my husband bore a striking resemblance to each other."

Prudence gave a start. "Is that so? When did you see him?"

"'Two nights ago, was it? Castleton had him brought round. They were talking in the library for quite some time before the Bow Street Runners arrived. During a momentary distraction, Mr. Roark took the opportunity to escape—he just jumped on one of our horses and fled!"

Prudence quickly concluded that had been the night of Lady Penelope's Ball. She thought he had forsaken her, but he had only been detained and had further risked Lord Castleton's ire by escaping. He had kept his promise to her even when it had been nearly impossible to do so.

This man loved her. She loved him. All that stood in their way was his deception, the uproar of society, the law, and Lord and Lady Castleton.

"My point, Miss Payton, is that I suspect that my husband and Mr. Roark are half brothers. One is the rightful heir and the other is lowborn. I cannot in good conscience let him lock up his own brother, but if he is the sort of shifty fellow who will constantly embarrass us and cause us anxiety, then I shouldn't hesitate to have Castleton lock him up and throw away the key. There are such awful men in the world—did you see that letter in *The London Weekly* this morning?" Lady Castleton looked sad and placed her hand over her heart before shuddering at the likes of such despicable creatures roaming free. Prudence merely nodded, feeling queasy at the thought of it. Lady Castleton continued, "Thus, I have come to you to learn of his character."

There was something heady, weighty, slightly thrilling, and a little bit terrifying about possessing power over another person. It left her feeling awed and even afraid of what she could do. In this moment, Prudence understood that she held John's fate in her hands by the words she chose to say next. Oddly, Prudence thought of Dudley and how he must have felt when he'd hurt her. Had he needed to diminish her to feel powerful?

If she was of a mind to, Prudence could say that a person ought to know their place in society and accept it. She could declare that nothing was more important than a man's good name—which is why the most damaging thing she'd done in her letter to *The London Weekly* was call out Lord Dudley by name. In stealing another man's identity and risking his reputation, John had committed a grievous crime.

Prudence had the power to say all of those things and thereby condemn John to life in prison or some other horrible fate. Of course she *wouldn't*. But for a girl who had so long felt powerless, it was a moment that required pause. She would use this power to lift up rather than drag down.

Lady Castleton sipped her tea, waiting.

Prudence finally spoke.

"Mr. Roark is, quite honestly, the best man I know. There isn't a doubt in my mind that he will cease using the name Castleton at once and will not plague or embarrass you again."

"I did hear that he was violent. . . ."

"Only to protect me from a man . . . like Dudley," Prudence said. She sipped her tea, while Lady Castleton took in the information that the faux Castleton protected young maidens from the worst sort of scoundrel. Prue then continued, "When I believed him to be Castleton, I saw him behave like a true gentleman, being constantly attentive to my comforts and safety. His manners to others were exceptional. He conducted himself like the best example of a peer of the realm, which is why I believed him."

"I see," Lady Castleton murmured. "You have given me much to consider, Miss Payton. I shall confer with Lord Castleton at once."

"Perhaps another time you might like to join me for tea with my friends, the Duchess of Ashbrooke and Lady Radcliffe," Prudence said, thus offering Lady Castleton the stamp of respectability that would certainly smooth her entry into society, plaguing rumors of imposters be damned.

Lady Castleton smiled. "I would like that very much."

There was just one last thing begging to be said. Prudence hadn't uttered those three words aloud yet, and she wanted John to be the first to hear them.

Eleven o'clock

John hadn't expected visitors at his cell in Newgate. Except perhaps for Prudence, but he didn't imagine that she—a lovely, highborn beauty— would make an appearance in this dank slum of a prison. Why would she? He had kept secrets from her when she had revealed everything to him. He had taken advantage of her trust. Worst of all, she had started to believe in goodness again, and he'd crushed her fragile belief.

He was no better than Dudley.

It didn't matter that he had wanted to tell her the truth of his identity. He'd been afraid that she would reject him, or leave him, or withdraw when she'd only just started to blossom. It had only been concern for her safety as he'd escorted her back to London that had kept him biting his tongue every time he had wanted to confess.

He should have told her the minute she'd confided in him.

Of course he had to realize this now, alone in his dark and damp prison cell.

But then he did have a visitor, one he least expected.

"Lord Castleton," John said by way of acknowledgment. The man's well-made, fashionable, expensive, and clean attire stood in stark contrast to the damp and crumbling stone wall.

"Mr. Roark," he replied with a nod.

"To what do I owe the pleasure?"

"It seems that in spite of being a mere footman, you have friends in high places," Castleton remarked, which struck John as interesting.

"That's news to me," John replied. To his knowledge, he did not have friends in high places. Or was this Prudence's doing?

"Like myself, these men also have wives who are equally determined to secure your freedom or make our lives a living hell should we leave you here. The choice, we are told, is ours. But I'm afraid it isn't much of a choice at all."

John smothered a grin. Definitely the work of Prudence and her friends. God, he loved her.

"There is nothing more vexing than a plaguing wife," Castleton continued. "A man knows no peace when his wife has her mind set on something. It's exhausting."

"Can you not escape to your club?"

"I find it's better to heed my wife," Castleton said wearily. "She has consulted Miss Payton about your character, and together they have determined that you are repentant and shan't cause the Castleton family any further trouble. My wife also has this idea that we may be half brothers."

Blue eyes glanced at blue eyes. They saw the same thing: a striking resemblance in their features and their mannerisms. And a polite determination to avoid mentioning it.

"There's no way of knowing, and I wouldn't expect anything of you because of some connection we may or may not have," John said. They weren't family. They might have been fathered by the same man, and they might have grown up in the same house, but they still inhabited different worlds.

Castleton seemed relieved that his lowborn half sibling would not call upon him for any favors. John didn't blame him.

"You just want to go free, I imagine," Castleton remarked, glancing around the squalid cell.

"A man can dream," John replied cautiously.

"We could allow this matter of fraud to go to trial," Castleton mused.

John tensed. Since he wasn't the begging or pleading kind, he replied, "Best not waste everyone's time with such a farce."

"Exactly. Which is why I'm dropping the charges," Castleton said. John's head snapped up in surprise. "That, and I fear for my sanity otherwise. Truly, I hope you know how bothersome wives can be. Nag, nag, nag . . . and something about tea with the duchess."

"I'd give anything to know," John said, thinking of Prudence. If he got out of here, there was a marriage proposal in Prudence's future. She might refuse him, but nothing would stop him from asking the question.

"How romantic," Castleton said dryly. He straightened, ready to depart now that his business was just about concluded. "Well, you shall now have the chance to be enlightened on the matter. However, if I hear of another Lord or Lady Castleton, my wife can nag all she wants, but I will see you hang."

And with that, John walked free.

Twelve o'clock

If one listened closely, one could hear the sound of many Mayfair hostesses dipping a quill in ink, tapping it ever so lightly on the side of the jar, and scratching the name *Lord Dudley* from their guest lists. Many had never liked him anyway, tolerating him only because the respected, powerful, and slightly feared Marquis of Scarbrough had demanded that his heir associate with the best society.

Well, not even Scarbrough could ensure his welcome now. Not when most hosts and hostesses were far more concerned about the safety of their lady guests, their daughters, their sisters, their mothers.

Many of the ton still championed the heir of the marquis. Many cast aspersions upon Miss Payton and whoever had penned that slanderous letter in the paper. Quite a few believed her and the author to be the same and wasted no time spreading rumors to that effect. She would be cut, of course. One did not attack the character of a peer of the realm without consequences. Thus, many hostesses did not revise their guest lists, except to remove the name of Miss Prudence Merryweather Payton. She was just a wallflower anyway. . . .

One might also hear the sound of heavy wooden doors closing firmly in the face of Lord Dudley. Butlers read *The London Weekly* whilst ironing it before placing it beside their masters' breakfast plates and finishing it after the family had taken turns reading it. Those who were not given the explicit orders to refuse entry to the Dudley family took it upon themselves to prevent such a cruel creature from darkening their doors. For they, too, had daughters and sisters and wives and housemaids who relied upon them for protection and to set an example.

Everyone understood that if Dudley had done such an unspeakable crime to one of his own class, then he very likely took advantage of lower-class girls, too.

At first Dudley thought it was a few butlers, who might find themselves sacked for refusing the future Marquis of Scarbrough. But when door after door after door after door shut firmly in his face, his long-simmering anger started to boil over.

He spewed curses and leapt on his horse, kicking the beast to a canter.

Dudley proceeded to White's, where the door was always open to its members. His father had put his name down on the waiting list the very day his name had been added to the birth registry. White's was his haven from the world, his home away from home, where he drank and gambled and held forth with his peers.

Some stuffy matrons might have had their corsets in a twist over that rubbish article in *The London Weekly*, but his mates would understand that the world was theirs to enjoy. It was in the bloody Bible—God granted *man* dominion over the animals and everything else. Why were females too feeble-brained to comprehend that? And what was so wrong about following the bloody scripture?

Dudley dismounted in front of the famous bow window at White's, tossed the reins of his horse to a boy, and told him to wait. Then he stomped up the four small stairs, pushed open the door, and stepped inside. His arrival in the foyer was noted by none other than the Duke of Ashbrooke, who had been embroiled in more scandals than Dudley had fingers.

The duke's expression darkened as he crossed the room and stood, arms folded over his chest, effectively blocking Dudley's entry into the club.

"Excuse me," Dudley said, politely ordering one of the few men who outranked him to get the hell out of his way.

The duke did not move.

But the duke was not alone. Lord Radcliffe, the man all of London had mocked as the Mad Baron, came and stood beside the duke in a similar pose.

Dudley glanced around wildly at the sound of chairs scraping against the wooden floor as they were pushed back abruptly. One gent after another came to stand with Ashbrooke, blocking Dudley's entry into the club.

There was the Duke of Hamilton and Brandon—he was always so damned *proper* and sensible it made Dudley sneer. Of course *he* would condemn Dudley. The Duke of Buckinghamshire stood, as did the scandalously heathenish Duke of Wycliff, who had done Lord only knew what with savage women during his travels.

All the dukes were out today, it seemed. Of all the damned days!

They were all judging him, too, when they had no right. None.

When that renowned rake Lord Roxbury stood,

Dudley felt a flash of rage. The man was known to have seduced half the women in London, and *he* was condemning Dudley because of one little incident? What was the bloody difference?

Even the Marquis of Huntley—a bigger rogue and scoundrel this town had *never* seen—stood and joined the others. As if he, who had ruined at least four women, had been one to judge.

Their message could not have been more clear: Dudley had done wrong. He was not welcome. Worse, he was not one of them.

What was he, then?

"This is a club for gentlemen," Huntley said. Dudley was receiving condemnation from *Huntley*?

They both had bad reputations, noble blood, and broken noses that hinted at past indiscretions. What was the difference? He didn't know. Wouldn't know. He could only sneer in response.

The hell with the lot of them. Dudley summoned all his strength to act as if *he* was the one shunning *their* company. Then he stormed out.

It was clear: he would not be welcomed in White's again.

Dudley was pretty damn sure he knew who had written that damned letter: Miss Prudence Payton. Who was she to ruin a good man's name?

Three o'clock

In spite of John's arrest, imprisonment, and subsequent freedom, the Duke of Ashbrooke and

Lord Radcliffe still received him when he called as planned. The men gathered in the duke's vast study, which looked like a duke's study ought to: large windows, suggesting funds to pay the necessary taxes on them, heavy and engraved wooden desks and tables, richly upholstered chairs and settees, bookshelves loaded with expensive leather volumes, plush carpets that one's boots sank into. Everything said *wealth*. Everything said *this man matters more than you*.

They took seats before the fire and began to converse about the invention, design, and construction of the Difference Engine.

"I think the engine is brilliant," John said, leaning forward as he did when he was excited about the conversation at hand, and as he done when he'd explained this to Prudence. He felt a pang of embarrassment that he should have been so eager about this engine, when she was well acquainted with it and its inventors. "But what excites me most is the path of innovation it blazes."

"Most people don't seem to see the practical applications," Ashbrooke said.

"Most people are idiots," said the former footman. The confidence he had used to pass himself off as a viscount wasn't entirely feigned. Every time he'd achieved something that no one ever expected from a man of his station, his confidence had increased until it was simply who he was.

"What is your plan for the engine?" Radcliffe asked. "Not that we'll agree to it. I'm just curious."

"I'd like to license the manufacturing of the engine from you," John explained. "I have secured the capital necessary to establish the factory. And then I'd like to sell them."

"What makes you think we haven't already made such plans ourselves?" Ashbrooke asked, lifting one brow in the challenging way only a duke could.

"Because you only just got the thing built and determined that it worked," John answered. "This is only the beginning. You could design an additional machine to print out the calculations performed. And who is to say machines cannot eventually do more than mathematical calculations?"

"You have grand ideas," Radcliffe said, but John could see he was already thinking about what those machines might be and how to build them.

"A man has time to think whilst he's standing at a door, waiting for a reason to open it," John said, alluding to his past service. There was no use hiding it any longer—everyone knew. What a relief it was. How freeing it felt. How exhausting it had been carrying that secret around, waiting at any moment for the world to find out. He thought of Prudence. He understood her now in a way he hadn't before.

"How did you come by the capital?" Ashbrooke asked. "And before you worry about the possibly nefarious means by which we suspect you came by it, be assured that it cannot possibly top what

I did to raise funds to build the engine in the first place."

"My money came from the usual sources of an idle gentleman: card games, wagers on stupid things with drunk lords, smart investments in the Exchange," John explained. He'd earned for the real Lord Castleton the reputation of a man who never overimbibed, who never wagered recklessly, and who always won honorably.

"And have you secured enough money to fund this venture with the engine *and* support a wife in the manner which she has been raised?" Radcliffe asked.

And then there was that.

There was no point in pretending he wasn't about to propose to Prudence immediately following this interview. Hell, he was glad that in the tragic event that she refused him, Prudence had powerful men to champion her and protect her. No matter what, she was not alone. He hoped she knew that.

"Yes, I can support a wife," John answered. "Perhaps not in as grand a fashion as this, but if Miss Payton accepts my proposal, she'll want for nothing. Especially love."

"A romantic," Ashbrooke said, grinning.

"You're the second person to tell me that today," John remarked. "What I'd like to know is if I'll also be the one to bring the Difference Engine to the people."

Ashbrooke and Radcliffe exchanged a glance

that seemed to say it all. And then the duke extended his hand.

"We're looking forward to doing business with you, Roark. Now go propose."

Four o'clock
Number 4, Mount Street

His father was not as empathetic or accommodating as Dudley had anticipated, based on prior experiences when trouble had found him and his father had made trouble go away.

"The thing is, you've gone too far this time," his father lectured. Dudley sulked in a chair, brandy in hand and a sneer on his face. "A highborn woman! You have to keep it in your breeches around the gently bred. That's practically the first thing any aristo learns. God knows I give you enough allowance to pay for a whore."

Dudley didn't know why a whore wasn't enough or why he'd pursued Prude Prudence. But he did remember feeling satisfied after. God, he'd felt in control, on top of the world, unstoppable.

She had resisted. And then she hadn't.

He had subdued her, made her want him and his cock, made her pliant in his arms and submissive to his will. He never felt like that in day-to-day life, what with his father calling all the shots about all and every estate matter, and card games never quite turning out in his favor, and all the entertainments of London easily obtained without much effort.

"It was years ago," Dudley muttered weakly in his defense.

"Well, the family name has been sullied in the papers *today*," his father thundered, his face reddening as his voice strained with anger. "It ruined my breakfast, I tell you! How am I to face my friends at the club, when they all know that my son was the one damned fool that didn't understand where and when to take his pleasure?"

Dudley decided not to mention the fact that his father might not be granted entry to White's in the near future.

"And what of your sister? She is still unwed. This will significantly diminish her prospects, if not ruin her entirely."

Dudley shifted in his chair, thinking of his sister. That his actions would affect her future never crossed his mind. There was Dudley and what he wanted and that was all. His sister was just a girl who would accept the proposal their father told her to accept—because when did a woman's wishes have to do with anything?

"It'll blow over when another scandal hits," Dudley replied, sipping his brandy and drawing upon the truth of life in high society. "Always does."

"God willing I will see the day," his father said. And then, leveling a hard stare at his son, he said, "But you won't. You will be in the West Indies. I have purchased you a commission."

"The West Indies? A commission?" Dudley asked, straightening in the chair. "That's practically a death sentence, and *I am your heir*."

His status as heir is what protected him from everything, particularly the consequences of his actions. After all, one had to protect the legacy.

"You are a disgrace. Your ship boards this evening."

Five o'clock in the afternoon
Number 12, Berkeley Square

Prudence was in the drawing room, alone, watching the minutes and seconds of her life tick by. She would go mad soon. Would he be free? If so, would John come to her or would he find another ship to America?

"By all rights, I ought to have given up hope for love and happily ever after," she continued softly under her breath. "But I haven't."

That was the thing of it: In spite of all her experiences, both devastating and exhilarating, she still had hope that maybe, just maybe, she would find that sense of wholeness she craved. And she had caught a glimpse of such happiness. She just had to believe.

Prue had done everything she could to ensure his freedom, short of marching down to Newgate herself. It wasn't entirely out of the question. Prue had learned that Ashbrooke and Radcliffe, at the behest of their wives, had spoken with Lord Castleton. It seemed that he was under enormous pressure to let John go. If only he would. . . .

The clock ticked. Callers—Lady Castleton, Emma, Olivia—had come and gone. Prudence was sick to death of tea and this drawing room and forever waiting for life to happen to her. But what could she do? There was precious little a girl could do on her own. Prue intently missed the freedom—terrifying, exhilarating freedom—of her wild adventure in the countryside.

"Farnesworth, my gloves and bonnet if you please." She didn't know where she was going, but she had to get out and feel the wind on her cheeks and breathe the fresh air and remember the times she was truly happy. On the run. With John by her side.

And then, suddenly, he was there.

A knock at the door.

Farnesworth opened it.

John, standing on her doorstep, lifting his head and gazing intensely. Blue eyes, the unruly dark hair, the slight grin, the broad shoulders . . . whether John or Castleton, he was the man she loved.

"Who may I ask is calling?" Farnesworth inquired.

"Roark. Mr. John Roark. For Miss Prudence Merryweather Payton," John replied to the butler without ever taking his eyes off Prue. She stood rooted to the foyer floor, unable to move and hardly able to breathe.

"I shall see if she is at home," the butler intoned. Even though she very clearly was at home. They gazed at each other until Farnesworth closed the door with a gentle click in the latch.

Before she could protest, the butler turned to her and asked, "Are you at home to this gentleman?"

A gentleman he was—in dress, in appearance, in the way he carried himself, in his actions and his goodness.

"Yes," Prudence said, smiling broadly and rushing forward to fling open the door and launch herself into John's arms.

She breathed in deeply, finding comfort and happiness in his scent and the imprint of his body against hers. She felt the soft strands of his hair entwined with her fingers and the lovely fierceness with which he held her close.

They were on the doorstep, where all of Berkeley Square and their spying neighbors could see. It didn't matter. Nothing else mattered, because he was here, and free, and they were in love.

Farnesworth's discreet cough reminded them that they were causing a scene. In his eyes, Prudence's reputation was still something to be handled with care. Hand in hand, Prudence led John to the drawing room. She left the door slightly ajar.

"You look beautiful," he said. She smiled faintly and blushed, still not quite used to being noticed, but liking it. "I don't know if I ever told you how beautiful you are."

She blushed again.

"You are quite fine yourself . . . ," Prudence said a bit bashfully in return. She clasped her hands behind her back. He was *here*. No one ever came for her, and he'd just been locked up in prison, yet he was here, in her drawing room, looking more handsome than she remembered.

"This footman cleans up well, doesn't he?" he said, the self-deprecating comment a test.

"Aye," Prudence agreed, allowing her gaze to roam from the tip of his shiny Hessian boots to his broad chest and handsome face that made her believe in happily ever after. She smiled and said, "But what girl doesn't fancy a man in uniform?"

John flashed a grin. The air between them was charged with electricity. Anticipating his touch, she had to rein in her racing heart. Then his expression became more serious.

"I have to tell you some things, Prue. But tell me to stop at any time."

"Don't stop," she said softly. She wanted to hear him. "Tell me."

"I am sorry that I let you believe I was Castleton. And I'm sorry that I'm not actually very sorry," he said, pausing with a faint grin, "because I'm afraid we would never have met or known each other otherwise. I'm sorry that I have to believe that, because it doesn't flatter you."

The truth was, she wouldn't have considered accepting a ride if he'd been driving a humble cart or a carriage. And the truth was, she didn't know if she would have allowed herself to fall in love with him if she hadn't thought there was a remote chance of marriage. But she didn't know then about how love mattered more than anything.

So she said, "Don't stop. Tell me more."

John exhaled and pushed his fingers through his hair, mussing it up.

"I am sorry that I didn't reveal my true identity to you when you confessed what you had suffered. You were brave enough to speak of your secret. But I wasn't. I admire you tremendously for that, Prudence."

She smiled slightly, basking in admiration instead of pity.

"You have no idea how you've made me brave or how much I've spoken up since," Prudence said. She would explain it all later if he hadn't seen the paper already.

"Here's the truth: I'm a lowborn bastard. I was raised in service but had dreams above my station. I stole candles and borrowed books from my employers so that I could teach myself something other than how to pour the port after supper or open a door. I've been violent, but only on behalf of women who couldn't defend themselves. I assumed another man's identity, attended house parties, horse races, you name it, as Lord Castleton. I let *you* believe it. The truth is, I'm a nobody with too many flaws to count. But I love you."

That was the truth, wasn't it? Everyone had their flaws and exhausted themselves trying to hide them. Nothing was perfect. One couldn't let that stand in the way of love.

"I love you, too," Prudence said, glad to finally tell him, even though those three little words didn't adequately express the enormity and intensity of her feelings for him. "The truth is, you have made me feel loved. You have given me strength, and happiness, and hope. And you are truly, in all the ways that really matter, better than every other man I know."

Prudence saw the tension fall away from him. She knew the feeling. When assured of love, one could have faith that everything would be all right. One could enjoy the comfort that love provides.

"I can't promise you that society won't shun us, but no matter what, I will stand by you," John said. "I struck a deal with Ashbrooke and Radcliffe that might make us ridiculously wealthy—or utterly penniless. Somehow, I will always provide for us. I can promise that I will do everything I can to make you happy. I promise to love you forever," John said. Then he took her hands in his and dropped to one knee.

"Prudence Merryweather Payton, will you do me the honor of becoming my wife?"

"Yes," Prudence said, the word a rush of breath across her lips. "Yes, I will, yes."

LADY DARE PEEKED through the drawing room door, which had been left slightly ajar, and saw a man on one knee and her niece looking splendid, gloriously happy, and madly in love. Rather than interrupt, she softly closed the door behind her, hummed a little song, and started to plan a wedding.

JOHN LOWERED HIS mouth to Prudence's. That kiss was sweet, like the sun coming out after the rain or like the first shoots of spring after a long, bitterly cold winter. That kiss was gentle, afraid this happiness was a fragile thing. After all, things could go horribly awry. But then again . . . everything had gone horribly awry and here they were, locked in a kiss that she felt from her head to her toes, and deep down in her soul. She felt safe enough to let go and enjoy the pleasure of the moment.

DOWN AT THE docks, Dudley boarded a ship bound for the West Indies. It relied upon navigational charts that were riddled with errors—which wouldn't have been the case had the calculations been done by the Difference Engine rather than former French hairdressers with little mathematical training who had become computers after the revolution. There was a very good chance that ship would not reach its intended destination. Meanwhile, Prudence said *yes*.

"YES," SHE WHISPERED. Until this moment, John hadn't known how one little word, whispered so softly, could be the happiest sound in the world.

He'd gone from nothing, to possibly everything, back to not a damn thing, and now he held Prudence in his arms for a kiss that undid him. She knew about him—*all* about him—and she still kissed him with the sweetness and passion he'd feared he'd lost forever.

His hands skimmed lower down her back, then up to the curve of her breasts.

"Yes," she whispered. He thumbed the center of her gown, above the fabric. A soft sigh escaped her. "Yes." She threaded her fingers through his hair and pressed up against him. Thank God she said yes. Now if only the wedding could happen *now*.

Somehow, without quite realizing it, they tumbled down to the settee with Prue beneath him.

"Yes," Prudence whispered, pushing a lock of hair out of his eyes. Then she gave a coy smile and writhed slightly underneath him. He groaned, thinking he was going to enjoy marriage. But first . . . there was a beautiful woman in his arms, and he was going to make love to her.

WHILE ALL OVER town people were still reading Prue's bold letter in *The London Weekly*—the housemaids who found it whilst cleaning, those who read it in the coffee shop or over afternoon tea, or those who reread it once more—Prudence said yes.

"YES," SHE GASPED, feeling alive everywhere

John touched her. Which is to say, she felt alive everywhere. Her skin tingled with pleasure under
his fingertips. She felt him, hard, at her entrance.
"Yes," she gasped again, wanting to feel him
inside, wanting to be one with him. Gazes locked,
he entered her slowly. "Yes," she murmured as
he began to move, and her hips moved with him
instinctively. She felt the muscles of his back flex
under her palms as she pressed him close. She
breathed him in until her breaths were shallow
and her heart was pounding and that exquisite
pressure was building within her. A moment ago
she'd had thoughts about trust, radiant happiness,
and feeling protected and loved—God, she felt so
thoroughly loved—but they flew from her head
until only one thought remained. "Yes," she cried
out as she came. John came, too, burying his face
in her shoulder to muffle the sound of his shout.

He held her close and she thought *Yes* to life
and love and happily ever after.

Epilogue

AFTER ROARK "JUST got" a factory, he "just happened" to manufacture the Difference Engine, which just happened to earn him a fortune. From there, he partnered with London's most famous newspaperman, Mr. Derek Knightly, now Lord Northbourne, to print new and correct editions of the reckoning books. With his hard-earned wealth, Roark invested in other promising ventures—which only seemed to bring him *more* money.

He also "just got" Amner Hall, a lovely, rambling country estate with a brick house covered with wisteria and plenty of bedrooms for his and Prudence's ever-growing brood of children. There were two boys and two girls and another on the way.

The estate was conveniently situated between the country residences of the Duke and Duchess of Ashbrooke and Lord and Lady Radcliffe. When the families weren't in town, they were often visiting each other.

This particular morning, the gents and their sons—and some daughters—were off in Roark's study, plotting more machines. There was talk of an Analytical Engine, which would perform even more complex calculations. Meanwhile, the ladies and their daughters were in the drawing room with pots of tea, along with plates of biscuits and pastries, fresh strawberries, and clotted cream.

"How is Caroline faring at Lady Penelope's?" Prudence asked, inquiring after Emma's daughter, who'd just begun at the school.

"I have already received missives from her teachers, who are concerned that she is exhausted in class after staying up late reading 'tawdry and inappropriate literature,' " Emma replied.

"Did someone say my name?" Caroline barely looked up from the book that lay open in her lap, which was absorbing nearly all of her attention.

"Like mother like daughter," Prudence quipped.

"What are you reading?" Olivia asked.

"*The Mad Baron*," Caroline replied, to the groans of the three mothers.

"She's also beginning to write her own stories," Emma declared. "*Romances.*"

"You must be so proud," Olivia replied with a grin. "But not as proud as I am of Miranda."

The three former wallflowers focused their attentions upon Miranda, whose pale blond hair had been awkwardly cropped short by her own hand because it kept getting in the way of climbing trees, dramatically reenacting the battle of

Waterloo with her brothers, and otherwise being
the most unladylike young lady in the history of
England.

Presently, Miranda was indulging in an unladylike number of scones, and her mother—who
had been raised to embroider, pour tea perfectly,
and paint watercolors of floral arrangements—
delighted in her little hoyden.

"I am so excited for your exhibition, Olivia,"
Prudence said. "I have a new gown and everything."

"I am so nervous!" Olivia said. "And I have no
idea what to wear."

"Are there really nudes?" Emma asked bluntly.

"No," Olivia replied, dejected. "Phinn would
never allow my portraits of him to be seen publicly. My exhibit should feature my landscapes of
Yorkshire."

"Remember how vehemently we opposed your
match to Radcliffe and your having to live in such
a remote location?"

"Shhh . . . ," Olivia said. "I don't want to give
Miranda any more ideas. She has enough already."

"Mama . . ." A little girl with reddish-brown
hair and sparkling blue eyes tugged on Prudence's
sleeve.

"What is it, Samantha?"

"Charlotte and I have a performance prepared."

"Well, let's see it," Prudence said.

"You must purchase tickets first," Samantha
declared.

"Takes after her father," Prue murmured. Roark had displayed a marvelous ability to make money, which kept their growing family comfortable. Meanwhile, Emma, Olivia, and Prue dug in their reticules for coins and scrawled IOUs on scraps of paper, which were promptly pocketed by Samantha.

Charlotte was a little more reserved than her older sister, but she still possessed an unshakable confidence in herself. In fact, she could be rather stubborn. Prudence never chided either of her daughters about being more agreeable or less outspoken or just . . . less. She knew what that felt like, and she never wanted her own daughters to feel so diminished.

Thus, they commanded the attention of the guests in the drawing room and put on a performance of an original mishmash of fairy tales in which at least three different heroines lived happily ever after. After a thunderous round of applause, the three women formerly known as "London's Least Likely" exchanged conspiratorial looks.

"Shall we?" Emma inquired with a lift of her brow.

"I'll fetch the writing materials," Prudence said. "Olivia, you still have the best handwriting."

"Don't forget the sherry," Olivia added.

"Now, where were we?" Emma asked.

"We were still debating the title," Prudence said. "*Advice To Young Ladies From Three Wallflowers* or

What Every Young Lady Should Know: Advice From The Wicked Wallflowers."

The former wallflowers and their daughters put the matter to vote, and the title was quickly decided.

"Now, onward to the book itself," Olivia said. "I distinctly remember writing the first few chapters."

"According to this list of contents we drafted, we are onto chapter four: Don't Be Scared Even When You Are Scared."

From there, the trio composed the chapter aloud based upon their own experiences. Each of them had received the perfect, quintessential ladies' education from a very respectable school and teachers who'd meant well. However, each of them had found their own education lacking in very distinct ways.

Prudence was resolved that chapter five would be When Not To Be a Lady. She and Olivia would share their experiences of how the strict rules of "ladylike behavior" had such devastating consequences. Meanwhile, Miranda availed herself of another scone and didn't hold the teapot properly when pouring for herself, and the world did not end.

Emma's favorite chapter had been Adventure Is Not Just for Books.

"Oh! I forgot to mention something!" Prudence exclaimed. "I had tea with Lady Northbourne—"

"—Dear Annabelle! I love her column," Olivia said.

"As we all do," Emma added.

"She loves the idea of our ladies' guide and mentioned it to Knightly. He has agreed to publish it for us. When we finish it."

"You might have led with that bit of news, Prudence," Emma remarked dryly, but she was smiling all the same.

"I vow my wits are scattered with this wee one," Prudence said, rubbing her belly affectionately.

"That is utterly fantastic news," Olivia said. "Though not completely surprising. We do know that he'll publish *anything*."

"Not *anything*. He turned down Lady Katherine's memoirs entitled *Queen Bee*."

"Ugh," Emma said, rolling her eyes. Olivia did, too, even though ladies did not roll their eyes.

"We must keep working. The husbands will return soon."

For the next hour—and during many other sessions—the former wallflowers sipped sherry and composed a conduct guide for young ladies, full of all the information they wished they had learned before they'd embarked on the great husband hunt, the marriage mart, and the wide, wide world. The book was dedicated to their daughters, who half-listened as their mothers wrote, discussed, and reminisced.

Their day's work concluded shortly after the arrival of their husbands. The families then embarked on a picnic.

"Remember our romantic picnic, darling?" Radcliffe asked Olivia, who laughed at the memory of that disastrous encounter.

"I believe that took place at the gazebo I constructed for my Emma," Ashbrooke boasted. "Remember that, dear wife?"

His dear wife blushed furiously, indicating that she did, indeed, remember.

Roark and Prudence had plenty of lovely memories, too, but they paused to create one more as the others walked ahead, leading a gaggle of children. Under the shade of an apple tree, he pulled his wife into his arms, and she melted against him. He had never tired of gazing into her warm brown eyes, and she loved how, after all these years, his blue eyes still sparkled when he looked at her.

"Remember that time I kissed you clandestinely in—"

"The stables? Yes," Prue said, laughing, remembering their very first, very brief kiss at the Coach & Horses Inn, in a town whose name they still weren't quite sure of.

"And—" Roark continued, but his clever wife beat him to it.

"On the side of the road somewhere in Wiltshire? Yes," Prudence said. That had been her first real kiss. Felt-it-from-her-head-to-her-toes kind of kiss. Changed-something-forever kind of kiss. No, she had not forgotten it.

Neither had Roark. A man didn't easily forget his last first kiss.

"And that time I kissed you under the apple tree?" Roark asked, pulling her even closer. She pressed her hand against his chest and leaned against him in a way that suggested a loving and easy intimacy.

For a moment, Prudence was confused. "Which time?"

"This time," he said with a grin and a mischievous sparkle in his eyes. He lowered his mouth to hers for a kiss that was no less sweet, or passionate, or yearning than their very first or all the ones in between.

"Something for you to write about in your book," he murmured.

"Perfect kisses and happily ever after," Prudence sighed. "Aye, I can write about that."

AUTHOR'S NOTE

On fact, fiction, and liberties taken . . .

THE DIFFERENCE ENGINE, which features promi-
nently in my three Wallflower novels, was real. It
was the invention of Englishman Charles Babbage
in 1821. He and his partner, Joseph Clement, spent
years and invested a fortune in their attempts to
build it. While known as the inventor of the first
computer, Babbage is also known for failing to
build his machines.

The Difference Engine wasn't successfully
constructed until 1991 (just in time for the two-
hundredth anniversary of Babbage's birth), when
a dedicated team from The Science Museum in
London endeavored to build it once and for all
from the original plans—to finally discover if it
would work. (It did! Brilliant!) I am completely
indebted to Doron Swade's book *The Difference
Engine: The Quest to Build the First Computer.* It was
a marvelous and riveting account of Babbage's
life and the modern-day quest to build the engine
using Babbage's original plans.

Babbage provided the inspiration for the Duke
of Ashbrooke (*The Wicked Wallflower*), and Clem-

ent the inspiration for Lord Radcliffe's character (*Wallflower Gone Wild*). While a few people did recognize the potential for the engine, Roark's character is not based on anyone in particular.

I have made my heroes successful in their endeavors to build and produce the Difference Engine because it's my historical world and I said so. Another liberty I took: the Great Exhibition did not actually take place until 1851, but I thought my heroes needed their own equivalent of Lady Penelope's Ball.

As I embarked on a series of interconnected historical and contemporary romance novels, I was deeply pleased to learn that the computer—of all things!—could be a link between Regency London and modern-day New York City. The hero of my corresponding contemporary series, *The Bad Boy Billionaire*, is a brilliant tech entrepreneur who, like so many men and women today, carry on the pioneering work of innovators like Babbage.

But an unfortunate link between the Regency era and our present day is the prevalence of sexual violence and the stigma and suffering of its victims. Though *What a Wallflower Wants* is a historical novel, it was influenced by the tragic and heartbreaking stories of sexual assault that are in the news far too frequently these days.

It's a topic I have also explored in the contemporary counterpart, *The Bad Boy Billionaire: What a Girl Wants*. These contemporary romances feature the romance of Duke Austen (the bad boy billionaire) and Jane Sparks, a modern-day Wallflower who is "writing" the Wallflower novels based on her own experiences.

Regency readers know that to be caught in a "compromising position" is to find oneself proceeding immediately to the altar. It's all quite romantic—unless it isn't. In parts of the world today, women are still forced to marry their attackers to preserve "honor." Or, just as horribly, they are murdered by their own families for some twisted notion of "honor."

The alternative was—and tragically still too often is—to be considered "ruined" and face social ostracization, harassment, slut-shaming, blame, or not being believed. Many keep their assault a secret. Many are driven to suicide. None of this is okay.

Romance novels are an escape, a fantasy, a pleasure. But these novels are also inspiring and empowering, and they have the potential to change hearts and minds with portrayals of two individuals finding healing and happiness in love. I wrote this story to perhaps provide hope. And as with every romance novel I have written, I write the change I want to see: relationships based on mutual trust, respect, and love.

For more information about my novels, please visit www.mayarodale.com.

To be notified of upcoming releases, please sign up for my newsletter: http://bit.ly/1kk95QP

Please help other readers find this book by leaving a review or telling a friend.

There's a story behind every story. . . .
*Happily ever after is in reach for Duke and
Jane . . .* almost. *Keep reading for an excerpt from*

The Bad Boy Billionaire:
What a Girl Wants

*The stunning conclusion to their whirlwind
romance.*

"This," I said angrily, waving my iPhone. I wanted to slam *this* down on the table, like I had done with the paper invitation to my high school reunion earlier this summer. But I wasn't about to risk breaking my iPhone over the Paperless Post invitation intruding upon my inbox.

I settled for firmly placing my phone on the bar. It just wasn't the same.

Roxanna reached for it, her red manicure a sharp contrast against the black screen.

"No way!" I snatched it back. "I'm not falling for that again."

Roxanna just grinned. "You're welcome for setting you up with the love of your life."

"Thank you," I murmured, pursing my lips and fighting a smile. It was the polite thing to say, and I was always polite. I suppose I did owe her a thank-you for her prank Facebook post announcing an engagement between me and Duke Austen, infamously known as the Bad Boy Billionaire. At the time of said announcement, he and I had met (and kissed) just once. That didn't stop us from a sham engagement, which led to a secret romance. Now we were really, truly in love.

"What is it this time?" Roxanna asked, flipping

her red hair over her shoulder. She was perched on a bar stool, sipping bourbon on the rocks. I took the seat next to her and sipped from the chardonnay she'd gone ahead and ordered for me.

"*This* is the invitation to the party celebrating the IPO of Duke's start-up."

"How fabulous. Where is it?"

"That's not the point. It doesn't even matter, because it's at the same time on the same night as my high school reunion."

Roxanna raised one eyebrow. It was one of the traits of hers that I was jealous of, in addition to her carefree attitude, her amazing alcohol tolerance, which allowed her to drink copious amounts of whiskey without getting ridiculously drunk, and the ability to talk herself into restaurant tables without a reservation.

"Are you actually torn between which event to attend?" Roxanna asked incredulously. "The hottest party in the city, celebrating the hottest business launch possibly of all time, with free booze and fascinating people. Oh, and your hot boyfriend. Or a party in an old gymnasium with the same old bores you've known for half your life. They'll probably just want to talk about their kids."

"It'll be on the terrace at the Milford Country Club," I replied, but unenthusiastically.

"Oh," Roxanna sighed. "The country club. Someone get the velvet rope to keep out the riff-raff."

I sighed. "I know Duke's party will be more fabulous. But why do I have this angst about missing my stupid high school reunion? I could just go home and hit the pizza parlor on a Friday night, and it'd be the same conversations with the same people."

"Might I point out that you don't ever go back to the pizza parlor on a Friday night? But I get it, Jane. This night is like some sort of finish line you have to cross."

"Exactly," I said. "That, and we had a deal. I would pretend to be his good-girl fiancée and keep him out of trouble. In return, he'd be my hot and successful boyfriend on a night when I'd sorely need a confidence boost. But we can't be in both places at the same time. And I held up my end of the bargain."

"You could go alone," Roxanna said, demonstrating that she was ballsier than me. "Since you do, in fact, have a hot successful boyfriend, *not to mention* your numerous best-selling books. You shouldn't need the confidence boost, Jane. You're fabulous already."

"Thanks," I said with a smile. "I know this is all silly."

"Have you talked to Duke about it?"

"Of course not," I replied. "That's the mature, logical thing to do."

"Are you not a mature, logical person?" Roxanna queried. I took a long sip of wine before answering.

"I am the kind of person so desperate for a date to my high school reunion that I faked a relationship."

"Point taken," Roxanna said before taking a sip of her bourbon.

My phone, still on the bar between us, buzzed and lit up with an incoming text message. I picked up the phone quickly in case it was something sexy from Duke. He was known to send Snapchats of himself without his shirt on or other flirtatious and naughty texts.

"Is that your bad boy billionaire lover?"

I frowned. "No, it's Sam. He's been texting me a lot lately. This one says, 'How do you feel about second chances?'"

"Weird. Has he forgotten that you two broke up?"

"I have no idea what's going on with Sam lately," I said with a sigh. "He was up for these two jobs, and I'm not sure if he's gotten them. I have no idea what's up with him and Kate."

"Your nemesis."

"Grrrr." I growled just thinking about Kate Abbott, who teased me all through high school and then, the minute Sam and I broke up, swooped in and claimed him. Not that I was too bothered about it these days. My breakup with Sam had nearly destroyed me, but already I could see that it was the best thing that could have happened.

"Are you going to answer him?" Roxanna asked.

"Maybe later." I got rid of the text and looked back at my email. The invitation was still there, awaiting an RSVP. "I have to talk to Duke about this party. But he's got a big trip to San Francisco coming up. Might not be a good time."

He tended to be really, really devoted to his business. It could be hard to tear him away from work, but once I did, that same intense focus was aimed at me. My toes curled in my black patent wedge heels just thinking about it.

"And he's not whisking you away with him?" Roxanna asked.

"No, you don't get the apartment to yourself," I answered with a laugh. "He's just going for a day or two, and I have to work."

Roxanna's iPhone buzzed with an incoming text. Like me, she snatched it up right away.

"Is that from your mysterious millionaire lover?"

"Yes," she said breathlessly. I tried to raise one eyebrow in an "I'm intrigued" sort of way, but I think I only managed a weird face. Either way, Roxanna was too busy smiling as she texted him back.

"Do tell," I said, sipping my drink.

"Oh, no. I won't have my romantic entanglements serve as fodder for your next book."

"Please?" I gave her my most sorrowful expression. "I have no idea what to write, and I have a deadline looming."

My first two historical romance novels had

been easy to write, since my real life provided all the inspiration I needed. The heroines of those two novels—loosely based upon myself—had a friend, Prudence, who needed a story, too. Also in my inbox: emails from readers asking when Prue's story would be available. I didn't have an answer for them. What I had was a bad case of writer's block and no cure.

"Your own romance isn't inspiring you?"

"Nope. My love life is wonderful, which doesn't exactly make for a very exciting romance novel. There's no conflamma," I said, using our made-up word for the awful mixture of conflict and drama. It was essential to any great story—the happy ending wouldn't be as sweet without it.

"Don't get all sappy romantic on me." Roxanna punctuated that with a big sip of her whiskey. "You have to promise not to turn into one of those awful, smug couples."

I laughed. "Well—I suppose there is some conflict. The dueling parties where he has to decide what matters more—his big night or mine."

"Or *YOU* have to decide what matters more," Roxanna pointed out. "Or which party is simply more fun."

My phone buzzed with another text. I hoped this one was from Duke. We'd planned to meet up this evening but hadn't confirmed when or where. I picked up my phone and frowned.

"Another text from Sam?" Roxanna asked after seeing my frown.

"Yeah." This one was weird and I didn't want to think about it, so I put my phone in my bag.

"Still haven't found your ring?" Roxanna asked, gesturing to my hands, where I was absentmindedly trying to twist my cubic zirconia "engagement" ring around my finger. Except it wasn't there.

"No," I sighed. "I could have sworn I left it in my jewelry box. You know me—I always put things away. But it wasn't there, and I can't imagine where I might have lost it."

"Good thing it wasn't real," Roxanna remarked with a grimace.

"Yeah. It still had sentimental value, though."

Roxanna's mystery love texted again. She smiled as she tapped a response with her red manicured fingernails.

"I have to go. It's for work," she said. But neither of us could keep a straight face, because it might have been her boss texting her, but it was definitely not about work. We both burst out laughing.

Roxanna and I parted ways outside the bar. She went off to meet her mystery lover and Duke texted, inviting me to join him and some of his team for drinks at a bar on the Lower East Side.

Since it was a gorgeous end-of-summer evening, I decided to walk.

I slipped on my headphones, played "Empire State of Mind," and started heading over to the bar where we'd agreed to meet. There was nothing like walking through New York City—letting your route be determined by red and green lights, dodging pedestrians on the sidewalk, flowing around cars stopped in the streets, moving in time to the city's unique rhythm—all while listening to a great song and getting lost in your thoughts. Tonight, I was thinking just how far I had come.

I arrived here a few months ago, a total mess. My boyfriend of twelve years, Sam, had dumped me, when I'd been expecting him to propose. Oh, and I had gotten fired that day, too. I'd had to move out of the house we'd shared. Rather than stay at home with my folks, and tired of too many awkward conversations with meddling neighbors at the grocery store, I'd declared I was moving to New York to write a novel.

Madness, that. I just wanted everyone— especially myself—to think I was running *to* something instead of just fleeing the wreckage of my life.

Then I met Roxanna, whose practical joke on Facebook got me involved with Duke. My relationship with him provided the inspiration I needed to write not one but two historical romance novels, which I published to great success.

With Sam I had my life all planned out. And to think . . . I would have missed living and loving in New York City if everything had gone according to plan.

I pulled open the door to the bar on Elizabeth Street and spotted Duke right away. There was just something about him—confidence, deter-

mination, drive—that declared him Someone
Important even though he tended to wear free T-
shirts from other start-ups, with perfectly broken
in Levi's and sneakers.

He glanced up and caught my eye. God, that
smile. So roguish. So mischievous. It was a smile
that made a girl believe in once upon a time and
heroes who swept a girl off her feet. It did things
to me every time. He stood and strolled through
the bar toward me. The crowds just melted out of
his way.

If I had gotten the life I had always planned of,
I would have missed *this*. Duke pulling me into an
embrace. His mouth crashing down on mine for
the kind of deep, passionate kiss that left no doubt
as to how he felt about me or what we would be
doing tonight.

Later I would think about this kiss and remember it as the one sparkling moment when everything was just *right* and my biggest problem was
which party to attend. It was the moment before
my past reared its ugly head, making happily ever
after seem unlikely. It was the moment before the
storm hit, leaving unfathomable destruction in its
wake. It was the moment before I got an idea for a
new story—but at a price I didn't want to pay.